D0823375

The One You Trust

Paul Pilkington

East Baton Rouge Parish Library
Baton Rouge, Louisiana

Published in 2014

UK English Edition

Copyright © Paul Pilkington

The author(s) assert the moral right under the Copyright, Designs
and Patents Act 1988 to be identified as the
author(s) of this work.

All Rights reserved. No part of this publication may be reproduced,
stored in a retrieval system, or transmitted, in any form or by any
means without the prior written consent of the publisher, nor be
otherwise circulated in any form of binding or cover other than that
in which it is published and without a similar condition being
imposed on the subsequent purchaser.

About the Author

Paul Pilkington lives in the UK. He has had material broadcast on BBC radio and ITV television, and was long listed for the 2004 London Book Fair Lit Idol competition. Paul was inspired to write his first suspense mystery, The One You Love, through his love of emotional mystery thrillers. He aims to create fast-paced, twisting and turning fiction that stirs the emotions. You can contact Paul via his website.

This novel is written in British (UK) English. British English words, spelling (favourite, colour, etc.) and grammar are used throughout.

By Paul Pilkington

The One You Love
The One You Fear
The One You Trust
Someone to Save You
Emma Holden and Me

For my family

Prologue

'Wake up.'

Peter Myers hadn't been asleep. Before he turned over to face the prison guard, he tucked the photograph that he had been gazing at into the waistband of his tracksuit, covering it with his top. If they knew he had it, they would take it off him straight away. There was no doubt about that. All the effort to which he had gone to keep the photo secret would have been wasted. And that photograph was one of the only things keeping him going in this place. Without it, he didn't know what he would do. It was the one thing that lifted him above the filth and the degradation of the life that festered within the prison walls, threatening to consume him.

'Come on, Myers, up!'

He climbed off the creaky, uncomfortable bed, with its damp odour, paper-thin mattress and unforgiving springs.

Without saying a word, he faced up to the guard with his bright green eyes. Despite the warder being half a foot shorter than him, their faces were only a matter of centimetres apart. Myers could smell stale tobacco on the man's breath.

'Look lively, Myers.' The guard liked to act tough, play the bully.

Peter Myers scratched at his greying beard, and continued to stare at the guard. He could sense his discomfort. No matter how well he tried to hide it, the man was afraid. He probably came to work every day with a sense of terror that someone would puncture the false bravado and show him up for what he really was.

But no matter how much Peter Myers wanted to be that someone, he knew he had to behave.

The guard watched from the doorway of the cell as Peter Myers brushed past him and moved along the corridor towards the washroom.

There was only one other prisoner in the cramped washing area — a man by the name of Carl Jones, who was awaiting trial for attacking his wife with a knife after he found her in bed with his best friend. Jones liked to think of himself as a bit of a joker; sometimes playing the fool, and at other times trying to make a fool out of others. Myers just found him annoying. He wanted to swat him away, like a persistent fly.

He didn't acknowledge him as he entered the room. Bending over the sink, he swilled his thin, angular face with ice-cold water.

'Hey, Myers, is this your girlfriend?'

Peter Myers, his face dripping, glared at Carl Jones in the mirror.

The man was holding up the photograph. It must have fallen from his waistband.

'Hey, she's a real looker!' he said. 'Nice pai—'

The word was cut off by Peter Myer's hand, which he had thrust out and wrapped tightly around the man's throat, pressing his thumb deep into his Adam's apple. 'Give me the photograph back, now.'

Jones relinquished it immediately, grabbing at his throat, gasping. His face was blood-red. Peter Myers tucked the photograph back out of sight. He stared down at Carl Jones, as he crouched, hunched over, still gasping for breath, and wanted to hurt him some more. But he had already done more than was sensible. He needed to stay out of trouble.

His plan depended on it.

PART ONE

1

Lizzy paused as she arrived outside Dan and Emma's apartment building. The weather was that of a typical early December morning – sunny but bitterly cold. She had her hands buried deep inside her winter coat, her strawberry-blonde hair covered by a woolly hat. She liked this kind of weather – it was Christmassy, and she loved the festive season.

Lizzy took a deep breath as she considered the events of the past two weeks, a feeling of dread rising within her, but she entered the apartment block anyway, glancing over at the post trays where the postman deposited the mail for each resident.

There were several letters in the trays, including a variety of Friday's newspapers. Hesitating again, nerves tightening, she shook off the feeling of dread, knowing she had to face up to things.

She leafed quickly through the mail. Thankfully, there was nothing to be worried about there.

Not like nine days ago.

The first letter had been waiting for her three days after her best friend, Emma, and her new husband, Dan, had left for their honeymoon in Mauritius.

Emma had asked Lizzy if she would mind the flat while they were away. She had only asked Lizzy to pop around once in a while, just to check that all was well, but Lizzy had found herself drawn to the place every day. Maybe after all that had happened, she just felt the need to be extra vigilant. Even though the nightmare was over.

Or so they had all thought.

The grey envelope containing the letter had been the only thing in the post tray that third morning.

It had been addressed to Lizzy, sent externally, first-class post. Inside had been a piece of lined paper, with just a single, taunting, typed sentence, in a Gothic font, centred on the page.

Who can you really trust, Lizzy?

Lizzy had never considered herself easily intimidated: she had always been somewhat thick-skinned, developed during childhood years of being playfully taunted by two older brothers; and then further hardened by surviving in the sometimes catty world of theatre. But this had certainly got to her; for the rest of the day it had remained uppermost in her mind. *Who sent this? And why?*

Whoever had sent it must have known that Emma and Dan were away, and that Lizzy was visiting the apartment building. She had found herself looking over her shoulder, wondering whether the person was watching, following.

But she had refused to be intimidated.

Defying her fears, Lizzy returned to the flat every day, making the post trays her first port of call. And, each day, she had expected to find another letter for her. But it had been another seven days before the next communication arrived. The modus operandi had been the same: a single typed sentence, in Gothic font, posted first class, addressed to her.

The one you trust is the one to fear. Who do you trust, Lizzy?

Lizzy had no idea what that was supposed to mean. It wasn't a threat, as such; it was more like a warning. But it was not a friendly warning – it was designed to unsettle her.

Again, the question is who . . .

The suspect was obvious: Sally Thompson. Two months before, Sally, masquerading as a girl called Amy, had planned to kill Emma's brother, Will Holden. A qualified skydive instructor, she had met and dated him, all with the intention of tandem-jumping out of a plane with him – and sending them both to their deaths. The motive had been revenge on the family: Sally blamed Emma for the death of her fiancé, Stuart Harris, who killed himself after his advances towards Emma, to whom he had once also been engaged, had been spurned. But, ultimately, Sally hadn't carried it through: she'd pulled back from the brink and hadn't, in fact, committed any crime. Which was why the police had only given her an official caution.

Maybe she was too obvious a suspect.

But if not Sally Thompson, then who?

Lizzy hadn't told anyone about the letters. She certainly wasn't going to let it spoil Dan and Emma's honeymoon. There was no way that she was going to let this individual ruin things. And she hadn't

12

told Will, because she wasn't convinced that he would be able to keep quiet if Emma happened to get in touch. She knew he probably wouldn't say anything, but it wasn't worth the risk. Lizzy had considered contacting the police, but it was probably just some loser with nothing better to do, who had been attracted to the case following the press publicity.

Lizzy climbed the stairs to Emma and Dan's top-floor flat. She entered, glancing back down towards the staircase as she closed the door. There was – of course – nobody there.

Once inside, she did her daily check of each room, moving quickly. Everything was as it should be. But being in the place, devoid of its owners, unnerved her, and she never stayed for more than a minute or so, always glad to leave.

Lizzy peered around the bathroom door. Again, nothing. But, inside her head, she heard Will's voice.

It's Richard. I think he's dead.

That image, of Will emerging from the bathroom, blood all over his hands, having found the battered body of Dan's brother, Richard, still haunted her – even though she knew Richard was safely up in Edinburgh now, getting on with his life.

She always left the bathroom until last.

Lizzy shivered, locking the door and turning to go back down the stairs. It wasn't getting any easier, but she *was* going to come back every day until Dan and Emma returned. She wasn't going to let her fears get the better of her.

By the time she reached the hallway, she was feeling better. But the sight of a grey envelope in Dan and Emma's post tray stopped her dead.

She looked across at the external door. There was no one. Moving over to the tray, she took hold of the letter. It was the same type of washed out grey envelope as previously but, this time, no stamp.

It had been hand-delivered.

Lizzy gripped the envelope. 'They've been here, just now.'

She was startled by the sudden sound of the outside door swinging open. It was Emma's elderly downstairs neighbour.

'Oh, hello.' Mr Henderson looked surprised to see her, although she'd seen him a few times over the past few days and had explained that she was looking after the flat. She wondered whether he, like his wife, was starting to lose his memory.

'Did you see anyone leaving the apartments just now?' Lizzy asked.

He looked confused, clutching onto a couple of shopping bags.

Lizzy tried again. 'Did anyone pass you, just now, as you were coming in?'

'Yes,' he said, his face brightening a little. 'A man, I think.'

'You think?' Lizzy bit her lip with frustration. 'What did he look like?'

'I don't know,' he replied. 'He was wearing a hat. A cap, one of those peaked caps. Seemed to cover his face. He was looking down. I didn't see his face.'

'Do you know which way he went?'

'Towards Euston Road. Is he a friend of yours?'

'I don't think so,' Lizzy said. 'What colour cap?'

Mr Henderson thought for a moment. 'Blue.'

Lizzy pulled open the door, still holding the letter. 'Thanks, Mr Henderson.'

She stepped out onto the pavement and peered down the road. There were a few people walking towards her, and another several walking in the direction of Euston Road, some way up the road. One of them looked like they might be wearing a cap, but it was too far to tell.

Lizzy set off up the road after the distant figures, walking at a pace just short of a jog. She wasn't sure what she was going to do if one of them turned out to be the person in the cap, but she wanted to do something.

She passed two people – a twenty-something girl listening to music through headphones, and a businessman texting on his mobile phone. And then, further ahead, she saw someone else. Striding purposefully, wearing a blue cap.

'Hey, you!'

Lizzy wasn't sure why she shouted, but it certainly got their attention – and confirmed her suspicions that this was the person who'd left the letter.

They turned their head at a low angle, just enough to see Lizzy, but still shielding their face beneath the cap.

14

And then they ran.

Lizzy gave chase, but the individual in the cap was just too fast and rapidly increased the distance between them. If she had been Emma, Lizzy thought, then maybe she would have had a chance. But Lizzy, although relatively fit, wasn't naturally sporty, and didn't run for fun.

She didn't give up, though, and pursued the person up towards the busy Euston Road, sure that the traffic would slow their speed. But the person in the cap just sprinted straight across the road, dodging buses, taxis and cars, and carried on across into Regent's Park.

Lizzy could only stand by the kerb and watch from the other side, punching the crossing button repeatedly in a vain attempt to stop the traffic.

She leant against the roadside railings to catch her breath and only then remembered she still had the unopened letter in her hand. She tore it open.

This time it wasn't just a message.

'What the hell?' she said to herself.

2

'I can't believe that tomorrow is our last full day.'

'Me, neither,' Dan said, as they sat down for dinner on the hotel's restaurant terrace. They were looking out over the stunning beach and a huge expanse of the Indian Ocean, bathed in a glorious sunset.

Emma closed her eyes and enjoyed the feel of the mild, strengthening breeze, which in the past hour had taken the edge off the humidity. Her skin had tanned a lovely golden colour since their arrival, bringing out the warm honey highlights in her dark brown hair. She reopened her eyes as Dan continued.

'It seems to have gone so quickly,' he said, subconsciously touching his dark hair, which he had cut shorter just before the trip. Emma liked the new style. 'Cheers to a wonderful honeymoon, Mrs Carlton.' He smiled and raised his glass of champagne to meet Emma's.

They'd come down early for the meal, before the later rush, so the restaurant was quiet, with only two other couples, seated some tables away. This dinner, in the smaller, Indian-themed restaurant, was a special treat arranged by Dan for the Friday night. Unlike the larger eating places in the hotel, he had had to book ahead, and the setting – for open-air dining by candlelight – was idyllic.

But, Emma thought, although this was an extra-special meal, in truth, everything about the holiday had been a treat. The hotel was amazing; it was a luxurious complex right by the best beach on Mauritius' east coast, complete with a number of swimming pools, several restaurants serving a vast array of food from around the world, and rooms that seemed palatial in their size and décor. And then there was the island itself. A real paradise, bathed in sunshine, and offering an intoxicating mix of cultures, sights and landscapes.

It was certainly the holiday of a lifetime.

'Em, are you okay?'

Emma snapped out of her daydream, releasing that she was absentmindedly twirling her chocolate-brown hair around one finger. She smiled at her husband. 'I was just thinking, on Sunday we go back to reality. Back to London, the flat . . .'

'It's not that bad, you know,' Dan joked, his attention taken for a second by one of the small sparrows that spent each day squabbling over the crumbs that fell from the tables.

'No, it's not bad at all.' She tried to smile.

'Everything is going to be all right,' Dan said, reading her mind. He reached across the table top and took her hand. 'Everything is going to be absolutely fine.'

Emma went to say something, then paused.

'What is it?'

'I don't want to spoil tonight,' she replied. 'We shouldn't let anything spoil it.'

'I know. But' – Dan looked at her – 'if you're worried about something, then it might be better to just get it out. We all know what happens when people keep secrets.'

'Okay,' Emma said, nodding reluctantly. 'Okay, I'll tell you. But, please, I hope you won't be upset.'

'Of course I won't, Em.'

Emma sipped some champagne to ready herself. 'Last night, I had that dream again.'

'Right . . .' Dan knew just what she meant. 'The nightmare at the church altar.'

Emma nodded. 'It was exactly the same as the other times. I was standing next to you, we were getting married—'

'And then I turn into your ex-fiancé, Stuart Harris,' Dan interrupted.

'Yes. And then he turns into—'

'Stephen Myers.' Dan sighed as he thought back over recent events. Just over three months ago, Emma had discovered that Stephen Myers, a man who had stalked her when she had worked as an actor on a soap opera in Manchester, had been murdered four years previously, by Stuart. Her brother, Will, had been pressured by Stuart to help him dispose of the body. And it had also resulted, this summer, in the kidnap of Dan by Stephen's father, Peter Myers, as he sought revenge on Emma and her family and friends.

Emma shook her head. 'I really thought that once everything was sorted . . . you know, after the wedding, then it wouldn't happen. I thought it was in the past.'

Yet she knew that the situation that had given birth to the nightmare wasn't in the past at all. Peter Myers had yet to be sentenced, and there was still the worry that he would one day reveal that his son had been murdered, and Will's role in that.

And then there was the unanswered question. *How did Peter Myers find out that Stuart killed his son?*

Dan was about to reply but was interrupted by a waiter. 'Sir, madam — are you ready to order?'

Emma and Dan exchanged a glance.

'Not quite yet,' Dan said. 'Another couple of minutes?'

'Certainly,' the waiter replied, and moved away.

Dan turned back to Emma. 'Why would I be upset about you having a recurrent nightmare?'

Emma shrugged, shaking her head. 'Because this dream, it's coming from inside me. I'm creating it. Inside, I must still be thinking about Stuart Harris and Stephen Myers. Doesn't that bother you?'

Dan nodded, reflectively. 'Yes, it does. But not in the way you think. It bothers me because I want you to be free of the bad memories, free of the nightmares.'

'Thanks.'

He thought for a moment. 'Last night, is that the first time you've had the dream since the wedding?'

'Yes.'

'I thought you seemed a bit distant today. I could tell something was bothering you.'

They'd been on an all-day, escorted tour of the island. It had been a lovely day, but Dan was right – Emma had been distracted.

'Look,' Dan said. 'Maybe the dream is down to worry – worry about going home. This past two weeks, it's been an escape. I don't know about you, but everything about being here . . . well, it's felt a world away from all the bad things that have happened to us recently.'

'I'd hardly thought of any of it since we arrived,' Emma agreed. 'We've been too busy having fun. It just seemed like a distant memory – as if it happened to someone else.'

'Exactly. And now it's coming to an end, we have to go back home, to where it all happened. We have to face up to the fact that it did happen, and we've got to deal with it, Em, no matter how difficult it is. And that won't be easy. It's understandable if your subconscious is unsettled.'

Emma nodded, relieved that Dan understood. She decided to tell him everything on her mind. 'In the past day, I've also been thinking about Firework Films. About whether they're still planning to finish that television programme . . .'

A dirt-digging production company, Firework Films, known for its exploitative reality TV shows, was making a docudrama of what had happened to Emma and Dan over the past summer.

'I think we have to assume that they will.'

'It's just that as we haven't heard anything more from Adrian Spencer, I thought it might be a good sign.'

Adrian Spencer, a researcher for the company, had been pestering them incessantly for information, but after they had complained directly to the company, his unwanted attention had stopped.

'I wouldn't bet on it, unfortunately.'

'I know. But I really wish they wouldn't.'

'Me, too. But we have no control over what they do, do we? All we can try and do is deal with it in the best way we can – try not to let it affect us too much. Though that's easier said than done, I know.'

'You're right,' Emma said, sitting up and taking a larger swig from her glass. 'We need to focus on the positives.'

'Yes. Like your new job.' Dan grinned at her.

Emma's new acting role in a West End play was, indeed, a really positive thing. Rehearsals weren't due to start for a few weeks, but she had received the script via her agent, and had already read it through several times. Each time, she had felt more and more excited by it.

Dan glanced up from his menu. 'And have you made a decision about the reunion?'

Emma had also received an invitation to attend a reunion event the following weekend for the cast of *Up My Street*, the soap opera in which she had spent five, largely happy, years. The event was to celebrate the twenty-year anniversary of the show and the move of the production to brand-new, state-of-the-art studios at Media City, a massive media development at Salford Quays, not far from their ageing base in central Manchester. She had made many wonderful friends during her time on the show, both in front of and behind the camera, so it would be amazing to see her old colleagues again.

'I'm still not sure.'

There were some things that made Emma hesitate in accepting the invitation: that time was, in many ways, the seeding ground for everything bad that had happened since.

It was where she had met and fallen in love with Stuart Harris. And it was where she had first come to the attention of Stephen Myers – the desperate, needy stalker who had made the latter stages of her time on the show an absolute misery.

Emma looked out at the ocean. A huge container ship was moving across the distant horizon, possibly heading for one of the big African ports. Their tour guide that day had explained how much shipping traffic passed through, either stopping off at the island or gliding past its shores. She noticed too that the sky was darkening purple and black in the distance – the guide had also warned them that a big storm would roll in that evening.

'Looks like the storm's approaching,' Dan said, seeing where she was looking.

The thought made Emma shiver a little: thunder and lightning always unnerved her. One of her first memories of childhood was cowering under her bedcovers during a storm, wishing that the noise would stop. Her parents had come to the rescue, letting her sleep in their bed that night.

'It's up to you, of course, but I think you should go to the reunion,' Dan said. 'It might be a good way to move on.'

'But aren't reunions about looking back to the past?'

'Maybe to deal with the past, you've got to face the past.'

Emma smiled. 'Maybe you're right. You think it might help stop the dream?'

Dan shrugged. 'Who knows? I'm not a psychologist. But, at the least, you should have a good time.'

'And what if Charlotte Harris is there?'

20

Charlotte Harris, Stuart's younger sister, had played a non-speaking part in the soap opera – Stuart had managed to get her the role of one of the children in the school that sometimes featured.

'She probably won't have got an invite. But if she is, then just try to ignore her.'

'I guess.' Emma certainly didn't relish the idea of seeing her again. Not after what Charlotte had said to her at their last meeting, two months ago – blaming Emma for Stuart's suicide and for the break-up of his relationship with his fiancée, Sally Thompson.

'Don't let Charlotte Harris stop you from going. If you really don't want to go, then fair enough, but if it's the thought of her being there that's putting you off, then that's different.'

'You're right. I will go.' Emma nodded briskly, smiling at him. 'And you're right about needing to face up to the past in order to move on. I'm thinking of maybe going to see a counsellor. Maybe the colleague of Miranda's that she recommended, the last time I was round with her and Dad. She said she'd see me on a more informal basis. What do you think?'

'I think you should do whatever you feel you need to do. I'll support you, whatever you decide.'

'And you? Do you think you might benefit from counselling?'

Dan smiled. 'I think I'll be okay.'

The storm hit just as they finished their meal. They ran back to their room as the rain began to fall heavily and, within minutes, water was cascading down the guttering and pooling across the balcony. Emma and Dan watched from the comfort of their room as the sky flashed and thunder boomed.

The intense, powerful storm raged on throughout the night, and Emma didn't sleep very well. But at least the dream didn't return. And, by morning, all was calm.

3

Will Holden and Katie left the cosy Italian restaurant in Soho after enjoying a wonderful Saturday lunch there. The December sun was shining, and all seemed perfect. They looked great together – Will in his smart Calvin Klein trousers and jacket, with royal blue shirt, and Katie in a lovely sequined black top and blue and black patterned skirt.

It was then that Katie asked him the question that marked the end of their brief relationship.

'Are you thinking about somebody else?'

Will ran a hand through his thick dark hair, shocked at her perceptiveness. But perhaps it had been obvious? He had spent most of the meal daydreaming, worrying about how he should deal with the thoughts that just wouldn't go away. It had been the same that morning, on a riverside walk. So, when challenged, there was no point in arguing.

He just nodded.

Katie smiled sweetly, kissed him goodbye on the cheek, and left. She crossed the road and disappeared from view without looking back.

And that was that.

Will stood there for a moment or so, collecting his thoughts. A young couple with whom they had shared the restaurant exited, holding hands as they moved away, laughing at a shared joke. He watched them walk to the end of the street and round the corner, then blew out his cheeks, his breath visible.

Katie was a lovely girl. Kind, intelligent, pretty. And they got on really well. They seemed to share opinions on the main things that mattered, and they made each other laugh. He should have been racing after her, telling her that the thing he was thinking about meant nothing compared to being with her. But, instead, he had let her walk out of his life without even a word.

He wandered around the streets of the West End for half an hour or so. By the end of his walk, he was sure. No matter how lovely Katie was, and how much they connected, there was a big problem.

He was still in love with someone else.

***

For almost the entire afternoon, Will Holden had been watching the girl from a safe distance, from the edge of Newington Green, a small park in Stoke Newington, north London.

He had been just down the street from her flat when he'd spotted her, making her way in the opposite direction. She had looked amazing – her blonde hair falling perfectly down the back of a long, red winter coat that reached down to her Ugg boots.

His first reaction had been to turn around and go back home – it had been a foolish decision to go there in the first place. But then he'd felt an uncontrollable urge to follow, to watch her, longing to be close enough to hear her voice.

My God, I'm behaving like a stalker.

He'd trailed her for a few minutes, hanging back as she'd entered the park in the middle of the square. It was there that she'd been joined by the man. A tall, ginger-haired guy wearing jeans and a bomber jacket, probably about Will's age. They'd walked side by side along the footpath, as Will had watched from behind a bank of trees.

Surely she hasn't found someone else so soon?

They weren't holding hands, but they had looked close – maybe brushing against one another as they walked. Will had felt sick, and jealous, although he really had no right to be. The two of them had sat down on a bench, next to the deserted children's play area, with their backs to Will.

He'd waited for them to kiss, or embrace, but they had just talked.

What the hell had he been doing there? If Emma ever found out, she'd be so angry.

Just after that West End walk, Will had headed for the tube. It was almost as if he'd been on autopilot, guided by his heart rather than his head. He'd known it was an incredibly stupid thing to do, and that it would probably only do damage, but he hadn't been able to help himself. If he didn't speak to her, and tell her how he felt . . . well, he knew that he'd regret it.

Surely Emma would understand that? And does she ever need to know?

The answer to the first question was maybe. The answer to the second was probably not. And, as much as Will didn't want to keep secrets any more, if it was for the best, then so be it.

He had waited while the two of them continued to talk. Then, just as he was beginning to wonder how long they would stay, the couple had stood up and parted company.

Without an embrace.

Were they lovers?

Will had shaken the thought from his head. It really was none of his business.

He had resisted the temptation to approach her on the way back to her flat, deciding it would just look too weird. So he had waited until she got back home, and then held back for another five minutes before approaching the door to the ground-floor flat.

Remember not to call her Amy . . .

The name she had used to deceive him.

The door opened just a few seconds after Will knocked.

He knew that his presence would be a shock, given the circumstances of their parting, but he hadn't quite expected the look of horror that flashed across Sally's face.

'Will! I . . .'

Will took a step back. 'I'm sorry for coming out of the blue like this, but I just wanted to talk to you.'

Sally looked both pained and sad. 'You shouldn't have come. You really shouldn't.'

Will nodded his understanding quickly, embarrassed. 'I'll go. As I said, I'm really sorry for turning up here like this.' He turned and began to walk away, his stomach still lurching from the sight of her.

She looked radiant. Just as he had remembered.

'Wait,' he heard her say. 'It should be me who's apologising.'

Will stopped and turned around. 'I didn't come for that.'

'Then why? Why have you come here, Will?' Sally had come out onto the pavement and now stood, arms folded tightly across her chest, looking at him.

24

Will pinched the bridge of his nose as he searched for the words. 'I came because . . . because I want to find out if the girl I thought I knew is really you.'

Sally nodded. She seemed to understand. 'Let's go and get a coffee. There's a place just around the corner; it's nice and quiet.'

***

'I'm so sorry, Will, for what I did to you.'

They were seated towards the back of the café, as far away from the counter as they could get, out of earshot. They were the only ones in the place.

'It's okay.' Will looked up from stirring his coffee. 'I understand that you weren't thinking straight. You were grieving for Stuart, I understand that. You were hurting, you were angry, you wanted revenge.'

Sally looked away and closed her eyes. 'I can't believe what I did. What I was planning to do. I am just so ashamed of what happened. So very ashamed. If there was a way I could make it up to you, then I would.'

'You don't need to.'

'How can you mean that?' she said. 'I led you on for weeks, I lied about who I was, and I was planning to . . .'

'But you didn't go through with it. You didn't do anything.'

'No, I suppose not.'

'Why *didn't* you go through with it?' Will had been desperate to ask this question ever since the revelations at the airfield. Why, after all that scheming, that thought, had she abandoned her plans – leaving him on the ground and getting into the plane without him?

Sally considered her answer. 'Because I liked you. I know it sounds pathetic, but I did really get to like you, Will. And I just couldn't do it. Especially after what you said to me when we were getting ready to board the plane for the jump. About how I'd changed your life for the better. I guess it just woke me up to the horror of what I was doing – how terribly, terribly horrific it all was.' She looked at him. 'Those weeks after Stuart's death, well, they're all a blur, really. I was in such a state, such a deep depression, that I

25

don't think I really knew what I was doing. It was like I was possessed.' She looked down, embarrassed.

'Were you still planning to kill yourself?' Will asked. 'If we hadn't radioed through to the pilot to land the plane, were you still going to go through with it?' Emma and the others had got to the airfield just in time, to alert Will, who was waiting bewildered in the changing area, to what Sally was planning to do.

'I was in a really bad place,' Sally replied after a pause, not quite answering the question.

'And now?'

Her smile seemed slightly forced. 'Better. Much better. I feel like I'm coming out of the darkness.'

'That's good. Really good.' Will watched Sally. She did look good; not like someone who was in the depths of depression. But then, how was he to really know the truth? She'd fooled him totally once before, and he had to assume that she could do so again.

They both took sips from their coffee, glancing over at the entrance as a mother and baby entered.

Sally broke the silence. 'I'm still confused, Will, about why you've come to see me. You've got every right not to want to remember that I even exist.'

Will laughed, shaking his head at the thought. 'Believe me, I've tried.'

'I don't understand.'

'Maybe you're right,' Will said, struggling for words. 'Maybe I shouldn't have come here.'

'You said back at my flat that you wanted to know if the girl you thought you knew was really me. What do you mean?'

Again Will shook his head, ruing the feelings that he had tried but failed to suppress. 'I . . . I fell in love with that girl . . . with Amy. I fell totally in love with her. She made me feel alive. I want to know, are you Amy?'

Will had thought this was going to be extremely difficult, but now he'd started, the words were coming freely; he felt emboldened. 'Are you the girl who I fell in love with?'

Sally seemed taken aback. 'I'm not Amy, Will.'

'But how much of Amy was *you*?'

'I'm not sure how to answer that.'

'Her personality, character, her likes and dislikes, sense of humour, her attitude and outlook on life – live for the moment, challenge your fears. Is that you, or was it just an act?'

'No, that's me.'

'Then it *is* you that I'm in love with.' Will sat back in his chair and looked at her, wonderingly.

Sally shook her head. 'You don't mean that. You can't be in love with me, Will.'

'Do you really think I'd be here if I wasn't?'

'It doesn't matter, anyway,' she said. 'After what's happened.'

Will wasn't giving up. 'I'm okay with being friends, if that's all that you want. I'll accept that. I promise that I will never pressure you for anything more than you're comfortable with.'

'Friendship requires trust, Will. How can you ever trust me, after what I did to you?'

'I do trust you,' he replied. 'Yes, I know it sounds crazy, but now that I've seen you again, spoken to you . . . I know that I can trust you.'

'And what about your family, Will? Will Emma trust me? Does she know that you're here, wanting to be my friend?'

'She'll understand.'

'And if she doesn't?'

Will didn't know the answer to that one.

***

Sally watched as Will turned the corner of the street, after their brief but friendly goodbye. She waited until she got back to the privacy of her flat before dialling the number. 'Hi. There's a problem. It's Will Holden. I think he was following me, and if he was, then he probably saw you.'

4

'So, you wanted to speak to me,' Adrian Spencer said, unsmiling, as he approached Lizzy on Saturday afternoon at their agreed meeting point, just down from Westminster Bridge, by the Thames. It was a halfway meeting point between the offices of Firework Films and the theatre Lizzy was working at.

Adrian, his balding hair shaved short, looked up at the darkening sky. 'Looks like it's going to rain.'

Lizzy nodded, noticing how his slate-grey eyes matched the sky. Following the events of yesterday, she'd thought of cancelling the meeting: concerns over the item left by the mysterious, capped individual were weighing heavily on her mind. But part of her wondered whether this would be her only chance; her only opportunity to try and convince Firework Films to drop the idea of the docudrama that they were planning to make about Emma.

Part of her also wondered whether she was crazy to even countenance the idea that she would be able to change their mind. They were a commercial company, with commercial concerns. They obviously thought that the programme had the potential to be lucrative. But, surely, it was worth a try? And what better present to give Emma on her return from honeymoon than the news that they had dropped the idea?

Lizzy tried a smile. 'Thanks for agreeing to meet me.'

Adrian Spencer had been curt but professional on the phone. In truth, Lizzy hadn't really expected him to agree to the request. After all, the last time they had met, he had been ambushed by Lizzy, Emma and Dan and faced uncomfortable accusations – that he was a researcher for Firework Films, not the newspaper journalist he had purported to be. Then he had seemed defeated, and deflated. On the run. But today, was that a hint of bitterness in his eyes?

'You've not got your friends with you today, then?' he said, looking over his shoulder pointedly. 'Dan Carlton isn't waiting in the wings, is he? Your knight in shining armour?'

Maybe the meeting *had* been a mistake. 'You know why we had to do that.'

Adrian surprised her by nodding. 'Of course I do.'

Spots of rain began to fall, and the clouds were thickening.

'Do you want to go for a coffee?' Lizzy said. 'There's the outdoor place just over there. It's got cover, and heaters.'

He shrugged. 'Whatever you want.'

The place was protected by a canopy, draped with bright, multi-coloured fairy lights. Not the sturdiest of structures, it was enough to keep out the light drizzle, and the outdoor heater was doing its job. They both ordered a drink.

'So, you didn't explain what you wanted to talk to me about,' he said, placing his gloves on the table between them.

'It's about the docudrama. I wanted to ask you if there was any chance that it might not go ahead.'

Adrian Spencer just looked at her.

Lizzy tried again, undaunted by the lack of reaction on his part to the initial question. 'Is it definitely going ahead?'

'Why do you want to know?'

'Because it's about us — me and my friends. And it's going to be very upsetting, for everyone involved, if it goes ahead. Why wouldn't we want to know what's happening about it? We have a right to know.'

'No, you don't,' he replied. 'You don't have any rights about it, not really.'

Lizzy bristled, and fought to keep her cool. *Is this why he agreed to the meeting, so that he could play games with me?* 'Just answer my question, please.'

Adrian laughed to himself. 'You've got this all wrong, you know,' he said, finally. 'You've got this all very wrong.'

'I don't understand what you mean.'

'I know you don't. And that's the problem, Lizzy.'

'Look,' Lizzy said, 'don't play games with me. *Don't* speak in riddles.'

'Okay, okay' he replied, holding up his hands in mock surrender. 'I'll tell it to you straight.' He paused, gathering his thoughts. 'First of all, do you really think that I've got any control about what goes on at Firework Films? Do you really think I've got influence?'

29

'Well, I thought . . .'

'Look, I'm a researcher. I was working for Firework. I was the hired hand. I don't have any control whatsoever.'

'But you must have some—'

'I have zero influence,' he interrupted. 'I was following orders, doing my job, trying to earn some money.'

'You were pestering us, refusing to leave us alone.'

'I was following orders,' he repeated. 'And because of your actions, because of what you did, the company fired me. I don't work for them any more.'

Lizzy kept quiet. She couldn't lie and say that she was sorry. And she was sure that he wouldn't want to hear that, either.

'So, you see, Lizzy, I have no influence whatsoever on what Firework Films do or don't do. And, frankly, I don't care. I really don't. All I care about is finding another job, so I can pay my bills.'

She had wasted her time. He'd be no help at all. But then she remembered something that Adrian had said. 'You said that we'd got this all wrong. What did you mean?'

'I mean just what I said.' He looked at her. 'You're worrying about the wrong things. You've got your eyes on what you perceive to be the threat, but creeping up behind your back is the real thing to worry about, the real danger.'

'You're threatening me?'

He paused. Whether it was to consider his response, or just for dramatic effect, Lizzy didn't know, but he certainly seemed to be enjoying casting out the bait and reeling her in. 'The reality, Lizzy, is that there is someone that you should all be worried about, especially Emma.'

'And that is?'

'Peter Myers.'

Lizzy blinked. 'Peter Myers is in jail. He can't do anything to us any more.'

'I wouldn't be so sure,' came the ominous reply.

'I don't understand what you mean.' Lizzy was starting to feel breathless.

'Look,' he said, 'through the research I've done, my dealings with Peter Myers, looking into his background, I'd be very worried about that man. I really would be very worried.'

30

'But as I said, he's behind bars.'

'For now.'

'What's that supposed to mean? You can't think that he'll get off, do you? There's no way they could find him not guilty, no way.'

'Of course not,' Adrian Spencer said. 'He's already pleaded guilty. The evidence is unequivocal. He *will* be found guilty, that's for certain. You don't need to worry about that.'

'Then what?'

'What about when he's released?'

'Well, that will be a long time off.' Lizzy suddenly realised that she hadn't, until that moment, actually considered that Peter Myers would one day be free again. Of course none of them had thought he'd be locked away for life, but it was still a shock to have this reality brought home.

'The sentence might not be as long as you think,' he said. 'As I said, he *has* pleaded guilty, and shown remorse, plus there are mitigating circumstances that the judge will take into account.'

Lizzy paused. 'What mitigating circumstances?' For a moment she nearly said it: *His son was murdered. Stephen Myers was killed by Stuart Harris, and his body dumped in a canal by Stuart, aided by Will Holden.* The realisation of what had happened had been the reason he had come after them; it had been the explanation behind it all, a justification even, for his extreme actions. But for some inexplicable reason, Peter Myers had kept the secret. She wondered whether he would choose to reveal it as the sentencing approached. *Would it result in a lesser prison term?*

'My research for the docudrama revealed that he'd been under a lot of stress over a number of years,' Adrian Spencer explained. 'His wife, Margaret, had been mentally unwell for some time and, as the sole carer, trying to keep his own business going, still dealing with the death of his son, it really took its toll. He'd been on antidepressants, among other things.'

Lizzy breathed an inward sigh of relief. Thank God he hadn't been referring to Stephen's murder. 'How long do you think he'll serve?'

'I have no idea. But one day, they will let him out. And if he behaves himself, then it will be sooner than you would want to believe.'

31

'And you think we should be worried when that happens?'

He nodded. 'Emma, in particular.'

'Why?'

'Because he's never offered an explanation for what he did.' Adrian took a sip of his coffee. 'He's never admitted that he is obsessed with Emma. That he wanted to make the connection with her, to be close to her, control her. And that kidnapping Dan, and later you, was part of this – at least, in his eyes.'

'But the police are sure that was the motive,' Lizzy said, hoping that he couldn't see her discomfort. Indeed, they had all stuck to that narrative when interviewed by the police: to suggest that wasn't the real motivation would potentially have placed the spotlight on Will and Stuart. So it had suited the group for Peter Myers to be labelled as the obsessive stalker – like father, like son, after all.

'Oh, I'm sure that was his motive. It's just that if he doesn't admit to why he did this, he won't get the right treatment and support in prison. He needs to face up to how he feels and what he's thinking, and talk to trained specialists. I think that's highly unlikely, though.'

'In which case . . .'

'He will leave prison still obsessed with Emma. And there's every likelihood that he will come looking for her.'

Just the thought of him being free again was frightening.

'What I still can't quite understand,' Adrian Spencer continued, 'is why now? After, what, four years? Why did Peter Myers reappear now?'

'I don't know.'

Adrian Spencer looked incredulous. 'You must have a theory. You must have talked about it between yourselves.'

'We have discussed it. But we don't have any answers,' Lizzy said, hoping that he couldn't see through the lie.

'Well, I have a theory.'

'Go on . . .'

'Something triggered it, I don't know what. Maybe a chance sighting of Emma, maybe he'd read about her in the newspaper – she'd just accepted that film role, so it's possible that he'd seen a story about it.' He shrugged. 'It's just a theory.'

Lizzy was impressed by Adrian Spencer's thought process. Without knowing the truth about Stephen's death, it was an understandable route for him to go down.

'Is all this going to be in the programme?'

'I don't know. As I said, I'm not part of that any more. It's just my theory, and I fed that back – before I was sacked. So they might choose to follow that idea, or they might focus on the others.'

'Others?' Lizzy looked up, alarmed. Did they know about Stuart and Will after all?

'Other theories.'

Lizzy fought to hide her true feelings. 'Like what?'

'There are other theories.'

'But you're not going to tell me?'

'You'll have to wait for the programme,' he said. 'But I'm just telling you what I think the explanation is, and what the implications of that are for you and your friends.'

'But you haven't offered any solutions.' Lizzy looked at him, eyes wide.

'Because I don't have any.'

'So why even tell me this? Are you just trying to scare us? To take revenge for us getting you sacked?'

'You really don't think much of me, do you?'

'I'm just going from past form.'

He laughed. 'Lizzy, have you ever considered that you might not be as good a judge of character as you think you are?'

'What's that supposed to mean?'

He stood up to leave, picking up his gloves. 'I mean, be careful who you trust.'

Trust. That word again. *Who do you trust, Lizzy?* The message in the note. She blocked his path with her arm. 'The man sending the letters, is that *you?*'

He looked genuinely confused. 'I have no idea what you mean. Now, please, I need to leave.'

'If it is you—'

'Remember what I said, Lizzy. You're at risk of missing the real danger. Now, please, I have to go.'

Reluctantly she conceded, and watched as he walked away through the rain.

As Adrian Spencer's words resonated in her mind, she pulled the envelope that the capped individual had hand-delivered out of her bag.

You're at risk of missing the real danger.

She thought about the contents of the packet.

Was the real danger much closer to home?

Just considering that possibility was the most terrifying thought of all.

5

David Sherborn looked at his watch again. It was mid-afternoon, half an hour after the scheduled arrival time of a mother and baby group at his studios. He'd tried to call the girl who had coordinated the group for the photography session, but there had been no reply.

'You okay?' His wife, Helen, stuck her head around the door that separated the purpose-built studio annex from the rest of the house.

He glanced at his watch again. 'They're probably not going to turn up.'

'Maybe they're running late?'

He shook his head. 'One person being late I can imagine, but a group of seven mothers and babies? At least one or two of them would have been here by now.'

She nodded her agreement. 'Sorry. What a pain – it's so annoying when people just let you down like that. Are you still okay if I pop out to the shops for a bit? You don't fancy coming along?'

'I'd better wait here.'

'I'll be back soon,' Helen said. 'See you in a bit.'

Just after Helen had left, David tried to call the woman again. This time she answered.

'Hi, is that Angie? It's David Sherborn here, from Sherborn Photography. You've got a session booked for this afternoon, and I was just . . . right, okay, yes, I understand . . . Well, maybe you'd like to rearrange? . . . Okay, I'll wait to hear from you.' He ended the call.

She'd apologised profusely, saying that her son had been unwell for the past few days, and although she'd called the rest of the group to say they shouldn't go ahead, she'd forgotten to cancel the appointment with him.

This kind of thing had happened before – it was an inevitable consequence of his policy not to charge any money up-front for his studio-based photography sessions. But it was particularly annoying on a Saturday – his busiest day by far, where a wasted appointment slot cost him hundreds of pounds.

At least he could make good use of the time, now he knew for certain that they weren't going to show up. He decided to do some housekeeping.

He powered up his computer, a top-of-the-range Apple Mac with a 17-inch screen. The machine was expensive, but cost-effective – it was amazing for taking clients through their images. Parents especially drooled at the sight of their children on the big screen, in stunning high resolution. The photographs sold themselves.

He decided to catalogue some images from the previous week, and then back-up some older images from the computer onto a portable hard drive. It was tedious work, but it had to be done. To lose any of the images would have been a disaster, both financially and from a professional point of view.

Pausing after half an hour to make a coffee, he yawned his way through to the kitchen. When he returned to the machine with his cappuccino, another digital folder of photos on the screen caught his eye. It was the photographs he had taken for Emma and Lizzy, which had revealed the identity of the man who had been following them.

He opened up a slide show and sat back as the images faded in and out, one after another. It was the first time he had gone back to them since his meeting with Emma and Lizzy, around eight weeks ago, and he didn't know now what was drawing him to look at them again. Maybe it was because he was proud of what he had done: the act had been reparation for his earlier behaviour, when, at the behest of a client, Guy Roberts, he had not only invaded the privacy of Emma and her friends, but also frightened her by taking paparazzi-style photos that were later splashed across the newspapers. The photos – taking advantage of the distressing circumstances surrounding Dan Carlton's disappearance – had been an attempt by Guy Roberts to stir up publicity for his up-coming film, in which Emma had been cast.

David knew that own behaviour, motivated by the need for money following a downturn in his photography business, had been shameful. But the photographs he had in front of him now had sought to put things right.

He paused the slide show and focused on one of the images. It had been taken in Windsor, just outside the castle. Emma and Dan were to the left of the photograph, and there, lurking behind a group of tourists, was the man who had masqueraded as Stephen Myers. Image after image, there he was – close to Emma and Dan, but far enough away to stay out of their immediate sight – Scott Goulding, the actor hired by Sally Thompson to impersonate Emma's stalker. Sally blamed Emma (unfairly David thought) for the death of her fiancé, Stuart Harris. She had used Scott Goulding as a means of taking revenge on Emma. .

David shook his head in sympathy for her, clicking on a different folder to be able to see the photos of the man talking to Guy Roberts on his Notting Hill doorstep. Yes, he was very pleased with these. The images might not have been perfect, they might not have had the visual impact of his portrait shots, but they had been far more valuable and rewarding.

They had enabled Emma Holden to identify her tormentor, and take action.

He wondered how Emma was doing. Emma and Dan had actually invited him to the wedding in Cornwall – as a proper guest, not a photographer. Unfortunately, he'd had a prior booking, but it had been nice to be asked, and a huge surprise. It had proved that in their eyes, he had make good his earlier damage.

He was about to close down the image folder when a thought occurred to him – something that his subconscious had seen in the photographs suddenly rose to the surface. *Is my mind playing tricks on me?* He opened the image again of Emma and Dan outside the castle.

'Can it be . . .?'

He clicked through another half-dozen photographs, his nerves tightening with each confirmatory shot.

There was no doubt at all about what he was seeing.

6

'Feeling better this morning?' Dan was sitting up in bed as Emma came through from the bathroom, a fluffy white towel wrapped around her. Waking early from her shallow sleep on their final Sunday morning in Mauritius, she'd decided the best thing was to get up and have a shower.

'More positive,' she said, perching on the edge of the bed. Following the Friday night at the restaurant, they'd spent a lazy Saturday around the hotel, lounging by the pool and beach, after which they'd talked again about their anxieties, trying to put things into perspective. 'I feel like we can put everything behind us, at last.' She looked across at Dan, his hair ruffled in the way it always was in the morning, and smiled.

Dan moved across the bed towards her and placed a kiss gently on her cheek. 'That's great,' he said. 'Fantastic. We have to move on, Em, we really do. Otherwise, we might as well be the ones in jail, not Peter Myers.'

Emma nodded, wrapping another towel around her still damp hair. 'And I've decided, I'm definitely going to meet the counsellor. It can't do any harm.'

'As I said, you should do whatever you think is best. I'll support you.'

'And maybe if she's as good as Miranda says she is, you might be tempted to meet her, too.'

'Maybe,' Dan said, rising from the bed and stretching luxuriously as he peered out of the glass balcony doors. 'Just look at the view out there.' He padded over to the doors, and Emma wondered whether he would ever take up the offer of speaking to someone about what he had gone through. Maybe he didn't need that kind of support. But his evasive reaction every time Emma mentioned talking to someone, and his continued silence on what had happened, pointed towards the fact that Dan *was* still struggling to come to terms with being imprisoned by Peter Myers.

'I'm really going to miss that view,' Emma said, as she joined him at the doors.

The sky was a flawless blue, and the sea sparkled like thousands of diamonds.

Dan slid the doors open, allowing cool air to drift in. 'Me, too. And it feels nice and fresh out there – perfect weather for a swim and walk on the beach. We should make the most of the morning, before we have to say goodbye to all this.'

'You're right.' Emma hurried to get dressed. The minibus was due to pick them up at one o'clock, delivering them to the airport in good time for their 4.30 p.m. flight back to Heathrow. Twelve hours later, they would land in a much colder and, probably, wetter England, with only the memories of this magical island remaining.

***

They headed down for their final champagne breakfast, which they enjoyed on the open-air decked area that overlooked the beach, then spent the rest of the morning walking along the golden sand, swimming in the warm sea, and making use of the all-inclusive bar – sticking to non-alcoholic drinks in view of their up-coming flight.

Emma sat up from the sun lounger as Dan handed her a glass of Mauritius Sunshine Surprise, a particular favourite of hers – a blend of orange and mango, and a number of other tropical fruits, served in a tall, frosted glass. 'Here you go.'

She took a cooling sip as she looked at the ocean. 'I'm really going to miss this.'

'What, the view or the drink?'

'Both.'

'Here,' Dan said, handing Emma a piece of paper. 'Something that might ease the pain of leaving. A little bit of Mauritius that we can take back to London with us.'

'They agreed to give you it!' Emma read down the ingredients list and instructions for making the cocktail.

Dan smiled. 'I managed to persuade the barman.'

'But how?'

The cocktail was advertised as a hotel secret special, and the barman, who was otherwise the friendliest, most helpful man you

39

could ever hope to meet, had, two days ago, refused to reveal exactly how it was made.

'Well, yesterday I tried asking again, nicely. Then I tried begging. And just then I made a deal.'

Emma pulled up her sunglasses to look Dan in the eye. 'A deal?'

'I swapped the recipe for something.'

'What?'

Dan hesitated. 'One of my Manchester United shirts.'

'You didn't—!'

'Afraid so. It was an old one, from a couple of seasons back. It doesn't matter.'

'The shirt they wore in the European Cup final?'

Dan looked caught out. 'Er, yes. I was hoping you might not remember that fact.'

'But that's one of your favourite things,' Emma said, her heart filling at what Dan had just done for her. 'You swapped that for the cocktail recipe?'

'It's just a shirt.' Dan laughed it off. 'It's no big deal.'

Just then Emma spotted the shirt. The barman was already wearing it, along with the broadest smile she had ever seen.

'Hey, look, I've made two people very happy,' Dan said, also noticing as the barman showed off the shirt to a customer. 'He's a huge United fan – said he's been supporting them for twenty-five years, and he watches all the games he can get to see on the TV here. His dream is to go to Old Trafford.'

Emma continued to watch, as the barman simulated scoring a headed goal. 'I can't believe you did it.'

Dan shrugged. 'I wanted to. Now you can make your drink at home – a little bit of Mauritian sunshine in soggy, grey London.'

Emma kissed Dan. 'You're a big softy, Dan Carlton. Thank you.'

'Anything for you, Em.'

***

The day passed quickly and, before they knew it, they were saying goodbye to the hotel and clambering aboard the minibus, which was already busy with fellow departing holidaymakers. The journey to the airport took less than an hour, and within no time they had checked in and found a couple of seats in the airport's waiting area. But it was only when they climbed the steps to the aeroplane and entered the cabin that reality hit Emma. This was the end of the honeymoon, and they were, indeed, returning to reality.

She watched from the window as they prepared for take-off. Dan cupped his hand over hers as the plane taxied away from the terminal, heading for the top of the main runway. He knew that she wasn't fond of taking off.

For Emma, it was definitely the worst part of any flight. *Maybe it's a family trait*, she thought, *given Will's similar, but worse, fear of flying.* The plane came to a halt for a minute or so, and she shifted uncomfortably in her seat.

I'm still your number one fan.

This thought was unexpected and unwelcome. Emma glanced across at Dan, who smiled reassuringly.

The noise level rose as the engines sped up and, seconds later, propelled the plane forward at unnerving speed.

I can't wait to see you again, Emma.

Emma gripped the arm rests of her seat as the plane rose into the sky, angling into the blue, leaving the ground far behind. She closed her eyes as the plane banked a hard right, gaining altitude as it turned.

I'm so glad you're coming back to me.

Emma tried to shut out the thoughts.

She would arrange the counselling appointment for that week, if at all possible.

***

Lizzy spent most of Sunday in her apartment, worrying about how she was going to tell Emma about what had happened while she and Dan were away. It was a conundrum. Was it fair to relay bad news just as she returned from her amazing honeymoon, and the start of her new life? She considered not telling Emma about the person who had been sending letters, and what he had left, but she knew she had to. What if she kept quiet and then something happened? She would never forgive herself. No, she had to tell her. The question was,

41

when? Ideally, she wanted to give Emma some time to settle back in – maybe a few days of ignorant bliss, before she burst her bubble.

She picked up the photograph again. 'There must be another explanation,' she murmured to herself. Except that she hadn't been able to think of anything.

She glanced at her watch. Emma and Dan would have taken off by now.

What if I just get rid of the photograph?

There was no doubt that the image, if it was how it looked, had the potential to jeopardise Emma and Dan's relationship.

Maybe it's better to talk to Dan first.

But that could be an even higher-risk strategy.

As much as she hated to think it, if the photograph showed what it purported to show, challenging Dan could be downright dangerous.

7

'Lizzy, great to see you!'

Emma and Lizzy hugged in the doorway to Emma's flat. Lizzy's smile masked her concerns about what she was about to do. After more consideration, she had decided that the best course of action was to tell Emma about everything as soon as practically possible, and take things from there. Anything else – leaving things to fester, or approaching Dan first – was just asking for more trouble.

'Recovered from the jet lag?' Lizzy asked, as she followed Emma inside.

'Pretty much, although I still don't feel one hundred per cent. I went for a run before breakfast, and my legs felt so heavy.'

Lizzy had given Emma and Dan the Monday to recover from the flight, calling first thing on Tuesday morning.

'How about Dan, was he okay for work?'

Lizzy knew that Dan was already back at work, which had given her the perfect opportunity to discuss this most sensitive of issues in privacy.

'Yeah, fine,' Emma replied, filling the kettle. 'I think he was quite looking forward to getting stuck back into things, to be honest.'

Lizzy took a seat at the table. She watched her friend preparing the tea, wishing that she wouldn't have to do this. She looked happier than she'd seen her in a long time. 'You look really good, Em.'

'Thanks. I feel good.' Emma smiled at her.

'So the honeymoon was fantastic, I assume?'

'Amazing. The best holiday ever. Lizzy, everything about it, was just, well, perfect! The hotel, the island, all the things we did—'

'I don't need to know about that,' Lizzy joked.

Emma grinned. 'You know what I mean. It was just paradise, Lizzy.'

'Sounds it. So you're not glad to be back, then?'

'In some ways, no. It's good to come back home, don't get me wrong, but we were just so carefree out there, as if nothing else mattered but just us – no external factors could affect our happiness. It was all under our control. But I guess real life isn't like that really, is it?' She handed Lizzy a cup of tea.

'No, it isn't.' Emma didn't know the half of it. 'So, you and Dan, you're still getting along well?' Lizzy hoped the question sounded light, rather than serious.

Emma looked at her. 'Of course!'

'That's great, glad to hear it.' Maybe she wouldn't tell her now. Maybe she just couldn't bear to do it at this point. To give her bad news so soon, it was just cruel, wasn't it?

But then she glanced at the table top, and saw a familiar-looking grey envelope on top of the small pile of letters there.

'Are you okay, Lizzy?'

'What? Er, yes,' Lizzy replied, caught staring dead-eyed at the letter. It was definitely the same handwriting as before. 'Your post,' she said. 'You've not opened it yet.'

Emma reached for the pile. 'No. I was just about to when you arrived.' She looked at the front and back of the offending letter, obviously intrigued as to what it was, and started to slide her finger under the seal.

'Don't!' Lizzy said, holding out a hand.

Her reaction shocked Emma into stopping what she was doing and staring at her friend.

Lizzy calmed her voice. 'Don't open it, please, don't open it yet. Not until I've had a chance to explain.'

'I don't understand. You know what it is?' Emma held the letter out towards Lizzy, as if asking for advice as to what to do.

Lizzy swallowed her fears. 'I know who sent it. Whatever's in there, it won't be good.'

Emma watched Lizzy's face, then realised what it all meant. She shook her head in disbelief and horror. 'Please, Lizzy, don't say that this isn't over . . .'

'I'm sorry, Emma, I'm so sorry.'

Emma's face was white. 'No, it's finished . . . we had the happy ending – the wedding, the honeymoon . . .'

Lizzy didn't know what to say. She felt sick. 'I know, I know.'

Emma was now holding the letter with a look of revulsion on her face. 'How do you know who sent this?'

'I don't know the identity of the person, but I recognise the handwriting – there have been other letters.'

Emma's eyes widened. 'More? To here?'

'While you were away. But addressed to me.'

'Why didn't you tell me?' Emma stared at Lizzy. 'And you don't know who they're from?'

'No,' Lizzy said. 'But I saw the person. They were wearing a cap. I interrupted them on Friday morning, hand-delivering one of the letters. They'd been downstairs at the post trays. I didn't see their face. I chased after them, but the person was too fast.'

Emma was shaking her head. 'My God. What did the letters say?'

Lizzy's heart was breaking as she watched her friend descend once again into the nightmare. A few sentences was all it had taken to destroy the happiness that had been flourishing in the newly married Emma Carlton.

'Not very much. Short messages, about trust.'

'Trust?'

'Warning me, asking me who I trusted.'

Emma was still struggling to take this in. 'And they were addressed to you, but delivered here?'

Lizzy nodded. 'Whoever it is, they knew that you were away, and they also knew that I would be coming over to your flat.'

Emma put a hand to her forehead. 'I can't believe that this is happening. I thought it was all over, I really did.'

'I know. Me, too.'

Emma looked up. 'Who do you think it is? It couldn't be Scott Goulding again, could it?' She shuddered as she remembered again how the actor who had impersonated Stephen Myers had stalked them as he had been convinced by Sally Thompson that he was auditioning for a part in the Emma Holden docudrama. But it was all just part of Sally's quest for revenge on Emma for the death of Stuart Harris.

'I'm not sure where the motive would be. Last time it was clear – he was tricked into doing what he did because of what Amy – I mean, Sally – told him. He was just playing a part, and it was for a specific purpose.'

'I agree. It wouldn't make sure. Unless this time he's being paid to do it. We know he was having trouble finding work.'

45

'Possibly. Although I wasn't sure the build of the person I chased matched him, but it was hard to tell, because things happened so fast.'

'And he did seem genuinely sorry for what he had done,' Emma said, now more convinced that Scott wasn't a likely candidate. After David Sherborn's photographs had identified him, which had led them first to Guy Roberts and then to Scott himself, he had confessed to what he had done and why, and had appeared to be extremely remorseful. And in fact, he had been the one to alert them to Sally's plans for the parachute jump.

'Say Scott Goulding isn't involved. Do you think this still might be Sally?' Lizzy asked. 'Maybe working with someone else?'

Emma still held on to the letter. 'She has the motive. But again, the police said that she's very remorseful over what she did.'

'Maybe she just said that, so the police didn't press charges.'

'You think?'

Lizzy shrugged. 'Well, she must have been in a terrible place to plan to do what she did. She was prepared to murder Will, for heaven's sake!' Lizzy shook her head. 'And she was a split-second decision away from carrying it out. Plus, it's been only a matter of weeks since what happened. Do you really think that she could be so much better in such a short space of time? Do you think all those feelings will have just gone away? Maybe they have, maybe they haven't.'

Emma thought about it. 'She's the prime suspect, isn't she?'

'I think so,' Lizzy said. 'What's the alternative? That there's yet another person who has taken against us? How many of these people are there?'

'Don't . . .' Emma said.

'Exactly,' Lizzy replied. 'It's just too horrid to consider. But it's also unrealistic, surely, to think that this is not connected to what's gone before. And then there was the fact that the person in the cap was so fast – much faster than me. We know that Sally is a sports teacher, so she's fit, sporty.'

'You've been thinking about this a lot,' Emma said.

Lizzy nodded. 'To be honest, this past couple of weeks, I haven't thought about much else. I've racked my brain about who could be doing this, and why.'

'Oh, Lizzy, I'm so sorry.'

'Why are you sorry? You've got no need to be sorry about anything.'

'I *am* sorry. While we were away, having such a fantastic time, you were here, dealing with all of this. And, ultimately, it's all about me, isn't it? If it wasn't for me, none of this would be happening.'

'Don't you dare start blaming yourself for anything,' Lizzy retorted. 'You've got *nothing* to feel guilty about. Nothing.'

'Thanks. But I am sorry you were having to deal with this on your own. Doesn't Will know?'

'I didn't tell him.'

'Because you thought he might tell me?'

'Yes.'

Emma shook her head, numbly. 'Lizzy, you shouldn't have tried to deal with this all by yourself. I know you're strong, but—'

'I agree,' Lizzy interrupted. 'I probably should have told Will. But I just didn't want to risk you finding out, because I really didn't want this person to ruin your honeymoon.'

Lizzy watched as Emma continued to shake her head in disbelief at what was happening. 'Are you okay, Em?'

'I'm okay. But I should call Dan.' She pulled out her mobile.

Lizzy interjected. 'Not just yet,' she said. 'There's something else I need to show you.' She steeled herself. 'I don't know what it means, but it's been really bothering me. Maybe you can explain it.'

She pulled out the photograph that had provoked so much anxiety in her.

Emma took it, gripping it harder when she realised what it showed. She looked up. 'Where did you get this?' Her voice was frayed.

'It came with the last note.'

Emma looked again at the image. It was a photograph of Dan. She could tell it came from the time just before they met, because of his hairstyle and what he was wearing. He was standing, beaming at the camera, a busy bar as a backdrop, a pint of lager in one hand. His other arm was wrapped around another man, who was also smiling broadly and holding a drink.

It was Emma's ex-fiancé, Stuart Harris.

8

Carl Jones came from behind, landing the first ferocious blow into the side of Peter Myers' abdomen. Myers folded and crumbled against the washbasin, pain rippling through him. Jones yanked his hair and slammed his head into the basin. Now on the cold, wet tiled floor of the washroom, another blow came – this time a stamp down hard onto the top of his right leg. Myers gazed up at his attacker, their eyes meeting for a brief moment. Jones was enjoying this. Myers nodded and the assault continued. Two other prisoners had created a diversion downstairs, feigning an escalating argument in the common room, so there were no guards to witness this.

As another kick connected with the side of his body and his vision starred, Peter Myers realised he couldn't feel a thing.

He just knew one truth – his plan was working.

9

'I don't understand this,' Emma said, still staring intently at the photograph. 'I can't understand what I'm seeing here.' She looked up at Lizzy. 'Dan knew Stuart before he met me—?' She looked stunned. 'Why wouldn't he have told me that?'

'Is the photo definitely from before you met? Could it be more recent?'

'No,' said Emma. 'It's definitely before we met.' She pointed at the image. 'His longer hairstyle. He'd had it cut shorter the week before we met, and the style hasn't changed much since. I can't believe this.'

Emma had met Dan at their local pub in Islington, just around the corner from where Lizzy and Emma were then sharing a flat. Dan had been there with a group of workmates, and one of them had approached Emma when she was at the bar, asking whether Lizzy and she wanted to join them for a drink. Following this, Emma had got chatting with Dan, and the two of them had hit it off: they'd been an item from that night onwards. It was only later that Dan had admitted his friend had done it as a favour for him, after he'd remarked how attractive Emma was. He hadn't had the courage to approach her himself, so his more confident friend, a marketing manager called Mike, had helped out.

'I don't know what to say,' Lizzy said now. 'I didn't know how I was going to tell you. I've been worried sick about what to do.'

Emma looked again at the image. 'What am *I* going to do?'

'I really don't know.'

Emma thought some more. 'You said the photograph came with a note. What did the note say?'

Lizzy got it out of her pocket and passed it across to her.

Emma read it out loud. '"Now who can you trust?"' Again, she turned to her best friend. 'Is this like the other messages?'

Lizzy had the others in her bag. She got them out and placed them on the table.

Emma inspected each one in turn. 'Always this thing about trust.' Then something seemed to strike a cord. She picked up the photograph again. 'You didn't want Dan here when you showed me this, did you? That's why you waited until now, until you knew Dan was at work.'

Lizzy flushed red. 'I decided it was best to tell you on your own first.'

'Why? Because you think this is about Dan?' It was hard not to make the sentence sound anything other than an accusation.

'I don't know, Emma, I just thought it was for the best. It would give you time to think things through, before talking to Dan about it.'

That made sense. 'I'm sorry, Lizzy, I didn't mean to get angry.' In fact, Emma realised, she had been directing the accusation at herself as much as her friend. She was challenging her own reaction; that this photo had terrible implications for her relationship with the man whom she loved and trusted. 'What does this mean, Lizzy?'

'Well, it means that Dan knew Stuart, and that he kept that fact secret from you.'

'But why would he do that?'

'Maybe he thought that if he told you he knew your ex-boyfriend, it would jeopardise your relationship.'

'Maybe.' It was a good hypothesis. In truth, during the early stages of their relationship, such a revelation would have certainly made Emma think twice. Her break-up with Stuart had been painful, even after several years, so the thought that there was this link could have made things feel very uncomfortable. And then, later, maybe Dan had decided that to say anything after years of silence would have just seemed too weird, and would have opened up old wounds and threatened their happiness. Then she had another thought. 'Or maybe there's another explanation.'

'Go on.'

'Maybe this photograph isn't real.'

Lizzy looked interested. 'Someone faked the photo, to make it look like Dan knew Stuart?'

Emma scrutinised the image. It certainly looked real, but she wasn't an expert. She just knew photographs could be manipulated in any way anyone could imagine these days. 'Surely it wouldn't be that difficult to add in Stuart, or Dan, to an existing image and create the impression that they were there together?'

'Sounds plausible,' Lizzy said.

'I mean, look at all these notes.' Emma fanned them out on the table in front of her. 'They all mention the word trust, but actually they're all about mistrust. Each note is designed to sow doubts in our minds about who we can trust. And this photograph is doing the same thing. Whoever sent this, whether it's a fake, or whether it's real, wants us, or me, to doubt Dan.'

'They want to try and wreck your relationship with Dan.'

'Exactly. Which feeds into the idea that Sally is doing this,' Emma continued. 'I destroyed her happiness with Stuart, as she sees it, so now she wants to do the same to me.'

Lizzy looked at her friend. 'So what do we do?'

'We let the police know what's been happening. And hopefully they can have a chat with Sally.'

'And what if it isn't Sally who's been doing all this?' Lizzy picked up a note. 'Do you think it could be Adrian Spencer?'

'Why would you think that?'

'Because he might have a motive. I met up with him the other day, and he told me he'd been sacked by Firework Films.'

'Because of our complaint?'

'I think so, yes.'

Emma sat back in her chair. 'But do you really think he'd do this?'

'I don't know, but it's just something he said to me. He said something very similar to what's in the notes, about trusting people. I asked him if he was the person sending the letters, but he denied it.'

Emma nodded, then asked, 'Why did you go to see him?'

Lizzy hesitated. 'I wanted to ask them not to go ahead with the docudrama.'

'But they wouldn't—'

'I know, they won't take any notice of us. I knew that really, before I even met him, but I just wanted to try.'

'And now he doesn't work for them any more.'

'Yes.'

'Did he seem hostile?' Emma spoke matter-of-factly.

'No, not really. He warned me about Peter Myers.'

'What do you mean?'

'Just like the police, he thinks Peter Myers is obsessed with you, and he said that when he's finally released from prison, unless he's admitted to how he feels and seeks help, that he'll . . . come after you.' She pulled an apologetic face at Emma.

'So he's trying to scare us?'

'He said no, but it seems like that.'

'So then it might be him doing this.'

'I don't think we can rule him out, but I think it's much more likely to be Sally.'

Emma glanced at her watch. 'I've arranged to meet Dan for lunch.' They had agreed a lunchtime meet-up at Perfetto, a lovely Italian café around the corner from Dan's office, to help sugar the pill of his first day back at work.

'Are you going to speak to him about this?'

'Yes.'

'Will you be okay about that?'

Emma nodded. 'I trust Dan. I'm not going to let this person ruin what we've got. Things are going to be okay. If the photo is real, I'm sure Dan will be able to explain it.'

'Well, I'll be on the other end of the phone, if you need me.'

'Thanks.'

'You haven't opened the letter,' Lizzy said.

Emma had forgotten about it. She opened it with a sense of trepidation. Inside was a single line, once again in the same Gothic font.

Ask Lizzy about her little secret.

She turned it around to face Lizzy.

'I don't know what that means, Em,' Lizzy protested. 'Honestly, I've got no idea what that's supposed to mean.'

'It's okay.'

'*What* secret?'

'Maybe it's referring to you not telling me about the photograph.'

'Maybe.'

'The person might just be wanting to make sure that you showed it to me. If I'd opened it earlier, then it would have prompted me to get in touch with you.'

'You're probably right,' Lizzy said, but she looked unnerved.

'Lizzy, don't worry. See, this person is trying to do it again – sow mistrust. But it's not going to work – I trust you, totally.'

Lizzy nodded. 'Thanks, Em, it means a lot.'

Emma's mobile rang. 'Hello? . . . Yes . . . Oh, hi . . . Okay, right . . . We'll buzz you in. Come right up.'

'Who's that?'

Emma looked perplexed. 'David Sherborn. The photographer. He's downstairs, and he wants to speak to me right now.'

***

Will was sitting at his desk at work, daydreaming about Sally. It had been three days since their meeting, and he hadn't been able to stop himself from thinking about her. He'd resisted the temptation to call, even though he still had her number on speed dial. It would probably be best to leave things for a few days more, to let things settle, give her time to think. He wondered whether, in time, they really would have a chance of making a go of things.

My God, am I delusional?

He could imagine Emma's reaction. And she would most likely be right. But, still, even though he knew pursuing a relationship with Sally – even a platonic one – was madness, there was an irresistible force driving him on.

He went back to tapping away on his keyboard, clearing out a few more emails as colleagues chatted in the background.

He remembered just a few weeks ago, when Sally – or Amy, as he knew her then – had called to ask about the parachute jump. It had filled him with a mixture of fear and elation.

But the plan had been to kill, not thrill.

And I want to be with this woman? I'm crazy.

Will played with a bitten-ended pencil, turning it over and over on the desktop, only checking himself when one of the senior managers ghosted past, afraid that he would pick up on his shocking lack of productivity.

'Will, you've got a visitor downstairs.' Will almost jumped as Collette, one of the PAs, appeared at his shoulder. 'I've told them you'll be right down.'

Will nodded, wondering whether he'd forgotten about an appointment. It wouldn't be surprising, given his wandering state of mind. 'Did they say who they were?'

'Sorry, I didn't catch it. You know what that intercom is like. I could only just make out that it was you they were here to see.'

'It's okay,' Will said, flicking to the right day in his diary. There was no appointment there.

He made his way downstairs, hoping that whoever this person was wouldn't spot his lack of preparedness. Turning the corner at the bottom of the stairs, he saw who it was.

His father, Edward, was waiting outside.

'Dad,' he said, opening the outer door. 'What are you doing here?'

Edward looked terrible, as if he'd been up all night. His slightly-too-young for him messy haircut drooped without its usual gel, and his trendy jeans were crumpled. 'I wanted to speak to you in person,' he said, 'without Miranda knowing. Now was the best opportunity.'

Will didn't like the sound of this. 'What's up? You don't look very good.'

Edward shook his head and whispered, 'I might need to find a lot of money, very quickly.'

Will looked at his father, startled. 'What? I thought things were okay again with your work.' He knew most of his father's clients had remained loyal, despite the police investigation into his possession and use of a firearm against Peter Myers. The dropping of the charges, on a technicality, had stemmed the small but still worrying outflow of clients.

'It's nothing to do with that, William. I'm being blackmailed.'

10

'Thanks for inviting me in.'

'That's okay,' Emma said, as David Sherborn entered the flat. She directed him into the living room.

He was holding a brown envelope, and it seemed eerily reminiscent of the day he had presented the photographic evidence that showed that Scott Goulding was following her.

Lizzy rose from the sofa to greet him, holding out her hand. 'Nice to see you again.'

He smiled. 'I just wish for once we could meet in happier circumstances.'

'Please, take a seat,' Emma said, her nerves growing taut. She waited for David to speak, but he seemed reluctant. It just made her all the more nervous. 'So, what's this about?' she asked, finally.

In the short time that it had taken David Sherborn to climb the stairs, Emma and Lizzy had had little time to speculate on the nature of his unexpected visit. But they'd both agreed that it was probably only bad news that would bring him there.

'Okay,' he said, seeming nervous. 'Listen, I might be wrong about this; I might be being over-cautious, but I thought that it was worth running this past you. At the weekend, I was doing some tidying out of my image files on the computer, and I got to looking at the photographs I took for you, when you asked me to try and identify the stalker. It was then that I noticed something.' He took a breath. 'As I said, it might be nothing.' Emma and Lizzy watched in silence as he pulled out a set of images from the envelope. He handed one to each of them. 'I think that there might have been someone else following you.'

'What?' Emma looked at the photograph of Dan and herself, outside Windsor Castle. 'Who?'

'In that photograph the person is on the far right. Wearing a dark-coloured peaked cap.'

Emma and Lizzy looked at each other.

Lizzy looked at her photo. 'I can see them in this one!'

David nodded. 'The person is in another couple of photos. At first I didn't spot it at all, because they're not in most of the shots. But the ones in Windsor, and one at the train station, there they are, in the background.' He shrugged. 'But, as I said, I might be overreacting, it might be nothing.'

'You're not overreacting,' Lizzy said, looking up. 'This is the person, Em.'

David looked between them for an explanation.

'While Dan and I've been on honeymoon, someone has been sending Lizzy letters. And they posted one to me, which I got this morning.'

'One was hand-delivered here,' Lizzy continued. 'I chased after whoever it was – I saw them leaving the building. They were wearing a blue cap, just like the one in the photos here. And the build looks right.'

'So I was right to be suspicious,' David said.

'Have you got any better images than this?' Emma asked. 'Closer-up shots, so we can try and see who it is?'

'Sorry, no,' he replied. 'In all the shots I was focusing on Scott Goulding, because I'd identified him as following you. So any time this other person is in frame, it's just luck. Particularly as they're hanging back, as you can see in those two photos. Of all the four images, these are the best ones.'

Emma looked closely at the photograph. It was impossible to identify the person, or tell their sex.

Lizzy gave the photo back to David. 'So, at times, there were actually three people following Emma? Scott Goulding as Stephen Myers, Firework Films' Adrian Spencer and this person in the cap?'

'It sounds ridiculous but, yes, sometimes there were three people following.'

Lizzy raised an eyebrow. 'Do you think each of the three people was unaware of the others?'

He shrugged. 'Well, I didn't see Scott Goulding or Adrian Spencer interact with anyone else whilst I was there. I certainly didn't see them talk to the person in the cap.'

'It *was* busy,' Emma said. 'I can imagine how they might not have seen one another.'

'Yes,' David said. 'It's not as if they were following you down quiet roads. Each of the three people could mingle with the crowds, blend in to some extent. And if you think that Adrian Spencer was only following for a shorter period of time, while the person in the cap was hanging back more – I think it's possible that they just didn't see one another.'

'There were actually four people following us,' Emma said.

Lizzy looked across at her. 'Four?'

'David,' Emma explained, gesturing at him.

'Yes, that's right,' he said, the thought obviously not having occurred to him. 'But what are you getting at?'

'Well, the three others didn't see you, so it's very possible that they didn't see one another either.'

He nodded. 'Good point.'

'There's another possibility,' Lizzy said. 'They might have been working together. Maybe not all three, but two of them could have been working as a pair.'

'You're thinking of Sally?' Emma said.

'Yes. We already know that she was telling Scott Goulding what to do, directing him. We thought it was just from a distance, but maybe sometimes she was closer to the action.'

'You could be right. And even if it isn't Sally,' Emma said, 'it still might mean that either Adrian Spencer or Scott Goulding knows who the person in the cap is.'

Lizzy nodded. 'You're right.'

Emma looked at David. 'What do you think?'

He was caught by surprise, lost in thought. 'I . . . I don't know, to be honest. It's possible that these people might have been working together. But I think it's equally possible that they weren't.'

'So what do you think we should do?' Emma said, a little desperately.

David Sherborn almost laughed. 'You're asking me? I'm just a photographer. I haven't got a clue with this sort of thing. Photographs, I'm your man, but anything else . . .'

He was right. He was a photographer, not a private investigator or law enforcement. It wasn't fair to expect him to be able to offer any solutions.

'I'm sorry I can't be of more help,' he said. 'I really am. You don't deserve all this, Emma. I wish I could do something.'

'Maybe you can,' Lizzy said. 'Em, why don't you show him the photo that came this morning? He might be able to tell whether it's real or not.'

Emma hesitated. She looked across at Lizzy, who nodded at her to go ahead.

Emma didn't feel completely comfortable sharing the image with David Sherborn before speaking to Dan about it, but it was an opportunity to gain some professional insight. She pushed away her reluctance and passed across the photograph. 'I received it in the post. We think it was sent by the person in the cap.'

David Sherborn inspected it. 'This is your husband, with . . .'

'My ex-boyfriend, Stuart Harris.'

'And what am I looking for?'

'Do you think it's real or could it be fake?' Lizzy said.

'Fake in what way?'

'Could it be more than one photo, combined, to make it look as though Dan and Stuart are together?'

He looked closer. 'It's impossible to say, with a hard-copy image. If I had a digital file I'd be able to examine it using some specialist software, and then I could say for sure. You can do that pretty easily now. But with a hard copy like this, well, there's an element of guesswork.'

'So, what's your best guess?' Lizzy asked. 'Is it real or not?'

Emma watched as David Sherborn looked at it some more. She almost didn't want to hear the answer.

Finally, he looked up. 'My best guess is that the photo is a single image.'

Emma's stomach lurched. She concentrated fiercely on the carpet for a moment or two.

'What makes you think that?' Lizzy asked.

'Well, as I said, it's an educated guess. But if you look at the light, especially the way it reflects here,' he said, pointing at Dan and Stuart's faces, 'and off the two glasses, then for me, it seems that the light source is coming from the same place, which indicates that it isn't an overlay of two separate images.' He looked hopefully at Lizzy and Emma. 'Is that what you wanted to hear?'

Lizzy looked at Emma, who was still staring straight down at the floor. 'Not exactly, no.'

11

'Archie, you'd better come quickly. It's Peter Myers.'

Slightly irked at the interruption of his morning break, Archie Turner looked up reluctantly from his copy of the *Sun* newspaper, clasping his cup of stewed tea.

Stephanie Steward, one of the more junior guards stood, breathless, at the door. He didn't show his irritation, as he was fond of the girl. She was a good kid – too good for working in a place like this. For him, it was far too late, but not for someone so young. He'd told her as much, on more than one occasion. 'What's he done?'

'He's not done anything,' she said. 'Someone's done something to him.'

Now Archie stood up. 'Attacked?'

'Yes.'

'How bad?' he said, already moving towards the door.

She followed him out. 'Pretty bad. He's not moving much.'

'Christ,' he said. 'Where is he?'

'In the washroom.'

They hurried in that direction. 'Is there anyone with him?'

'Johnny.'

Another young prison guard. Another good kid. Archie climbed the staircase and approached the washroom. He prayed that this wasn't going to be as bad as it could be. He didn't like Peter Myers, hadn't taken to him from the first few minutes after meeting him – the guy had no respect, for one thing. But that didn't mean he wanted something like this to happen. Archie prided himself on the fact that events such as these were extremely rare under his watch.

By now, there was a group of guards outside the entrance to the washroom, preventing interested prisoners from seeing what was happening.

'Is he dead?' asked one of the prisoners, grinning.

Archie ignored the comment, and breezed past as the guards stood aside. 'Bloody hell.'

Peter Myers was on the floor in the recovery position, unmoving, his face battered. It looked as if someone had given him a serious kicking.

Johnny was kneeling beside him.

'Is he breathing?'

'Yes.'

Archie knelt down and placed a hand gently on Myers' side. He groaned softly. Blood was trickling from his nose, and his left eye was already blackening. 'Have you called an ambulance?'

'No, sorry,' Johnny replied.

'We wanted to see what you thought first,' Stephanie explained.

'Well, call one now,' Archie said. 'This guy's in a bad way. He needs proper medical attention.'

***

'Hi,' Dan said, as he took a seat in Perfetto that lunchtime. 'Well, this is a nice treat. Just what's needed for the first day back at work after such an amazing time. And it's Tuesday – a short week!'

Emma smiled automatically, thinking that this was how Lizzy must have felt just a few hours ago, back in the flat, wondering how to break bad news to a person who seemed so happy. She had put on a brave face since meeting Dan outside his office, and he didn't seem to have noticed that anything was wrong.

'I'll go and get some drinks. Orange juice? Mineral water?'

'Juice would be great.' Emma watched as Dan went to order. She slid a hand into her pocket, where she could feel the photograph that showed Dan with Stuart. Or that purported to show them together. Despite what David Sherborn had said, Emma wasn't totally convinced that the image was real. Or maybe she was just blinding herself to the truth?

Despite what she had said to Lizzy about there having to be a reasonable explanation for it, Emma felt extremely uneasy about the possibility that Dan had known Stuart Harris, and kept that fact from her.

'Here you go,' Dan said, returning with the drinks. He slid into the chair opposite hers. 'I need this. You know, I've been back in the office a matter of hours, and it feels like I've never been away.'

Emma decided to avoid the hard questions for the moment. 'How was the meeting?' Dan had had a 9.30 meeting with new clients who were looking to develop a dating website. It certainly wasn't the most original of ideas, and the market, already extremely crowded, had seen its fair share of failures over the past few years. Dan's job would be to design the site to make it stand out from the crowd, and give it every chance of not only surviving but prospering.

'It was more interesting than I thought it would be,' Dan replied. 'The guy I met, he's got some great ideas. He wants to target the university market – link students in a university to one another through shared interests, connecting to existing social networking sites like Facebook and Twitter. His idea is that it could facilitate finding the right people for one another in those first few weeks at university.'

'But don't people join societies and clubs for things like that?'

'Yes, I guess. But he thinks this could add value.'

'Add value.' That made Emma genuinely smile, and for a second she forgot about her problems and the difficult conversation to come.

'He also sees it as a way of connecting students across universities that are located within the same city – for example, university students in and around London or Leeds. Because they rarely ever mix.'

'I can see the value in that. But where's the money?'

'Paid-for link-ups with entertainment and leisure providers in the cities – pubs, clubs, cinemas, that sort of thing. They would come up as personalised suggestions – with discounts – for places to go, based on the likes of the members.'

'What are the timescales?' Emma realised she was grasping at straws – she was going to have to confront Dan with the photo. *But not yet. He's so excited* . . .

'Challenging. He wants it up and running before next September, and it will need extensive testing.'

Emma sipped her orange juice. 'So you'll have to hit the ground running.'

'You could say that.' He puffed out his cheeks and looked at her. 'What I wouldn't give to be back in Mauritius. Just you, me, the beach, the sea and the sunshine. No worries, no problems.' He grinned. 'But I guess unless you're a millionaire, that's not very realistic, is it?'

Emma's mask slipped as her face crumpled momentarily.

Dan leant forward, shocked. 'Em! What's wrong?'

She searched for the words. This was going to be so difficult.

'Em, what's happened?'

She wouldn't start with the photograph. Instead, she would tell him about what had happened with Lizzy and the person with the cap. It seemed easier. 'Lizzy came around this morning. While we were away, someone has been sending her sinister letters.'

Dan brought a hand up to his forehead and closed his eyes. 'Dear God, not again.' Emma just watched, not knowing what to say to make it better. Then he seemed to recover his composure. 'What did they say?'

'The messages were pretty cryptic. Things about trust.'

'Trust?'

'Yes, warning her about not trusting people.'

'What people?'

Emma shrugged. 'Her friends, I guess.'

'You mean us?'

'I think so, yes.'

Dan shook his head. 'It makes me so angry, that people won't just leave us alone,' he said, almost to himself. 'Does Lizzy have any idea who's doing this?'

'No, but she saw the person.'

'She saw their face?'

'No, it was hidden by a cap. She ran after them; they were in the entrance hall to our apartment building, hand-delivering a letter.'

Another angry shake of the head. Emma thought for a moment that Dan was going to thump the table, but he didn't.

'It's okay,' she said. 'It's okay to be angry about it.'

'I just feel so useless, Em,' he burst out. 'I don't know what to do to help. I don't know what to do, to make all this go away.'

Emma reached across the table and took his hand. Dan looked like he was on the verge of tears. 'Please, Dan, try not to be upset. We're all struggling to know what to do.'

Dan nodded and smiled ruefully. 'Looks like the honeymoon is well and truly over.'

Emma again felt the photograph in her pocket. She considered not asking Dan about it, but there would never be a good time. 'The person also sent Lizzy a photograph,' she said, her voice cracking with nerves.

She brought it out and passed it to Dan, afraid of where his action might lead.

He stared at the image, unspeaking.

Emma knew Dan so well, thought she could recognise every tic, every expression. But his reaction threw her: she couldn't tell what he was thinking, how he was reacting. For those few seconds, he even looked somehow different from the man with whom she had shared the past few years.

It reminded her of the time her mother had been pumped full of drugs during the latter stages of her cancer fight – the times when she just didn't look quite herself, as if an impressive but imperfect imposter had snuck in to take her place.

'Are you okay, Dan?'

'This isn't real,' he said, finally. 'Whoever sent this, they've faked it.'

It was the answer that Emma had longed to hear. 'So you never knew Stuart?'

'No.' He looked again at the image. 'No, I didn't know him.'

'The image looks so convincing,' Emma said. 'David Sherborn couldn't tell whether it was real or not.'

Dan's reaction was instant and shocking.

'You went to *him* about this?' His raised voice drew the attention of several customers, and the young server behind the counter.

'Let me explain. He—'

'I can't believe you went to him before speaking to me!' Dan continued. 'Don't you trust me at all?'

'I do trust you.'

'Really? Like when I was kidnapped and tied up by Peter Myers, and you thought I'd just had second thoughts about marrying you?' His voice dripped sarcasm.

Emma scrambled mentally for cover. 'That's not fair, Dan.'

'Isn't it?' He made to stand.

'Dan, please, don't go like this!' Emma looked at him, shocked. 'Let's talk about it.'

He shook his head, slapping the photograph onto the table as he stood up. 'You might need this, in case you want to get it analysed.'

Emma stood up to stop him as he turned away. 'Please, Dan, don't . . .'

He shrugged her off with surprising force. 'I need to get back to the office,' he said, bitterly.

Emma could only watch as he stormed out of the café.

***

Dan strode away from Perfetto and turned down the next side road. Stopping abruptly, he leant against the wall and pinched the bridge of his nose tightly. Kicking out, his heel connected with brickwork. It hurt. He pulled out his mobile. There was only one person who could help him at this moment.

It rang and rang. 'Come on, come on.'

At last they picked up.

'Hi, it's me . . . thank God, I thought you weren't going to answer . . . No, I'm not okay. I've just done something really, really stupid.'

PART TWO

12

Some years earlier

'Excuse me, can I have your autograph?

'Sure,' she said. 'No problem.'

'Thank you so much,' he gushed, as he handed Emma the pad and pen. He was so excited to be this close to her, within touching distance. He had waited outside the gates for two hours to get the chance to meet her. An hour ago, a heavy rain shower had drenched him, but he hadn't wanted to run for shelter in case he missed her. And now it had all been worth it. The wonderful Emma Holden was talking to him! 'I'm so grateful to you for doing this. I thought you might be too busy – I know you're busy – but it's great that you can take time for me.'

'It's no problem, honestly,' Emma replied, holding the pen ready to write.

The biro was about half its normal size; the plastic at the end was cracked and splintered. He hoped that she wouldn't mind the sticky tape that was wrapped around the top – he had a habit of biting pens, especially the plastic ones. Sometimes they would crack, leaving him to fish the plastic splinters out of his mouth. The teachers at school used to chastise him for it, but he didn't see the harm. It helped him when he felt upset; like when he had been bullied by his classmates.

'I'm your number one fan,' he said. 'I didn't watch the programme that much, but since you've been in it, I haven't missed an episode. If I'm out when it's on I record it. Sometimes I record it anyway, so I can watch it back as much as I want.' He watched her, waiting for Emma to write a message.

'What would you like me to—?'

'I think you're a fantastic actress.'

'Thanks.'

She was looking at the pad, so he ducked down to see her face. Maybe she was shy, like him. He loved shy girls the best. He hated those girls who knew how beautiful and talented they were, and expected everyone to love them. There were plenty of girls like that – girls at his school, and girls on the TV show – but Emma was different. 'I'm your number one fan,' he said again. He wanted her to understand that these weren't empty words. He meant them more than anything. He moved forward slightly, unable to resist getting just that bit closer to her. 'I know everything about you.'

'I hope not.' Did she sound a bit strange when she said that?

'Your favourite meal is lasagne, your favourite film of all time is *Dirty Dancing*. You're a black belt in karate. You started training at your school when you were eleven, because a girl started bullying you in your art class. It only took you five years for you to get your black belt. This year you're fighting in the British Championships in Birmingham, but you're finding it difficult to fit in the training now you're working on the show. You've always wanted to be an actress, and you'd love to work on a film, but you don't think you're ready yet.'

He could see that Emma was impressed. 'How do you know all this?'

'I read it,' he said. 'I always look for articles about you in the magazines. I never buy the magazines though – I read them in the newsagents. They let you go there and read magazines for as long as you like – you can stand there all day and it's all free. I like going there, especially when there are articles about you.'

'Oh, the magazine article. You read the interview in *Celebrity Goss*.'

He nodded and smiled. 'I like reading articles about you.' He visited the shop regularly, to scour all the magazines for articles about his favourite celebrities. He knew the days that each new edition came in stock – he had all the dates written in his notebook. He catalogued all the articles he found, listing them by magazine, date of publication, page number, and date he read them. He was already on his third notebook in just a year or so.

'What would you like me to write? Emma said.

'Whatever you like. My name's Stephen.'

'Okay, Stephen.'

He watched intently as she wrote down a short note on the blank page in his autograph book. He was so excited that she was holding his book, using his pen. She handed the book back to him, and he studied the message. '"To my number one fan, love from Emma."' He looked at her and smiled. It was such an amazing message. 'Thank you. You're not just beautiful – you're really kind. I think we're going to be really good friends. I knew we would, from the first moment I saw you.'

She seemed to like that. 'Thanks. Look, I'd better get going now. Nice to meet you.'

'Just a second,' he said, nearly forgetting in his excitement to take the photograph.

Emma put up a hand to block the shot. He'd read that she was camera shy, but she shouldn't be. There could never be enough photographs of Emma Holden.

'No, Stephen, please don't.'

He would prove to her how beautiful she was. 'It's okay, it's done now.'

'I have to go,' Emma said.

He watched her as she walked away, into the studios, longing to stay close to her. He waved, but she wasn't looking. She had a lot to concentrate on, he knew that. 'See you again soon!'

***

'Emma,' he said, as he saw her appear at the gates to the television studio building that afternoon. He'd been waiting for just under an hour, running through in his mind how she was going to react to his surprise. He smiled as she approached, but she just walked straight past him, as if she hadn't seen or heard him. 'Emma!' he shouted. 'What's the matter?' He raced up behind her, his camera bouncing on his chest. It hurt. 'I've got your photo.' He struggled to keep up with her. 'Here it is.' She didn't stop to look. 'I'm going to put it up on my bedroom wall.'

'Please, Stephen, I need to get home,' she said.

'Are you okay?' He had to start jogging to keep up. But he wasn't very fit, and he felt tired after the first few steps. 'Has someone upset you? Did *he* upset you?' She looked so worried, scared even. He felt so sad that someone was making her feel that way.

'I'm in a hurry,' she said.

'Going home to your boyfriend?'

Emma stopped. 'Look, Stephen. You seem like a nice guy, but it's getting dark and I've really got to get home..'

'To your boyfriend, to Darren.'

'Darren?' Emma had no idea why Stephen was referring to a character on the show.

'Yes, Darren . . . Darren Clarke.'

He was a nasty piece of work. Stephen didn't understand for one moment why someone as lovely as Emma would be with such a person. He was someone who couldn't be trusted; he lied, cheated and broke the law, but still she forgave him, because that was the kind of person she was.

'His real name is Stuart,' Emma said, 'and I don't live with him.'

'I think you can do better than him,' he said. 'You shouldn't be going out with a criminal – not someone like Darren. What do you see in him?'

'Please, Stephen, I have to go now.' She turned and began walking off.

He couldn't hold his feelings in any longer. Now was the time to let her know how much she meant to him. 'Emma, I love you!' She didn't turn around, but Stephen had no doubt that she would be thinking of those words very carefully as she made her way home. He smiled. Today had been a good day.

***

Stephen Myers unlocked the front door as quietly as he could and crept down the hallway. He could hear his mother cooking, could feel the heat from the steamy kitchen and smell the meal that was being prepared. It was Monday, so that meant burnt sausages and instant mashed potato. After that it would be an under-cooked sponge pudding and lumpy custard. He groaned at the thought.

'Stephen, is that you?'

She'd heard him. And he'd tried to be so quiet. He paused at the base of the stairs, waiting for her to say more. But she didn't. Taking his opportunity, he put his foot on the first tread, but was unable to stop the stairs from creaking.

'Stephen, is that you?'

He ignored the second call and tiptoed up the rest of the stairs, across the landing towards his bedroom. Pushing open the door, he surveyed the wall on the left, which was covered with photographs, and beamed.

So many lovely girls that he had met and spoken to. They seemed to look back at him and smile. There were times when he spent hours just looking at their beautiful, kind faces. It made him feel so happy, so alive.

His mother didn't like him looking at the photographs. She said it wasn't healthy, and that he should spend less time on his own, otherwise he might go mad. She said she wanted him to meet a nice girl, a girl who was a good match – the right girl for him. But she just didn't understand.

He pulled out his latest photograph which, in his opinion, was also the best of all. Emma was such a natural beauty. 'I do love you, Emma.' The other girls just didn't compare to her. He cradled the photograph in one hand. It captured her beauty perfectly. Her skin, her eyes, the way her hair framed her face . . .

'What are you doing, Stephen?'

Stephen tensed. *He's back already?* Now there would be trouble. He kept his eyes down. 'Hello, Dad.'

Peter Myers stood in the doorway. 'Look at me when I'm speaking to you.'

Stephen pulled his eyes up from the floor. His father's face was stern. It scared Stephen when he looked like that.

Peter Myers took a step forward. 'I said, what are you doing?'

'I'm . . . I'm just . . .'

'Did you not hear your mother calling you?'

Stephen again faced the ground. 'I did, but—'

'But you chose to ignore her, because you wanted to come up here and be in your own little world.' His father sighed, explosively. 'When are you going to stop being such a loser?'

'I'm sorry, Dad.'

'You think any of the girls on that wall like you?'

'I . . . maybe. I don't know.'

His father laughed. 'What have you got there?' He snatched the photograph out of his son's hand with sudden force.

'Please, Dad, be careful with it!'

'Get downstairs, now,' he ordered. 'Before I do something I might regret.'

'But, Dad, please don't dama—'

Peter Myers swiped his son hard across the side of the head.

Stephen cowered. The side of his face was stinging. But it could have been much worse. It had sometimes been much, much worse.

'Now look what you made me do,' Peter Myers said. 'Get downstairs, now.'

'Yes, Dad, I'm so sorry. I'm sorry I made you do that.'

'If you tell your mother about this, I won't be responsible for my actions,' his father warned. 'I'll be down in a few minutes.'

Peter Myers waited for his son to start descending the stairs before he looked again at the photograph. He nodded to himself. 'Well, Stephen, you've excelled yourself this time,' he said softly to himself. 'You've really excelled yourself with this little one.' He picked up the notebook – Stephen always put it in the top dressing-table drawer – and flicked to the most recent page, reading the message intently.

By the time he came downstairs, the dinner was cooling, but he didn't mind that at all. In fact, he didn't really notice.

His head was full of fantasies of the beautiful girl with the chocolate-brown hair.

13

Present day

'Hi,' Will said, greeting Sally with a slightly awkward smile as she approached him in the middle of the bustling concourse at Waterloo Station. At six o'clock on a Tuesday evening, it was filled with commuters.

He hugged her, but pulled back, suddenly feeling as though the embrace may not have been welcome. 'It's great you could come at such short notice.'

Sally smiled, her shoulder bag tucked down by her side, and brushed back a strand of hair. 'I came straight from work. So, what's this about, Will?'

'You'll find out in a few minutes.' He smiled, hiding the nerves that had kicked in as he'd waited for Sally to arrive. Part of him had wondered whether she would turn up. After all, he had only called her a few hours before, during what he knew would be her lunch hour, requesting that she meet him later, at Waterloo. He knew it was on her normal route home, and had hoped it might sway her decision to take him up on the offer. To his surprise, she'd accepted, without many questions.

'This is all very mysterious,' she said, searching Will's face for clues.

'Come on,' Will said, in reply. 'Follow me.'

They walked side by side out of the station, crossing the road and heading up towards the river. Night was drawing in, and the lights from the London Eye shone brightly as they turned towards the big wheel.

Will paused as they neared the structure, and Sally waited for an explanation. 'I loved that surprise trip you booked on this for me,' he said, peering up at the pods. 'So this evening, I'm repaying the gesture.'

75

'But why?' Sally asked, surprised.

It wasn't quite the reaction Will had been hoping for, but it could have been worse. And, to be honest, it was to be expected.

'Because I want to show you what you did for me, and I wanted to say thank you.'

She appeared confused. 'Okay.'

'C'mon,' he said. 'I'll explain more in a few minutes.'

***

'You're joking,' Sally said, looking first at the waiter in the open pod with the bottle of chilled champagne, and then at Will.

'I wanted to make it special,' he explained.

Sally hesitated. 'This is too much, Will. Remember what I said?'

Will held up his hands. 'I know it looks like a romantic set-up, but, honestly, that's not my intention. I just wanted to do something different, that's all. And I remembered what you said last time we went on it.'

She smiled. 'That I've always wanted to sip champagne at the top.'

'Exactly,' Will said. 'So, please, just accept it as a present from a friend.'

Quite uncharacteristically for Will, or least the old Will, he'd arranged the trip as a spur of the moment decision that afternoon. And it was looking as though it had been a good plan.

Sally looked back at the pod. 'I don't deserve this.'

'Rubbish,' he said. 'And we'd better get on board, before we miss out!'

She nodded and they entered the pod, to be greeted by the waiter, who handed them a glass of champagne each. He then exited, leaving the rest of the bottle in a chiller bucket on top of the table in the centre of the pod.

The doors closed and the pod began its ascent.

As they climbed higher, Sally and Will watched the illuminated city of London in silence from their private pod. Last time, on the trip booked by Sally to challenge Will's fear of heights, they had shared the space with a dozen or so tourists, young and old. Will had welcomed their presence, as it had calmed his nerves that there were others, including small children, wandering up and down the pod, unconcerned by the experience. But this time he was relishing the opportunity to be alone with Sally – and he no longer needed the support.

'I'll never get tired of looking at that view,' Sally said, peering off into the distance. 'Especially at night, with all the lights. It just seems so alive, so vibrant.'

'I love London, too,' Will said, cradling his champagne glass. 'Especially from this height. And, because of you, I can do this. I can be this high up, without panicking. I can book a trip on the London Eye without worry. Without your encouragement, I wouldn't have been able to do this. I might never have done this, and experienced this feeling.'

Sally looked away. 'You're underestimating yourself, Will. You would have done this eventually, without my help.'

'I don't think so,' Will said, taking a sip from his glass. The champagne was cool and refreshing. 'You see, I'd always been the same. I'd always set these boundaries, and barriers – things that I either thought I didn't want to do, or wasn't capable of doing. Even when I was really young, I used to be the same. I was always the one at school staying in the background, sticking to my comfort zone. But then you came along, and you changed everything.'

Sally put her head on one side. 'I think you're seeing me through rose-tinted spectacles.'

'Not at all. You've transformed the way I think about things, what I want to do, what I think I can achieve.'

'What, even now that you know the truth? I'm not the person you thought I was, Will. I'm Sally, not Amy.'

'Amy is Sally. Sally is Amy. It's just a name. The person is the same.'

She looked away again. 'Maybe.'

'I must admit, when I first found out the truth, I was devastated. I felt so hurt, and I was also grieving, in a way, for the person I thought I was in love with. She'd just gone. It was as if the whole thing had been a dream. But I couldn't stop thinking about you, and what you'd gone through. And I thought, well, maybe things weren't as bad as they looked. I decided that I had to see you, to speak to you, and let you know how I felt.'

Sally blushed. 'I don't know what to say.'

'Just say that you'll give us a chance. And I don't mean a relationship; I mean as friends.'

'But you said you love me.'

'I know, I know. Maybe I shouldn't have said that.' Will sighed. 'I didn't really intend to say it.'

'Friendship in those circumstances isn't easy.'

'Yes, I understand that. But it happens all the time, it must do. There must be thousands of people around the world in the same position.'

'Unrequited love?'

He seemed unhurt by that phrase. 'Yes, I guess. Where a man and a woman are good friends, but one loves the other, and would ideally want to take things further.'

Sally exhaled, thinking this through. 'I'm not ready for another relationship yet, even if I wanted to.' She sensed Will's disappointment. 'I'm not saying that I would never want to, but not yet, and maybe not for a long time. Are you sure you'd be able to handle that?'

'Yes,' Will replied. In truth, he desperately wanted to continue with the relationship that, even though it had been false, had made him so happy. 'I want to try and be friends.'

Sally thought about that briefly. 'There's still the issue of trust. Do you really trust me, Will?'

'Yes.'

'On what evidence? Why would you trust me, after what happened?'

'Because I just have a feeling.'

'And that's good enough?'

'It is for now, yes.'

Sally smiled, suddenly relieved. 'You don't know how much that means to me, Will. You might think that I've given you all these things but, believe me, I've gained so much from you, too. And to hear that you'll put your trust in me, well, it means the world. It's been so hard, since Stuart . . .' She stopped.

'You can talk to me, you know, about him. I don't mind.'

She seemed to close down a little. 'You don't want to hear about that.'

'I really don't mind,' Will said. 'I knew him well too, remember. There was a time when we were pretty close.'

'I know,' she said. 'And thanks. One day I will be ready to talk about it, but not just yet, okay?'

Will nodded. 'Of course.'

'It's just all so raw. I still don't really know what to think. Part of me hates him for what he did to me – acting on the feelings he still had for Emma, and then taking his own life – but I don't want to hate him, Will. I know he wouldn't have done that unless he wasn't in his right mind. He would never have wanted to hurt me.'

'I know.' Will placed a hand on her back.

'Thanks,' she said. 'That day, at the airfield - when I said you were a good man, Will, I meant it. It is great, to have you to talk to. I really enjoy your company.'

Will smiled. 'So, friendship it is?'

She nodded, and they clinked glasses.

'And about that parachute jump,' he added. 'I'm still on for it, if you are.'

***

Will was buzzing. He couldn't believe how well the night had gone.

Following the trip on the London Eye they had strolled along the Thames for a few minutes, before having a quick bite and drink in a nearby pub. Sally had then headed off home, and he was returning to his flat by bus.

Now, he wondered how he was going to tell Emma about what was going on. He hadn't seen her since she and Dan had returned from honeymoon, but that wasn't a good excuse. It might be uncomfortable, but he'd decided that he wasn't going to keep this a secret for any longer. No, if he and Sally had any chance of working, then there could be no deception. There had been enough of that to last a lifetime.

He pulled out his phone and considered calling her there and then, but then decided against it. He needed time to construct the right words, and he didn't want people listening.

He scanned the other bus passengers: people from all backgrounds, all living their own lives in their own worlds yet, for a few minutes, sharing this small space as they stopped and started through the streets of London. What highs and lows were his fellow travellers dealing with themselves, right then?

As he stepped off the bus, his thoughts turned back to what his father had told him earlier that day. Arranging the London Eye trip had been surprisingly effective as a diversion tactic, as he hadn't thought about blackmail at all during the evening – maybe that was why he had arranged the spur-of-the-moment event, to stop him from thinking about what might happen, and to grasp another piece of happiness, in case things all caved in? But now, alone again as he put the key up to his front-door lock, he couldn't ignore it any longer.

Was this really it? The thing that he had been dreading but hoping would never come? Was his secret about helping dispose of Stephen Myers' body finally going to be made public, for everyone to judge and condemn him?

But maybe it wasn't about him at all. Maybe it was something else entirely; something related to the father rather than the son. *After all, they targeted Dad, not me.*

He turned the key in the lock and pushed open the door. Waiting for him on the mat was an envelope. He bent down and picked it up.

And then he knew – it *was* all about him.

14

Emma waited by the window of the flat, looking down on the street below. Dan was usually home by now. And he wasn't answering his phone. She glanced again at her watch. About ten minutes or so later than normal. But that could be explained by a delay on the tube, or a last-minute job to do at the office. She wandered back into the kitchen and made sure that the evening meal – a stir fry and rice – wasn't spoiling, before returning to her vantage point.

Emma had spent the afternoon replaying the events of lunchtime in her head. Dan's reaction had shocked her, yes, but, when she thought about it, it had been understandable. From his point of view, it probably did look like she doubted him, or didn't fully trust him.

And at least she now knew for certain that he still felt hurt by what he saw as Emma's lack of trust in him when he was imprisoned by Peter Myers.

But, still, she had expected him to call. They very rarely argued, but when they did, they were quick to make things up. Dan especially always said that he never liked prolonging any disagreement. He had suffered from warring parents during childhood – their arguments could go on for hours, even days on occasions. The bitterness and recriminations had poisoned a large part of his home life, tainting what should have been a happy time. He'd promised himself never to follow down their path.

What if he isn't coming home?

She tried to dismiss the thought, but it was strong. In an attempt to rationalise it, she pulled out her phone and called Lizzy, keeping her eyes on the street below, scanning for signs of Dan's arrival.

'Hey, Lizzy, you okay to talk?'

'Sure,' Lizzy replied. 'You all right? How did things go with Dan?'

'Not good. I told him about the person leaving the notes, and then I showed him the photograph. He got really upset and walked off. I haven't heard from him all afternoon, and he's not back from work yet.'

'Oh, Em, I'm so sorry. I feel responsible.'

'Well, you're not. It's okay, I'm sure it will all be fine.' She thought she saw Dan for a moment, but when the person turned to cross the road she realised it was just someone with a similar build and hair colour.

'Did Dan say anything about the photograph?'

'He said it must be fake.'

'But David Sherborn said—'

'David said he couldn't be sure whether it was real or not,' Emma interrupted.

'Yes, but on balance, he thought—'

'I know, I know. But that's what Dan said, and I believe him. He got so upset and angry about it, thinking I was accusing him. Particularly when he heard that David Sherborn had taken a look at the photo. I thought he was going to thump the table.'

'It's really out of character, isn't it, for Dan to react like that?' Lizzy commented.

'I've never seen him like that,' Emma agreed.

There was a pause on the other end of the line. 'Em, please don't hate me for saying this, but maybe Dan reacted in that way, not because you accused him of something that wasn't true, but because he was confronted with the truth.'

'You can't mean that, Lizzy.'

'It's just that it reminds me of how my cousin was when we were little – whenever she was accused of something, if she hadn't done it, she'd just deny it. But if she was being confronted about something that she actually had done, she'd react in just the same way as Dan did. She'd blow her top, scream, shout, say all kinds of things, and then a while later would calm down and admit that she was guilty.'

'You're comparing a child to a grown man. It's not the same, is it?'

'She's still like that now, though.'

'But Dan isn't your cousin.'

'I'm not saying I think that's what's happened, but I just mean it's a possibility. I know David Sherborn said he couldn't tell for certain, but he did offer his professional opinion.'

Emma didn't know what to say. She could understand what Lizzy was saying, but to entertain the possibility that Dan had just lied to her wasn't pleasant. 'I trust Dan, Lizzy, I really do. If you can't trust the person you've just married, then what have you got left?'

'I know you trust him. And so do I. Dan is a great guy – kind, loyal, and I don't doubt that for a second. But sometimes even the people we trust the most keep things from us. There might be a very good reason – being afraid of what the other person might think, not wanting to upset the other person, a whole number of reasons. It doesn't mean that you can't trust people, because everyone has their secrets.'

Emma thought about that. *Everyone has their secrets.* To what secrets was Lizzy referring? 'But there are some secrets that you shouldn't keep from those closest to you.' Just then she saw Dan across the road. 'Dan's here, Lizzy. Thank God. I'll let you know how it goes.'

'Yes, good luck, Em. And I'm sorry, I don't mean to sow seeds of doubt. I'm just trying to look out for you.'

'I know, Lizzy, I know.'

***

Emma heard Dan's key in the lock as she stood by the door. She was nervous, but so grateful that her worst fears hadn't been realised, and that Dan had come home.

He seemed surprised to see her waiting on the other side. 'Em, hi.' He looked drained and sheepish. He placed his bag down on the floor and stood there, his arms down by his sides, hangdog. 'I'm so sorry, Em, for behaving the way I did earlier. And for not calling you this afternoon. I feel really bad about it all.'

'It's okay,' she said, moving forward for a kiss. 'Honestly, it's fine.'

He pulled back. 'No, it's not, Em. It's not okay.'

'What do you mean? It was just a misunderstanding – it's fine, forgotten. Look, I'm sorry I accused you. I do trust you, Dan, I really do. I believe you.'

He ran a hand through his hair, reaching for the right words.

The gesture made Emma's stomach lurch. 'What is it, Dan?'

83

'We'd better sit down,' he said.

They took a seat at the kitchen table. In the first few moments of silence, Emma felt the need to make small talk. 'The meal is ready. I just popped it in the oven to keep it warm.'

Dan didn't seem to be listening.

'Please, Dan, tell me what's wrong. It'll be okay.' She reached for his hand, and bit her lip when he pulled back from her.

'Will it?' he replied. 'You might not think so after you've heard what I've got to say.'

Emma nodded her understanding. 'The photograph is genuine,' she said. The earlier words of advice from Lizzy echoed. Her best friend's instincts had been right. 'You did know Stuart before you met me, didn't you?'

Dan nodded, reluctantly. 'It is me and Stuart together in that picture.'

***

Edward Holden ended the call and started to pace around his study, playing through various scenarios in his mind. He didn't know what the hell he was going to do, but one thing was for certain: he couldn't afford to pay the blackmailer.

He glanced over at the clock. Miranda would be wondering where he was.

She looked up from her chair as he entered the living room. 'Are you okay, Edward?' Miranda was blooming with pregnancy, her blonde hair gleaming in the soft lights of the room.

He nodded and sat down, taking a sip from the glass of whiskey that he had poured himself whilst taking the call upstairs. He had needed to calm his nerves.

'It's not work, is it?'

'Everything's fine,' he lied. 'Nothing's wrong, I'm just tired.' He reached across for the newspaper.

A minute's silence, and then: 'You would tell me if there was anything worrying you, Edward, wouldn't you? Remember, you promised. No more secrets.'

He hid behind the newspaper, pretending to read the business pages, when in fact he was indeed thinking of his predicament.

84

Miranda's last statement resonated, cutting through his thoughts. He *had* promised that there would be no more secrets. And he had meant it. He had meant it more than anything. But now, after just a few short weeks, he was again shutting her out from the darker parts of his world.

Miranda wanted a response. 'You promised, didn't you?'

He brought the newspaper down. 'Yes, I promised. And I meant it.'

'Then why do I feel that you're not telling me something?'

He couldn't tell her what was happening. He just couldn't. If he said anything, then it would bring Miranda into the conspiracy, and there was no way that he was going to let that happen. She didn't need to know about William's involvement with Stephen Myers. Especially not when she was seven and a half months pregnant. He thought quickly. 'Okay,' he said, 'there is something.'

'I knew it,' she replied. 'I knew there was something wrong. These past few days, you've just retreated back into yourself. You'd been so happy and relaxed since the charges were dropped but, suddenly, things just seemed wrong again.'

'I'm sorry,' he said. 'I should have told you. It's William. He's in danger of losing his job.'

'Oh, no, really?'

'There's a big restructuring going on, with lot of cuts, and he's been told he's one of those in the firing line.'

'That's terrible. How is he?'

'You know Will. He's not the strongest of individuals. He seems convinced he's going to be made redundant, and he doesn't feel very hopeful about getting another job.'

Edward watched Miranda as she took in the news, and felt genuine remorse for the lies. But this time he wasn't just doing it for himself: he wanted to protect her from the truth. And, in some ways, it was a half-truth: William probably *would* lose his job if this problem wasn't solved.

Miranda moved out of her chair and lowered herself down next to Edward. 'You shouldn't keep these things to yourself,' she said, nestling into his side. He rested a hand on her substantial bump, and felt a movement. 'The baby knows its daddy,' she said.

He felt a swell of emotion. 'I'll never let anything bad happen to either of you,' he said. 'I'll always be there.'

'I know you will.'

He brushed back some stray strands of hair and kissed her forehead. 'Just like I'll always be there for Emma and William.'

He had decided what he would do.

15

Even though Emma had tried to ready herself for the possibility that Dan had known Stuart before they had met, the admission was still a shock.

'I'm so sorry, Em, for lying to you.'

The smell of the meal from the oven was making her feel nauseous. 'But you're going to tell me the truth now, aren't you?'

'Yes, of course.'

'Then that's what matters.' She wasn't sure that she meant it, but it felt like the right thing to say. *Things might never be the same after this.* She desperately hoped not – she wanted to give them the best possible chance of getting through this, and that meant supporting Dan through his confession as much as she could manage.

Dan smiled, looking hopeful. 'I don't deserve you.'

Emma just waited for the explanation, hoping that it wasn't something that would test their relationship in the way that Dan had suggested.

'I met Stuart Harris through a mutual friend,' he said, finally. 'He started dating my housemate, Kelly. Do you remember her?'

Emma nodded. She did remember Kelly. She'd only met her a couple of times, as she'd moved out pretty soon after Emma and Dan had started dating. Kelly had worked in the City, in PR, for a major accountancy firm. She had seemed pretty quiet, and appeared to like to keep herself to herself, but she hadn't been unfriendly.

'They only went out for about six months,' Dan continued. 'I don't think she was ever that serious about him, but Stuart and I became quite good friends. Sometimes we'd go out without Kelly, just a few of the lads, for a pint or two. There was a nice pub just around the corner from where he was living. That's where that photo was taken. I remember it, because Stuart gave his camera to a Spanish girl I'd been chatting to during the evening to take the picture.'

Dan searched Emma's face for a reaction, but she just wanted to listen. She didn't want to say much, in case she said something that she might regret.

'It was only a few months later, just before he and Kelly split, that I realised Stuart had a drink problem. I'd noticed he was drinking more and more on our nights out, and then he seemed to be already drunk by the time we met up with him. One night I was out with just him, and he was on his tenth or eleventh pint. He was really out of it – couldn't stand up on his own. I had to carry him out of the pub and back home. That's when he told me about you.'

Emma hadn't wanted to hear that. She'd hoped that Dan knowing Stuart, and Dan meeting her, had been a coincidence – that Dan had met her not knowing of the link with Stuart.

But he *had* known.

Dan could sense Emma's discomfort, but she nodded as a cue for him to go on, and he continued. 'He told me about what had happened. About how Stephen Myers had stalked you, and how you'd come down from Manchester to London, to try and start a new life. He blamed Stephen Myers for breaking up your relationship. He admitted that he was relying more and more on drink to try and cope with it all. I hadn't realised until then just how low he was.'

'Did he tell you about what he'd done to Stephen Myers?'

'No, he didn't. I swear, he didn't tell me anything about Stephen Myers having died.'

Emma took in the revelations. It was a reshaping of history; everything that she had believed about the origins of their relationship had been false.

It had all been built on this secret.

'So the evening that we met in the pub, and your friend called me over, you already knew who I was.' Emma was finding it difficult to look at him. *He knew how much Stuart hurt me. And he's been keeping their connection secret, all this time . . .*

He nodded. 'Stuart talked about you quite a lot, particularly towards the end of his relationship with Kelly. I'd heard so much about you, so many good things, that I wanted to find out more. I must admit, I wasn't familiar with you before that – you know I don't watch a lot of TV – so I found out about you on the internet. And when I saw you walk into the bar, I recognised you straight away.

You were even more beautiful than in the photos. I made a comment to my friend, Mike, and, well, you know the rest.'

'Were you still in touch with Stuart when we met?' She dreaded his response to this question, and prayed for the desired answer.

'No. We'd lost contact a few weeks after he split with Kelly. That was some months before we met.'

'How many months?' Emma wasn't sure why this mattered, but it did.

'Oh, it must have been five, six months.'

'So not long, then.'

'No, I suppose not. We stayed friends for a time after the break-up. Kelly got fed up with his drinking – that's why she broke up with him – and so did I eventually, to be honest. It can be pretty draining to be around someone who drinks so much, and is so unhappy. I just couldn't be his friend any more. It was taking too much out of me.' He looked at her. 'I know it sounds selfish.'

'No, I can understand that; it wasn't being selfish. You did what you had to do. And you swear that you didn't see him or speak to him after we started dating.'

'I swear. I didn't see him, or speak to him.'

'But why didn't you tell me about the connection?' she said. She already knew the answer to this, or thought that she knew, but she wanted to hear it from him. 'Why didn't you tell me that you knew Stuart?'

He paused. 'I nearly told you, right at the beginning. Not when we first met, but on our third date . . . You remember we went to the theatre—'

'To see *Les Misérables*, yes.'

'Well, before that, at the restaurant, I planned to tell you. It had been bothering me that I was keeping it from you, and I decided it was best to just come out with it, but . . .'

Emma closed her eyes. Things were now making sense. 'That was the evening I told you about how much he'd hurt me, and how I'd tried to move on from it all.'

He nodded.

'And then that put you off saying anything.' She hadn't for one second intended to tell Dan all about her history, at least not so soon in their relationship, but she'd felt so comfortable with him that she hadn't been able to help herself. And it had come out so naturally. 'You thought that if you told me there was a connection between you and Stuart, I'd end the relationship.'

'You were saying how you and I seemed like such a fresh start, a real break from the past. I got scared that you'd end it if you knew the truth. I didn't want to risk losing you, because I knew from the start how much I felt for you.'

Emma wondered what she would have done if Dan had told her the truth on that third date. The honest answer was, she didn't know. But it would certainly have made her think twice about continuing with the relationship. At the very least, the relationship would have felt very different than it had otherwise done. 'I can understand why you didn't tell me.'

'I nearly told you a few times after that, but the longer it went on, the harder it seemed to get. I just felt that if I came out after months, years, saying this, it might wreck what we had – what we still have. Can you understand that?'

'Yes, I can.' Suddenly a thought occurred to her. 'Stuart must have known. After you were kidnapped by Peter Myers, and I met up with Stuart again, he must have known that it was you – that you were the Dan Carlton he'd been mates with.'

Stuart had appeared on the scene shortly after Dan had disappeared. It was then that Emma had discovered that Stuart had recommended her for the part in the film that she had landed at that time, as he knew its casting director, Guy Roberts. Stuart had also declared to Emma that he still loved her, and had wanted to rekindle their relationship.

'I assume so, yes.'

'But he didn't say anything. He never said a word.'

Dan shrugged. 'I guess he was just concentrating on winning you back. He had no reason to tell you that we'd known one another.'

'No, I suppose not.' But Emma still felt uneasy. 'Would you have ever told me about you and Stuart?' she asked.

'To be honest, not now, no.'

Emma appreciated the straight answer. It would have been easy for him to say yes, but this answer was much more believable. 'So why are you telling me now?'

'I panicked in the café, and lied. But straight afterwards I spoke to Richard, and he made me see sense.'

Richard knows? 'So your brother knows?'

'Yes, he's always known.'

There was a pause. 'Are there any more secrets?'

'No, I promise, there are no more secrets.'

'Good.' Emma reached out and took Dan's hand.

He smiled. 'We're going to be all right, then?'

'Yes. Now let's eat. I've just got my appetite back.'

***

Emma waited on the sofa, listening to the radio, while Dan finished the washing up. It was his turn to do it, as she had prepared the meal.

'Finished,' Dan said, sitting down next to her. 'Thanks for dinner, it was lovely. Pity you couldn't finish yours.'

'It's okay, I wasn't that hungry after all.' Quite a bit of her meal had gone to waste, as her appetite hadn't returned in the way she had thought.

'I'm so sorry,' Dan said again. 'About everything.'

'I know.'

'Not just about the Stuart thing. I'm still really sorry I left you on your own today. You'd just told me that there was someone else out there, bothering us, and I ran out on you.'

'You were upset. You weren't thinking straight.'

'Yes, but I shouldn't have done it. What if something had happened to you? What if this person had been watching, and chose to take advantage of what went on?'

'Now that's scary.' Unconsciously, Emma picked up a sofa cushion and hugged it to her chest.

'Sorry, I don't want to scare you, but what I'm saying is that my priority should have been protecting you, not myself.' Dan shook his head with disgust.

'You're a human being,' Emma said. 'None of us is perfect, are we? We all do things we regret. The important thing is that we recognise what we've done, and we make amends.'

'I will, Em, I'll make amends. And it won't happen again.'

'I don't want you to beat yourself up about this. I just want things to be normal.'

Dan nodded. 'So, what next?'

Emma shrugged. 'We hope that this person gets bored and leaves us alone, or the police catch them.'

'Of course!' Dan smacked his forehead with the heel of his hand. 'I'm sorry, Em – I didn't even ask if Lizzy had been in touch with the police.'

'She hadn't up until this morning, but she said she might give them a call later. You know Lizzy, though. She doesn't think much of them.' Suddenly Emma had a thought.

'What is it?'

'The photograph was real, and you said it was Stuart's – that girl took the photo for him. Which means that the person who left it for Lizzy has had access to Stuart's possessions.'

Dan nodded slowly. 'Yes, that has to be right.'

'So that lends credibility to the idea that Sally is involved in this. She and Stuart lived together, so she would have had easy access to his things. Assuming he'd kept the photograph, which he must have done, then she may have seen it, either before or after he died.'

'While she was sorting out his stuff,' Dan said.

'Possibly, yes. It makes sense, doesn't it?'

'Yes, it certainly does. She's still the one with the motive, and doing what this person is doing – trying to hurt us – well, it fits with her earlier behaviour. So what now?'

But before she could answer, the phone rang.

It was Will. 'Em, I know it's late, but can I come over to yours now? There's something I have to tell you. And can you ask Lizzy to come over, too? We all need to be there, as it involves all of us.'

16

Detective Inspector Mark Gasnier walked the short walk from the bus stop to the stadium, mingling with the crowds of good-spirited supporters, most of whom were clad in the claret and blue of West Ham United Football Club.

He himself wasn't dressed in a replica shirt. Despite being a lifelong fan, he owned only one club jersey: a signed shirt from the early 1970s that he had won in a competition, and which was kept in a frame on the wall of his spare room. Mark Gasnier wore suits to matches. Although he was off duty, it paid to be prepared, just in case. He didn't want to turn up to a crime scene or emergency meeting dressed like a football supporter.

'Quiet night, I expect,' Gasnier said to a young uniformed officer, who was standing on the street corner with a female colleague. He recognised him as a friend and colleague of his nephew, Matthew. When his nephew's training cohort had started, Gasnier had taken Matthew and a few of his fellow recruits out for a drink, to give them some advice about how they might want to manage their careers, including a few do's and don'ts. They were good kids, and had seemed to appreciate it. Of course, Matthew had ignored his original piece of advice of not joining the force, but then Gasnier's father, a former Met officer himself, had once said the same to him. The result had been the same and, in many ways, Matthew reminded him of himself when he was that age.

'I'm hoping so,' the officer replied, and then smiled when he realised who he was talking to. 'DI Gasnier. Matthew told me he'd managed to get you a ticket.'

Gasnier nodded, embarrassed at the situation. Tickets for the evening game – a European Champion's League tie against the mighty Real Madrid – were like gold dust. Matthew, who often policed games, had obtained a ticket for his uncle via his network of contacts at the club. Gasnier didn't believe in abuse of position, but he was willing to make an exception in this case. 'Hopefully it won't be quiet inside the ground,' he noted. 'Do you think they can do it?'

'Not really, no,' the officer replied. 'The Hammers beating the Galácticos? I just can't see it, sir.'

'Me, neither. Miracles do happen, though.'

'Never say never, sir.'

'Indeed. Is Matthew around? I was hoping to catch him before I went in.'

'I think he's down at the South Stand entrance, sir.'

Gasnier turned. 'I'll see if he's there. Have a good night, officer.'

He made his way around the stadium, taking in the atmosphere. He really needed this. It had been a hard few weeks, with a particularly gruelling murder case taking its toll.

The noise from the stadium was already immense, with air horns sounding and team songs being sung. Around the stadium, there were lots of Real Madrid merchandise to be seen, all being sold by the street vendors, while local entrepreneurs had worked quickly to produce 'half and half' scarves featuring the colours and names of both clubs. In an uncharacteristic act, Gasnier stopped and bought one, placing it around his neck. He couldn't find Matthew, and time was ticking by, so he headed for the correct gate.

He was just about to pass through the turnstile when his phone rang. He wouldn't have noticed it, given the noise levels, but he'd put it on vibrate. He looked at the caller display, irked by the interruption. It was DS Christian Davies, his colleague.

He stood back from the turnstile entrance, his finger hovering over the green receive button. Davies knew he was at the game. *What's he doing calling now?* But DS Davies had no appreciation of football; he wouldn't understand the importance of the match at all. Gasnier's finger switched to the red reject button, suddenly feeling a little like the US president with his finger ready to fire nukes.

Maybe he was calling because something significant was happening. *But can't it wait for a few hours? Even for just over ninety minutes?* Evidentially not, as he then rang again. If it could have waited, Davies would have given up by now. *Damn it.*

'DI Gasnier . . . Christian, hello. Yes, I'm just about to go in now . . . What! When did this happen? . . . Okay, thanks for letting me know . . . No, you were right to tell me . . . No problem, we'll speak again later tonight.' Gasnier cut the call and stood with his back to the stadium wall as the supporters filed past. He looked at his ticket, and then towards the entrance, mulling over his next move. Then he strode away. The call of the game was strong, but the call of the force was stronger.

He made eye contact with a boy in his late teens, a bright yellow charity collection box slung around his neck.

'Spare a bit of change for the local children's hospice?'

Gasnier stopped. 'Do you have a ticket for tonight's game?'

'No way, you must be joking! They sold out so fast, and who can afford it, anyway?'

'Well, take this then,' Gasnier said, handing him the ticket. 'Think of it as a well done for what you're doing for the charity.'

He didn't wait to hear the thank you. He spotted a man walking towards him, accompanied by a young boy, probably about seven or eight years of age. He lifted the scarf from around his neck and handed it to the man as they passed. 'They've been giving them away,' he explained. 'I've already got one.'

The man clutched the scarf, open-mouthed.

Gasnier picked up the pace, trying to banish the disappointment of missing out on the game of a lifetime. He knew that the issue in the phone call could have waited. He knew that he could have enjoyed the football match, and then dealt with it first thing tomorrow morning. But that wasn't his style. No, he needed to speak to Emma Holden as soon as possible.

17

'Em, it's so good to see you.'

Emma embraced her brother in the doorway. He was trying to put on a brave face, but she could tell he was really worried about something. 'Great to see you too.'

'Sorry I haven't been around since you got back,' he said. 'I've been meaning to, but things have been busy.'

'It's only been a couple of days.'

'I know, but it feels like longer.'

She pulled back. 'Everything's okay, isn't it, Will?'

'Not really,' he said. 'Is Lizzy here?'

What on earth can all this be about? 'She arrived a couple of minutes ago. She's in the kitchen, with Dan.'

He nodded. 'That's good. Then I can tell you all now.'

'We've also got something to tell you,' she said.

Dan and Lizzy were chatting at the kitchen table. They both said hello as Will and Emma joined them.

'There's no easy way to say this,' Will said, 'so I might as well just come out and tell you. I'm sorry,' he said to Emma and Dan, 'this is going to spoil what should still be a really happy time for you two.'

'It's a bit late for that,' Dan replied.

Will looked across to Emma for clarification. 'I'll explain in a minute,' she said. 'You go first.'

'Okay,' he said. He gathered himself. 'I'm being blackmailed.'

'What?' the group said in unison.

'Well, it's Dad who's being blackmailed, but it's about me.'

Emma's stomach felt as if it had gone into freefall. She had dreaded this moment ever since they had decided to keep quiet about Will's role in the disposal of Stephen's body. She had always feared that the truth would come calling, and her little brother would be dragged back into its jaws. 'About Stephen Myers?'

He nodded. 'They said they'll tell the police if we don't pay them.'

'How much?' Dan asked.

'Fifty thousand pounds.'

Dan shook his head. 'My God.'

'Do you know who the blackmailer is?' Lizzy said.

'No.'

'How did they get in touch?'

'They called Dad on his home phone a few days ago. It was a man, but he didn't recognise the voice. He said that he knew about everything I'd done. He didn't say what, but he said they've got proof.'

Dan looked incredulous. 'What kind of proof?'

'No idea,' Will replied. 'They just said they had evidence that they could take to the police.'

'And then they asked for the money?' Dan said.

'Not on the first call. They called later in the day, and outlined what they wanted.'

'But they still didn't say what they knew about you?' Lizzy said. 'Couldn't they just be bluffing?'

'Dad thought that too. He came to see me at work this morning, and explained everything. We just hoped that it was a prankster, trying it on, and that they didn't really know anything. But tonight, when I got back to my flat, there was a letter waiting for me.'

Lizzy leant forward. 'It gave details?'

'Yes,' he confirmed. 'The letter said that they had proof that I'd helped to dispose of Stephen Myers' body. It also repeated the ransom demand, and this time it gave a timescale.'

'Of what?'

'Two weeks.'

'Fifty thousand pounds,' Dan mused, 'in two weeks. That's serious money to find in such a short space of time. Does your dad have that much?'

'I don't think so,' Will said, 'and I wouldn't want him to pay it – I've told him I don't want him to pay a thing. It's my actions, I helped Stuart to commit a crime, and I'm not going to let other people suffer for it.' He turned to look at Emma. 'Are you okay, Em?'

Emma had been only half listening, in stunned silence, but Will's last statement had hit home. 'You're just going to tell the police?'

'I don't think I have any other choice, do I?'

'If I had any money, I'd gladly contribute,' Lizzy said. 'I wish I could help.'

Will smiled his appreciation. 'Thanks, Lizzy, but it's not just about getting the money.'

'Will's right,' Dan said. 'I mean, we have some savings – not enough by far – and we'd be happy to contribute. But I doubt that even if we found fifty thousand pounds it would be enough.'

Emma nodded. 'You reckon that they'd come back for more?'

Dan smiled, grimly.

Lizzy was thinking. 'So if we find fifty thousand, they'll think, hey, they can find fifty, so let's ask for another twenty?'

'That's it,' Dan replied. 'If they know that we're prepared to pay fifty thousand pounds in order for them not to go to the police, then why wouldn't we pay sixty, seventy, eighty, one hundred thousand pounds?'

'Because we wouldn't be able to afford it,' Lizzy replied. 'It's unlikely we could ever find that amount of money.'

'In which case, the person could just tell the police anyway, and they've still got their fifty thousand pounds. Or they could leave us hanging, ready to come back in a few years, when we're likely to have more money. They've got the information, the power, and they'll use it to their full advantage.'

Emma sat back and stared at the ceiling. 'So there's no hope.'

'Which is why I have to take away the power they have,' Will said, 'and go to the police myself.'

***

For the next half an hour, still sitting on the sofa with Miranda tucked in beside him, Edward Holden considered his next move.

Then he spent another couple of minutes rehearsing his lines.

'Damn,' he eventually said. 'The papers for Clive Munroe – I forgot to drop them off this afternoon.'

Miranda raised her head. She'd been dozing. 'Is that a problem?'

'It is. Clive needs them early tomorrow morning for an important meeting.'

'Can't you drop them off early tomorrow then?'

'The meeting is in Sheffield, and he's leaving really early.'

'Oh.'

'Exactly,' Edward said, standing up from the sofa. 'I'll have to drive over now, there's no other option.'

Miranda nodded. 'Your clients come first.'

Edward didn't know whether that was an accusation or not. 'Well, I wouldn't say that, but . . .'

Miranda pulled herself upright. 'Oh, I didn't mean it badly. I just mean that you can't afford to let them down. We know what it's like when clients start to drop off, how fragile it all is. We don't want to go back there, do we?'

'Yes, you're right, we certainly don't.' Edward smiled briefly at Miranda, appreciating her understanding. Even if it was misplaced. He shifted uneasily. 'Especially not now we've just bought the rental property.'

They'd recently purchased a small buy-to-let house in Croydon, south London. It was an investment that Edward had pushed for. The dwelling was a repossession, so they'd got it for a good price.

'Any idea how long you'll be?'

'No longer than half an hour. Maybe forty-five minutes if we get talking.'

Miranda nodded. 'I'll go and have a bath. Then do some reading in bed. I'll probably be asleep by the time you get back. I'm so tired recently.'

Edward smiled and kissed her goodbye. She was so beautiful, so trusting, and he didn't like lying to her. 'I'll be as quick as I can.'

***

Edward headed over to Will's flat, knowing that his son had said he was going to visit Emma that evening. Edward had cautioned him against telling her about the blackmail, but he doubted whether Will would heed that warning. He wasn't very good at keeping things to himself.

That had been the problem from the beginning.

'If only you hadn't told me about all this,' he said himself now, as he clasped the steering wheel and looked across the road at Will's place. 'You could have dealt with all this yourself.'

Will had told his father how he had helped to dispose of Stephen Myers' body just a few weeks after it had happened. He had been desperate to tell someone, but Edward had never been sure what Will wanted from him: reassurance that he wasn't a bad person; comforting words that the police would never find out what had really happened; or maybe someone who would convince him that the best course of action was to come clean? If it was the latter, then Will had been disappointed; there was no way he was going to allow his son to go to jail.

Edward got out of his car and headed over the road to Will's flat.

He rang the doorbell, just in case Will had changed his plans. No answer. He knocked. 'William, are you in there?' Still no answer, and no signs of movement from inside.

So he used the spare key that Will had left him in case of emergencies, and entered the flat.

He knew what he was looking for. William had an old-style address book – a habit that he had inherited from his mother. It didn't take long to find it. And there was the name, address and telephone number he had been looking for.

'Perfect.'

He copied down the details and replaced the address book in the drawer where he had found it.

18

It was a quarter past nine, and Emma, Dan, Lizzy and Will were still discussing the blackmail. 'There must be another way,' Lizzy said. 'We've got two weeks, right? Two weeks to find another solution, which doesn't involve paying them, or you going to jail, Will.'

'I can't see what other option there is,' Will said. 'I appreciate what you're saying, and I'm really grateful to you all, but I've been preparing for this. I've always thought I was on borrowed time.'

'I don't like you talking like that, Will,' Emma said. 'It makes me feel so sad. You're not a criminal. Stuart lied to you, and you made a stupid mistake, but what good would it do to anyone if you went to jail?'

'Lizzy's right,' Dan said. 'There must be another way. Or at least we must have hope that there is. And, as you said, Lizzy, we still have two weeks to come up with something.'

Will didn't look convinced. 'Like what?'

'The first thing,' Dan said, 'is that we need to find out who these people are, so that we know who we're dealing with. Who might be doing this?'

'Well, it sounds obvious, but someone who knows what I did,' Will said.

'And who knows?'

'All of us. Then there's Dad. And Peter Myers. That's it. There's no one else.'

'But there *must* be,' Dan said. 'They're just the people you know about. What if other people found out?'

'Maybe, yes,' Will acknowledged. 'But it wouldn't have come from any of us, would it?' He looked at the other three, who nodded their agreement.

'None of us would breath a word,' Lizzy added.

'What about your dad?' Dan asked. 'Do you think he's told anyone?'

'No, no way,' Will said.

'Not even Miranda?'

'No way,' Will repeated. 'Dad wouldn't say anything because it looks bad on him that we didn't tell the police. He would be too scared that if he told someone else, the truth would come out.'

'I don't think Dad would have told anyone,' Emma agreed.

Dan seemed satisfied. 'Then that leaves two other people.'

'Two?' Emma said. 'Peter Myers and—?'

'Stuart Harris,' he stated.

'Of course,' Lizzy said. 'Stuart may have told other people before he died.'

Dan nodded. 'Or left evidence that someone found after his death.'

And then Emma realised. 'I see what you're getting at. The person who had access to the photograph of you and Stuart could also have been told what Will did, by Stuart.'

'Exactly,' Dan said. 'If we assume that the person who sent the photograph is also the person who is doing the blackmailing, then it narrows down our list of suspects, potentially.'

'I don't understand,' Will said. 'What photograph?'

Dan had forgotten that Will didn't know anything about what had been going on. He glanced across to Emma, who nodded at him to explain. 'Someone has been sending letters to Lizzy, including a photograph showing me with Stuart Harris. It was taken a few years ago, before Emma and I first met.'

Lizzy, open-mouthed, looked across at Emma, who hadn't had a chance to tell her that Dan had confirmed that the photograph was genuine.

Emma smiled reassuringly. 'It's okay, we've discussed it and it's fine.'

'The person, whoever they are, is trying to cause trouble,' Dan said. 'They're trying to wreck things.'

'But we're not going to let them,' Emma continued. 'We have to stick together.'

Will looked troubled. 'You didn't tell me this was going on.'

'I was going to tell you,' Emma said. 'This week.'

'So do you have any idea who this person is?' Will said.

'Yes,' Dan replied. 'Sally Thompson. Or Amy, as you knew her.'

Will sat back abruptly in his chair and shook his head. 'I don't think it would be Sally.'

'Why?' Lizzy said. 'She lived with Stuart, so she would have had access to the photograph, plus it's possible that Stuart told her about what he had done – including your role in it.'

'I don't think so,' Will said again. 'I don't think she knows anything about what Stuart did to Stephen Myers.'

Dan was unconvinced. 'We don't know that.'

Will was thinking. 'What about Peter Myers? He could have told someone else, maybe someone he met in jail, or someone on the outside.'

'But that doesn't explain how the person got hold of the photograph,' Dan said. 'Peter Myers wouldn't have had access to that, unless he knew Stuart.'

Will turned to his sister. 'What do you think, Em?'

'I don't know if Sally's behind all this. But it would make sense, after what she did last time.'

Will seemed deflated by Emma's response.

'Why don't you think it's Sally?' Lizzy asked him.

'I just don't,' he said. 'The person who called Dad was a man.'

'But Sally worked alongside a man last time,' Dan said. 'She could just be doing the same now.'

'Maybe,' Will said. And suddenly he was thinking about the ginger-haired man whom he had seen talking to Sally in the park. Could she be doing this? Could he have been deceived, for a second time? *Have I been taken for a complete fool?*

Emma noticed his consternation. 'What are you thinking, Will?'

He breathed out. 'I don't quite know how to say this. You'll probably think I'm an idiot.'

'We won't think that,' Emma reassured.

'You haven't heard what I've done yet.' He took a breath. 'I've, um, been seeing Sally.'

Everyone in the room was stunned into silence.

'Seeing . . . as in, *dating?*' Emma said.

'Well, yes, no – I mean, not dating, but meeting up.'

Emma watched her brother struggling for an explanation. She felt sorry for him, as he looked very uncomfortable, but she genuinely couldn't understand what she had just heard. 'I don't understand, Will. Why would you meet up with Sally?'

He closed his eyes. 'Because I still love her.'

Emma just wanted to hold him. 'Oh, *Will* . . .'

'I know I'm an idiot,' Will said. 'And I know it probably makes absolutely no sense to you all, after what happened, that I'd get in touch with Sally. But I just had to see her, and find out what she had to say, and how she felt about me.'

'And what did she say?' Emma said.

'She said she was really sorry for what she did; that she was ashamed of herself. She said how she'd been in a terrible depression since Stuart's death, and that she hadn't been herself. And I believed her.'

'Did you tell her how you feel about her?'

'Yes.' Will swallowed. 'I didn't really mean to, but it just sort of came out as we were talking. I suppose I couldn't help myself.'

'So what did she say about that?'

'Well, she didn't say that she felt the same way,' he said, with some regret. 'But I think she does want us to be friends.' Will noted Dan and Lizzy's continued silence. 'You both think I'm crazy, don't you?'

'Actually, yes, I do,' Lizzy replied. 'But I also think you're very sweet, and a romantic. If that's how you feel about her, then I can understand you doing what you did. I wish there was someone I loved that much, to do something so crazy.'

Will looked at Dan. 'How about you?'

'You're definitely crazy,' Dan said. 'But I know how I feel about Em, and if you feel the same way about Sally, then I can totally understand. Even though it does sound like madness that you would want anything more to do with the woman who had planned to send you plummeting into the ground without a parachute.'

Will nodded, sadly. 'But now you think that she's behind the blackmail, and the letters. And you're probably right. In which case, she's playing games with me again, making a fool out of me.'

'I'm so sorry, Will,' Emma said. 'She might not be doing this, but she is the obvious choice.'

104

'So what now?' Will said, looking at each of the three in turn. He seemed drained of emotional energy, and looked completely defeated. 'You're going to tell the police about your suspicions of Sally?'

'Did you call them today?' Emma directed her question at Lizzy.

'No,' she replied. 'I was going to, after I got back from work, but I decided to wait until we'd had chance to talk about it all a bit more.' She shrugged. 'I don't know why I didn't call them. But you know how much I dislike dealing with the police. I should probably call them first thing tomorrow – unless we just call them now?' She looked across to Emma for a response.

'Maybe it's not such a good idea at the moment,' Dan said, before Emma had a chance to reply.

'How do you mean?' she said.

'Well, if Sally is the blackmailer, and she knows about what Will did, then maybe it's not a good idea to go to the police right now. We might need to think about things more carefully before taking that step.'

'Why?' Lizzy said. 'Because the truth might come out?'

'Maybe,' Dan replied. 'She might decide to just tell the police if she thinks we're on to her. If she's still feeling low and that maybe she has nothing to lose, then she might take Will down with her.'

'If it *is* Sally,' Will added.

Dan nodded. 'Yes, of course, if it is her. But do you really want to take that chance – antagonising her, and risking everything?'

'No, I guess not,' Lizzy said.

'Then what do we do?' Emma said. 'Nothing?'

'No, not nothing,' Dan said.

Lizzy was interested. 'Go on, then. What do you think we should do?'

'Well, as I said, I don't think we should do anything to rock the boat. But we've got two weeks to decide what to do. And, Will, I think you could really help.'

Will looked hopeful. 'How?'

'Well, you're the only one of us who can get close to Sally without her becoming suspicious.'

'I don't like the sound of this.'

'It's okay,' Dan said. 'I don't think you should do any more than you've been doing.'

'I'm not sure I understand what you mean.'

'I mean, just keep seeing Sally, meeting her, talking to her. She might reveal something, let her guard down.'

Will sighed. 'I did see something,' he said, reluctantly. 'I saw Sally talking to a man. I was watching from a distance, so I don't know what it was about. It might have been nothing, but I guess it may have been linked to this.'

'You didn't recognise him?' Emma asked. 'It wasn't Scott Goulding?'

'No, it definitely wasn't him. This guy had ginger hair, and he was taller and broader shouldered than Scott Goulding. But I don't know who it was. I didn't ask her about it, of course.'

'And would you be okay,' Emma asked, concerned, 'seeing Sally, with the possibility that she's lying to you?'

'Yes,' he replied, 'because I'm still not convinced, and I want to give her a chance to prove us wrong. I don't want to assume the worst.'

'You just need to keep your eyes and mind open,' Dan cautioned.

Will nodded.

'And what about you, Lizzy?' Emma said. 'Are you okay not going to the police yet? After all, you're the one this person has been targeting the most.'

'I'm okay with that,' Lizzy said, nodding. 'I don't really feel that threatened by what's happened so far. If I'd been bothered, then I would have gone to the police straight away, wouldn't I? Maybe I've just become accustomed to this kind of thing, after everything that's happened.' She rolled her eyes dramatically, attempting to lighten the mood. 'And, to be honest, compared to what happened with Peter Myers, it's just irritating. How do you feel, Em?'

'I've got to admit, I feel uncomfortable about it all. But if you're all okay with it, then I'm okay. On one condition.'

Dan raised an eyebrow. 'And that is?'

'If this person gets any more threatening, then we go to the police straight away.'

They all agreed.

***

They opened a bottle of wine and tried to talk about other things. And, despite the near-impossibility of the task, the atmosphere improved significantly, with talk of the honeymoon in Mauritius, and the latest celebrity gossip. Even Will seemed to forget his problems, laughing and joking along with the others.

It had just turned ten o'clock when the friends were quietened by the landline's shrill ring. Emma's reaction was the same as that of the others: unexpected phone calls at that time of night were instinctively unsettling. She answered, praying that it wasn't bad news.

'Hello?'

'Hello, is that Emma Holden?'

The voice was familiar. 'Yes, it is.'

'Good. Hi, Emma, it's Detective Inspector Mark Gasnier. I'm very sorry to call you at such a late hour, but I'd like to come over and see you now, if that's okay. You're living at the same address?'

'Er, yes, that's fine. What's happened?'

'I'd really like to speak to you in person.'

Emma looked over to the others. They were all radiating anxiety. 'Okay, that's fine.'

'Excellent. I'll be there in ten minutes. I'm not far away.'

Emma replaced the receiver. She had been unnerved before picking up the phone, but she felt sick now. 'That was Mark Gasnier. He's coming over here right now. I don't think it's good news.'

19

Edward Holden rapped on the door and waited for an answer. He had been certain of what he was doing up until that point, but now he was having second thoughts. *What if I've jumped to the wrong conclusion?* If he had, what he was about to do could backfire badly. But it was too late. He could hear someone coming.

'Who is it?' a girl's voice asked on the other side of the door. It didn't have a spyhole, so it was prudent of her to want to know who was there, particularly at this time of night.

He thought about lying, but decided against it. It would be interesting to see her reaction to the truth. 'It's Edward Holden. Will's father.'

There was a pause. He was about to speak again when he heard the lock click, and the door edged open.

Sally peered around the half-open door. She was dressed in a blue T-shirt and pastel pink lounging trousers, her blonde hair pulled back into a loose ponytail. Edward could see why Will had fallen for her. She was effortlessly attractive. 'Why are you here?'

'I need to speak to you,' he said.

She was obviously puzzled. 'But it's really late. Anyway, how did you get my address?' She pushed the door ever so slightly nearer to the closed position.

'I got it from Will,' he said, telling a half-truth.

'It's really late,' she repeated.

'It's important,' he said. 'I wouldn't be here at this time of night if it wasn't.'

Sally looked behind her towards the inside of her flat, then nodded and opened the door.

Edward wasn't invited to sit down, but he preferred to stand anyway; he wasn't planning on being there long. 'I've come to tell you to stop what you're doing. I know what's going on.'

'Pardon? Stop what?'

Edward searched her face for a trace of guilt. She just looked confused. *God, I hope I've got this right.* 'You know what I'm talking about.'

'I'm sorry, but I really don't.'

'Just leave my family alone. You've done more than enough to hurt us, so please just have the decency of disappearing from our lives.'

Sally's face cleared a little. 'I'm afraid that's not your decision. Will is big enough to decide for himself what he wants to do.'

Edward shook his head. So he *was* right. 'Look' – he pointed at her – 'you're not getting a penny from me or my family, do you hear? Not a single penny. We were very good to you – we could have pressed the police harder for charges to be brought, and this is the way you repay us, with a seedy attempt at blackmail? I don't know how you live with yourself.'

'Money? Blackmail?' The girl looked genuinely shocked. 'I have no idea what you're talking about. I'm not blackmailing anyone.'

'Don't bother denying it.' He could hear his voice rising.

'I *am* denying it!'

Edward could feel himself sliding into a hole. Either she was lying, or he had indeed made a costly rush to judgement. He had to pull things back, fast, otherwise it could all unravel and he would be left sinking in the pit. 'But I thought . . .'

'I don't know what you thought, but you're wrong. Look, I've done some bad things, but I'm really sorry for what happened, and as far as Will is concerned, he's happy to accept that and move on.'

Edward was taken aback. 'You've spoken to Will?'

'Yes, of course. I thought he must have told you.'

'No, no, he hasn't. You've been seeing one another?'

'A couple of times, yes. But you should really talk to Will about this, not me.'

Edward was perturbed. 'You're dating?'

'You need to talk to Will,' Sally repeated, 'but we're not dating, no. We're just friends.'

'*Friends?* After what you did?'

Sally's face closed. 'I'd like you to leave now, please. I need to go to bed.'

Edward considered holding his ground, but then backed down. He turned at the doorway. 'Just don't hurt my family again.'

'I understand how you feel, Mr Holden. But I have no intention of doing that. You've got nothing to worry about, as far as I'm concerned.'

'I hope that's true,' he replied. 'For your sake as much as ours.'

20

'Emma, sorry again about the late visit.' DI Mark Gasnier looked just as Emma had remembered — the towering build, the movie-star smile and olive skin. And the dark suit. Even at this late hour, he cut an impressive figure.

'You, too. Come in, we're in the living room.'

Gasnier walked ahead of her. He took in the sight of Dan, Lizzy and Will, who were sitting pensively on the sofa. They all nodded their hellos. 'I didn't expect a welcome party,' he said. 'Sorry to interrupt.'

'Would you like a drink?' Emma asked. 'Tea, coffee, water?'

'I'm okay,' he said, sitting down in a single chair opposite the three. 'I've just had a coffee back at the station.'

Gasnier had spent the past hour and a half finding out more information; he had wanted to know the full facts before presenting Emma with the bad news. He knew he would need to be able to answer all her questions, or at least all those that could possibly be answered at this early stage.

He had also kept half an ear on the radio: West Ham had beaten Real Madrid by two goals to one. The commentator had described it as one of the club's greatest ever victories. Matthew had sent him a text shortly after the final whistle, asking what it had felt like to be there.

Emma sat down next to the others and waited for Gasnier to explain.

'You look well, Dan,' he said. 'Much better than the last time I saw you.'

'Thanks,' Dan replied. 'I feel a lot better.'

'That's good, very good.' He tracked slowly from right to left across the occupants of the sofa. 'You all look well. It's nice to see people get through very difficult times. You've all done really well.'

Emma watched him. The small talk was just making her more nervous. He was building up to something, and she had a very strong feeling that she wasn't going to like it at all.

Gasnier appeared to notice her discomfort. 'I'm sorry,' he said. 'I should tell you what I'm here about. I'm afraid there has been a worrying development. But I want to try to allay any concerns you may have.'

Emma closed her eyes, preparing for the guillotine to come down. It was something about Peter Myers, it had to be. *Has he reversed his plea to not guilty?* It would mean making them all endure the pain and hurt of a protracted court case, she knew that. She had been afraid that it might happen, despite his decision to admit his guilt shortly after his capture. But her worst fear was still that he would take the opportunity to reveal the truth about Stephen Myers' death during the trial, as a mitigating circumstance. And in doing so, point the finger squarely at Will. Emma felt Lizzy grip her hand in support.

'This evening the news came in that Peter Myers has escaped from custody.' He watched carefully for a reaction from the four. 'There are a lot of officers out there looking for him, and they hope that this will be a quick operation. I don't expect it will be long before he's back behind bars.'

Dan was the first to speak. 'When did he escape?'

'This afternoon.'

Lizzy was next, looking pale. 'But how *could* he escape? He was in a secure prison, wasn't he? You can't just walk out of those places, can you?'

'Well, unfortunately, it has happened in the past,' Gasnier replied. 'Although, thankfully, it's rare. But Peter Myers didn't escape from prison. He was being treated in hospital at the time.'

'What for?' Lizzy said.

Gasnier hesitated. 'I'm afraid I can't pass on that information.'

Dan shook his head in disgust. 'Even criminals have a right to privacy.'

'Something like that, yes,' Gasnier said. 'But the reason for his admission to hospital is not really of any significance. What is significant is that he is currently out, and it's important that you should know.'

Now Emma mustered the strength to speak. She hadn't expected this news, and the thought that Peter Myers was out there, somewhere, was truly frightening. 'What should we do?'

She had expected Gasnier to shoot straight back with a list of advice, but he just sat there for a few seconds, considering his response. His hesitancy was worrying – she wanted him to have all the answers on the tip of his tongue. He usually seemed so certain, so confident.

'Well,' he began, 'I know it's very worrying, but the first thing to say is that the great majority of offenders who escape are caught within the first twenty-four hours of their so-called freedom. So I do expect that he will be back in custody within a relatively short period of time. And when the escape is opportunistic, they're often caught within a matter of hours, because the offender has no plan, no safe house, no shelter. There's a national alert out across all the forces, so if he's out in public, there's every chance that he'll be spotted pretty quickly.'

'Is that what you think?' Emma said. 'That it was just opportunistic?'

'That's the assumption at the moment,' Gasnier confirmed. 'He was in the hospital for a genuine reason, so the officers on the case are working on the basis that he just took advantage of the reduced security. He had guards with him, of course, but it's obviously less secure than a prison.'

'I just don't understand,' Lizzy said. 'How could he get away from the guards? Weren't they watching him at all times? I mean, this guy is dangerous. He shouldn't be left alone to walk around a hospital.'

'It's a matter that's under investigation. But the priority is to find and recapture him, as soon as possible. Recriminations can come later.'

'Should we be worried?' Dan said. 'Do you think we're in danger?'

Gasnier paused again. 'The honest answer is that we can't rule that out. We know what he's done in the past, and he is dangerous. So it's wise to be cautious. But, and this is a big but, it would be very unusual for Peter Myers to target any of you. His priority will be to evade capture, and heading straight here, for you, wouldn't be a very wise decision. He knows that this is one of the places we'll be monitoring, so he would be mad to come here.'

'But that doesn't mean it couldn't happen,' Lizzy said.

'Again, working on what's happened in the past, it's very unusual for an offender to seek out their previous victims during an escape. I can only think of a handful of instances when that happened, and there are usually special circumstances – for instance, the victim was a family member who could also offer shelter.'

'So do we really just have to stay here and hope that he doesn't come looking to finish what he started?' Lizzy asked. 'It just sounds crazy to me, whatever you say about how unlikely it is that Peter Myers will come.'

Gasnier opened his palms. 'It's your decision whether you stay, or whether you go somewhere else until he's re-arrested. But, as I said, I'm not expecting that it will be that long before he is brought back into custody.'

'Can you protect us better here?' Emma asked. 'If we stay, then you and your officers, they'll be able to protect us, in case he does come?'

'We'll do what we can,' Gasnier replied. 'We'll certainly make patrols, be on the other end of a phone, assign you a link officer. But I'm afraid we can't provide twenty-four-hour protection.'

Lizzy wasn't happy with that response. 'So if Peter Myers does come looking for us, we'd better hope that it's during one of your patrols.'

'I'm afraid, Lizzy, it's just the reality of what we can resource. There are a lot of people in London who would like one-to-one protection, believe me. And a lot – with all due respect to your situation – who are at more risk of harm than you.'

'So we should go somewhere else, where Peter Myers won't be able to find us.'

'As I said, that's up to you.' He glanced at his watch. 'Look, I'm sorry, I have to go now. But I'll be in touch again first thing tomorrow, hopefully with good news. In the meantime, if anything happens, or you're worried about anything at all, call me on my mobile. Whatever time of the day or night, just call me. I really don't mind.'

***

Emma closed the door behind DI Gasnier. The others were standing at her shoulder, and Dan placed a hand on her back.

'I can't believe this,' she said. 'I can't believe he's out there, free to do whatever he wants. It's the worst nightmare.' She turned to her friends. 'What should we do?'

'Well,' Dan said to Will and Lizzy, 'it's up to you guys, but I think you should both stay here tonight. Then we can talk about it more in the morning. Lizzy, you can share with Emma; I'll sleep on the floor in the living room with Will. We've got sleeping bags and spare blankets and pillows.'

They both nodded.

'That's good,' Emma said. 'We need to stick together and get through this. Because it doesn't matter what DI Gasnier says to try to reassure us, I'm really frightened.'

21

The girl lay on the bed and gazed at the ceiling. She reached out to the man lying beside her and stroked his back. 'This feels so good. You and me, like this.'

The man turned to face her. 'I couldn't agree more.' He kissed her deeply, and they entwined under the covers.

'I really think this could be the start of something special,' she said, afterwards, as the man dressed. She waited a few seconds for a response. 'Don't you?'

He looked at her and smiled as he picked up his shirt from where he'd put it carefully over the back of the chair, slipping his arms through the sleeves and buttoning up the front. 'Of course I do.' He turned to the full-length mirror and carefully checked his hair. 'Let's talk more about this later, after my meeting. I'd also like to speak to you more about what I suggested earlier.'

'Okay,' she said, snuggling back down under the covers and nestling into the pillows. 'Hurry back.' She waited for a response, but when she turned to look, he'd already left the room.

As she closed her eyes, her thoughts turned again to what he had said in his sleep.

It probably meant nothing . . .

PART THREE

22

Emma lay back in the warm water of the deep bath as Dan massaged her neck and back, moving his fingers delicately across her wet skin.

'What are you thinking?' he asked, pressing his fingers in deeper.

Emma arched her back as the pleasurable sensation ran down her spine. She felt his legs wrap around her body.

Baths for two were always a treat.

'Of us,' she said, closing her eyes and playing with the tap using the tips of her toes.

'What about us?'

'Oh, I don't know. Our future, I guess.'

He began kissing the back of her neck, sending shivers through her body.

'What future?' he whispered in her ear.

Emma opened her eyes. 'What do you mean?'

She felt his breath against her skin, tickling the small, fine hairs around the nape of her neck.

'You'll wish you'd never met me,' he said.

She twisted around to look at him. He looked serious. 'Don't be silly. Of course I don't wish that.'

'No, you *will* wish you'd never met me.' He stopped the massage but kept a hand on each shoulder. 'There's no future for us, Em. I'm so sorry.'

The pressure on Emma's neck increased.

'Dan, you're hurting me.'

'I'm so sorry,' he repeated. 'Please, don't forget that, will you?'

She tried to raise herself from the water, but with his grip it was impossible to move anywhere but down.

'Dan!' she protested, hearing the fear in her voice. She wanted to lash out and grab him, anything to stop this from happening, but her arms simply flayed about, unable to get a grip.

'Relax,' he said, still holding her firm. His voice sounded different, alien. Again he began kissing her, but this time it was not tender, the kisses almost violent in their intensity. 'I'm sorry you can't trust me.'

'Dan, please, stop it, you're really scaring me!' Emma arched away from him, but he pulled her back. 'Dan!'

'I'm your number one fan, Emma. I always have been.'

It wasn't Dan. The voice, the feel of his hands. It was *him*. 'Stephen, please, let me go, let me go.'

Emma felt an immense pressure being applied to her head and, before she knew it, she was under the water. Soapy water gushed into her nose and mouth, cutting her breathing dead.

She threw out her legs and arms against invisible targets, desperate to get out, and tried to scream, despite knowing that she would choke faster that way. But she didn't know who she was hoping would hear her cries. Dan had gone. And there was no one else. It was like she was trapped in a whirlpool that was dragging her down, deeper and deeper. The depth of the water was amazing.

She opened her eyes. Through the water, at the surface, she could see the silhouette of Stephen Myers looming over her.

It was over.

Suddenly tired of fighting, she relaxed into her fate, her eyes fixed on the figure above.

'Emma, are you okay? Emma?'

The image was fading.

'Emma, please, wake up.'

Emma opened her eyes. Lizzy was sitting over her in the semi-darkness, concerned.

'You must have been having a nightmare,' she said. 'You were thrashing around, mumbling things.'

Disorientated, Emma pulled herself upright. She glanced across at the clock, its dial casting a familiar orange glow over her bedside table. It was half past four in the morning.

'Can you remember what you were dreaming about?'

Emma yawned. She felt so groggy. 'Stephen Myers.'

'Oh, I'm so sorry, Em, that's awful.'

'It's okay. It was just a dream. Did I wake you up?'

'No, I've been awake for ages. I can't seem to get back to sleep.'

'Worrying about Peter Myers?'

'Peter Myers, and everything else. Do you really think he's a threat to us?'

'I don't know,' Emma said. 'I really don't know. I'd love to believe what Mark Gasnier says, but I'm scared, because we know how dangerous Myers is.' She yawned again.

'Sorry,' Lizzy said. 'I shouldn't be discussing this in the early hours of the morning. You'll never get back to sleep with me talking about him.'

'It's fine. If I'm going to have another dream like that, then I'd rather stay awake.'

'I can understand that. It must be horrible for you.'

Emma pulled the duvet up to her chin. 'These nightmares, they're not a surprise really. It's just a reaction to the stress of everything that's happened. I know that when things settle down, then the likelihood is that they'll stop.'

'Yes, but that doesn't make them any easier to deal with, does it?'

Emma shrugged, then continued reluctantly: 'The nightmare, it wasn't just about Stephen Myers. It was about Dan, too. He was saying all these strange things, about not trusting him, and about there being no future for us.'

'Right. That's probably because of what happened yesterday, with Dan and Stuart, and the photograph.'

'You're probably right.'

'How do you feel about Dan having known Stuart?' Lizzy looked at her friend in the half-darkness. 'We haven't had chance to talk about it yet, have we?'

Emma sighed. 'I don't really know how I feel. To be honest, it doesn't seem that big a deal now. Stuart had been dating one of Dan's housemates – that's how they had got to know each other. Stuart had talked about me to Dan when they went out together, and he'd checked me out online. Then, months later, after losing touch with Stuart, Dan recognised me and we got talking.'

'It all sounds pretty reasonable.'

'You think so?'

'Yes.'

Emma blew a deep breath out. 'I'm glad you think that, Lizzy. It means a lot to me, because I really trust and value your opinion.'

'Ditto.' Lizzy reached for Emma's hand and squeezed it. 'Did Dan explain why he hadn't just come out and told you the truth?'

'He said he'd wanted to, but he was scared that it would put me off him if I knew about the connection.'

'And is he right?'

'Maybe. I probably would have been put off, if I had found out that he knew Stuart.'

'So again, that's a reasonable explanation.'

'Yes, it is.'

'But you're dreaming of Dan saying those things to you, about trust and there being no future.'

'Meaning?'

'Well, I'm no expert, but maybe the dream reveals that the experience has unsettled you in terms of your relationship with Dan.'

'Possibly.'

'I might well be reading too much into it,' Lizzy said, 'but when everything else is over, when Peter Myers is back behind bars, and this other person has stopped bothering us, then you might have to address it again with him, to make sure that things don't fester.'

Emma nodded. 'I know.'

Lizzy looked over at the clock and grimaced. 'Not quite five yet. Maybe we should just get up, even though I'm sure we'll regret it later.'

Emma agreed. But within a few minutes, they had both fallen back to sleep.

***

Emma woke to the smell of bacon. Lizzy was still fast asleep next to her, mouth open like a fish on a slab. Their early morning conversation seemed almost dream-like, but the reality of what they had discussed was fresh in her mind. Lizzy was right. Dan's concealment of his friendship with Stuart probably would take time for her to come to terms with, and she shouldn't just try to bury her feelings. But she was determined that it wouldn't overly affect things, either.

She swung her legs out of bed and planted her feet on the floor, stretching, feeling surprisingly refreshed despite the disturbed sleep.

Padding across the room and out into the passageway, Emma was met by Will, who had just come out of the bathroom. He was fully dressed, but not all of his clothes were his own – she recognised his blue shirt as one she'd bought for Dan as a birthday present the year before.

'Hi, Em. You like it?'

'Good choice,' she said. 'How did you—?'

'Dan sneaked into your bedroom to get it. You and Lizzy were both dead to the world. I was going to wear the one I had on yesterday, but Wednesday's the day I've got a couple of regular morning meetings to go to. So he offered me one of his.'

'It suits you. Lucky you're the same size.' Emma had already offered Lizzy the choice of her clothes – again, it was fortunate that they were both size eight; it made the last-minute stay-over idea much easier.

'Is Lizzy still asleep?' Will asked, looking over Emma's shoulder towards the bedroom door.

She nodded. 'We were awake for a while in the early hours, so I guess she's catching up.'

'We both woke up early too,' Will said. 'Just before six. We had a chat for a while, tried to get back to sleep, and then decided to just get up. Even had time to nip out for some bacon.'

'I noticed. It smells delicious.'

'I'm surprised it hasn't woken Lizzy,' Will joked. 'You know how much she likes bacon.'

They entered the kitchen, where Dan was buttering some toast. He too was dressed. 'Hey, Em. Hungry?'

'I am now,' she said.

'Great. Lizzy's up?'

'Still aslee—'

'No, I'm here,' Lizzy said at the doorway, rubbing her eyes. Her curly hair was wild. 'Couldn't resist the smell.'

Will winked at Emma. 'Told you.'

They all sat down around the table and tucked into the food. Dan flicked the radio on and they let the jovial voice of the breakfast DJ fill the silence.

They all knew that it was simply a prelude to facing reality, but everyone was happy to take the opportunity to just sit down and enjoy breakfast. However, it was getting towards eight, and although Lizzy had a free morning, Emma knew that soon both Dan and Will would have to leave for work.

They would have to start talking soon.

'I have a suggestion,' Dan said finally, as he swallowed his last bite of toast. 'I discussed it with Will this morning, but of course we've all got to be happy with it, especially you, Em.'

'Go on.'

'Why don't we all go up to Salford this weekend, to Media City?'

'Really?' Emma had fully intended to call the organisers of the *Up My Street* reunion that morning to let them know that she could no longer attend. The thought of travelling up there on her own, with Peter Myers on the loose, had seemed neither sensible nor appealing.

'It seems like an ideal solution,' Dan said. 'I really don't like the idea of us staying just where Peter Myers expects us to be – as unlikely as it might be that he'll come here, I don't want to risk it. If we go up there, stay two nights, say, and keep in contact with the police, hopefully we'll be able to return knowing that Myers has been recaptured.'

'But we'd be going closer to where he comes from,' Lizzy said. 'Do you think that's wise?'

'I know it sounds counterintuitive, but surely that's the one place he won't expect us to be – he won't be looking for us in the North West.'

'You're probably right,' Lizzy said. 'It's definitely an idea. And, I've got to admit, the thought of getting away from London for a few days is very appealing.'

'Can you even get the time off?' Emma asked. 'Haven't you got performances tomorrow?'

'I could pull a sickie. It's not like I don't have a good reason to not want to perform. I could tell them the truth, and try for compassionate leave, but they might say no.'

'And if someone found out?'

'They wouldn't.'

'But if they did, you'd probably lose your job.' Emma looked unconvinced.

'They won't find out, don't worry.'

Dan could understand her reluctance. 'As I said, Em, it's just an idea. We would all need to be happy about it.'

'I'm just not sure I'll be in the mood for a reunion,' she said.

'Of course.' Dan nodded. 'I guess, ultimately, if we go up there and you decide you don't want to go, then we'll just do something else. The trip will still serve the same purpose.'

The idea was starting to sound more appealing. As Dan had said, they would be away from the place where Peter Myers would come looking and, secondly, they would all be together, finding strength in numbers. There was a lot to be said for that. 'What do you think, Will?' Emma asked.

'I think as long as you're okay, we should do it.'

'What about the other problem?' she said. 'That hasn't just gone away, has it? There's still someone out there, blackmailing Will and Dad, and trying to wreck our relationships – someone who knows secrets about us.'

'You're right,' Lizzy said. 'We can't afford to forget about that.'

'I agree,' Dan said, 'and we won't. But, at the moment, I think our priority has to be what's happened with Peter Myers, and to protect ourselves from that. The other situation, it can wait.'

'Dan's right,' Will said. 'We need to put the Myers situation first.' He looked at them all in turn. 'Even if it means going to jail, I don't care. I just want us all to be safe from that man.'

'Okay,' Emma said, slowly. 'Let's go.'

Dan looked pleased. 'Great. We can head off first thing tomorrow morning.'

23

'You okay?' Lizzy asked. She had returned from the bathroom to find Emma resting her head on her hands at the kitchen table.

'Bored,' Emma said, getting to her feet. 'I'm desperate to go for a run. Especially with it raining. There's nothing better than running in the rain for clearing your head. I really feel as though I need it.'

It was ten thirty. Will and Dan had long since left for work, and time was ticking by at a snail's pace. They'd watched TV for a while, but the choice was mind-numbing and more than a little depressing. So they'd turned back to the radio, and had both been reading the trashy celebrity magazines that Lizzy had in her bag. But there was only so much gossip you could look at.

'Maybe you should do it,' Lizzy replied, sitting down at the kitchen table too. 'I'll come with you.'

'Do you think it'd be wise?'

Dan had been adamant that he thought it would be best if Emma stayed in the flat, no matter how unlikely it might be that Peter Myers would be in the vicinity. Will had also been cautious, but Lizzy appeared more relaxed.

'Look, I'm as worried as you about the thought of Peter Myers being loose, but we'll go mad if we stay in here all day, listening to the rain hitting the windows. And surely we'd be safer out there than in here, which is just where he'd come looking for us.'

'Don't,' Emma said, hardly baring to consider that possibility.

Lizzy grimaced, immediately regretting having brought that up. 'We could just go out for a few minutes, stay close by.'

But Emma was having second thoughts. 'Maybe we'll go out later, after lunch.'

'Of course,' Lizzy said. 'Your decision, totally. I'll go along with whatever you think is best.'

Emma smiled her appreciation.

'Em, are you sure you're okay about going to the reunion? I mean, if you're not, maybe we could go somewhere else, instead.'

'It'll be okay. And as Dan said, if I decide I don't want to do it when we get up there, then I'll just leave it.'

'Do you think it might be a bit uncomfortable, you know, if anyone talks to you . . . about Stuart?'

Stuart had been one of the stars of the show for quite a few years and, with Emma, they'd been the golden couple. It was only natural that she would be forever linked with Stuart when it came to *Up My Street*, and his absence would be noticeable and significant.

'I've thought about that. I'm prepared for people to talk about Stuart and, to be honest, I would be sad if people didn't mention him. He should be remembered at the reunion. But hopefully I won't have to break any bad news. Most people will probably know what happened, because word gets around quickly in our business, doesn't it?'

'Probably. I remember that when this girl, Abigail, died in a car accident over in Australia, it got back to us almost immediately, even though she'd left the show I was in a few years before.'

'Exactly.'

'And what if you run into you know who?'

'Charlotte? Then I'll say hello and be nice. It's such a shame she feels the way she does, because we were close for so long.' Emma sighed. 'But I can understand why she feels upset and bitter about what happened. She's lost her brother, and she thinks it's my fault.'

'But it wasn't!'

The unpleasant altercation eight weeks before with Stuart's little sister, Charlotte, where she accused Emma of ruining her brother's relationship with Sally, was still fresh in Emma's mind. 'I know, but she's looking for an explanation as to what happened, and, as far as she's concerned, I'm it. I hope she comes around, and it would be great if we could be on friendly terms, but if not, it won't spoil things – there will be plenty of other people to catch up with. The cast I worked with were lovely, so it would be great to see some of them again.' Emma's voice warmed as she began to see the reunion in a more optimistic light.

'Sounds like it could be an ideal distraction, then. How many people are they expecting?'

'I've got no idea. I don't know very much about it as it's all come through my agent. But I expect there should be quite a few people there, seeing as the show has been running for so long, and the cast turnover is pretty high.'

'Cool,' Lizzy replied. Then, 'So, where's the hoover?'

'Hoover?'

'Yes.' She smiled. 'If we're going to stay inside, I want to keep busy.'

'Oh, don't be . . .'

'No, I mean it. Just show me where it is, and I'll make a start.' She looked down and around at the floor. 'I mean, this place could do with a clean.'

'It's in the bottom of the main wardrobe, in our bedroom but, really, Lizzy, I don't expect you to do our housework!'

But Lizzy was already out of the door, and within a few seconds had come back out of the bedroom, dragging the vacuum cleaner by the hose. And then she was off, vacuuming down the hallway like a pro.

Emma watched her, feeling lazy. She decided to join in and, locating the polish and duster in the cupboard, went to work on the photo frames in the lounge.

She paused at the photograph of her and Dan, taken just one year into their relationship, holding hands, the Eiffel Tower their backdrop. Dan had booked the three-day break as a surprise for their first date anniversary. They'd travelled first-class on Eurostar, having got a great last-minute deal which had included an upgrade, and had stayed in a lovely little hotel called the Hotel Louvre. They'd been taking the photograph, with Dan stretching his arm out and turning the camera back on themselves to try to get them both in shot, when a passer-by, a local Parisian student, had offered to take their picture.

It had only been a few years ago, but they both looked so much younger, and so carefree. She wondered just how much they had aged in the past few months.

Lizzy entered with the vacuum, the machine still whirring noisily, and stopped as she saw Emma staring at the photograph.

'I'm just reminiscing,' Emma explained, over the noise.

Lizzy nodded and carried on cleaning, getting on her knees as she manoeuvred the hose around the base of the sofa. 'You know, this is really rather satisfying,' she shouted over the noise, her head almost disappearing under the sofa. 'It's much more fun cleaning someone else's home!'

Emma gave the Paris photograph a final wipe with the duster and placed it back on top of the mantelpiece. She was just about to pick up the next photo – a family shot of a five-year-old Emma with her mother and father at a holiday camp in Wales – when she heard a jarring noise coming from the cleaner.

Lizzy extracted herself from under the sofa. 'What the—?'

'Something's caught,' Emma said, pressing the off button with her foot. She crouched down and took the hose from Lizzy. A quick waggle of the hose revealed that whatever had been sucked up had now travelled up into the bag. Which was a pity, as it would be a messy job to recover the item.

'Probably money,' Lizzy said. 'Happens to me quite a lot, but unfortunately it's always one or two pence pieces. Never a pound coin.'

'It sounded like metal,' Emma agreed, opening up the vacuum cleaner's casing and easing her hand into the bag. She felt around among the clumps of dust and fluff, pushing her hand in as far as it could go.

'My hands are a little smaller,' Lizzy said.

Emma stretched just that bit further. 'It's okay, I've got it.' Like one of those grabber machine games at the funfair, Emma clung on to the item firmly as she drew it slowly back through the opening.

As it emerged from the inside of the cleaner, she couldn't quite believe it. She picked off the dust that masked the gold band. 'It's Dan's wedding ring.'

'Wow,' Lizzy said. 'Lucky we realised. I wonder how it got there.'

'Fallen off, I guess.' But Emma was perturbed, and Lizzy could see it.

'Is it too big, then?' she said.

Emma slipped the ring onto her own finger. 'No. At least, I didn't think so.'

Just then Lizzy's phone rang from the kitchen. Emma sat on the sofa, inspecting the ring, as Lizzy took the call.

Around the inside of the ring were Dan and Emma's names, along with the date of their wedding. It had been such an amazing day – the most brilliant day of her life so far. She closed her eyes and pictured the stunning Minack Theatre in Cornwall, its stone amphitheatre bathed in golden sunshine, as the ocean sparkled blue behind it. It had felt like the happy ending that they all deserved.

But what if our story isn't going to have a happy ending?

'I'm really sorry, Em,' Lizzy said, hurrying back into the room. 'I've got to go down to the theatre. The producer's called a full cast meeting. They won't say what it's about, but they want us there right now.' She looked at her friend. 'Will you come with me? It'd be absolutely fine, although I don't know how long the meeting will last.'

'It's fine, I'll be okay here.'

'Are you sure?' Lizzy looked doubtful. 'I suppose as long as I come straight back . . . I won't hang around afterwards.'

'I'll watch one of the box sets,' Emma said. 'Or carry on cleaning. Honestly, you just go, and don't worry.'

'Thanks, Em,' Lizzy said, kissing her friend goodbye. She headed for the door. 'I'll be back in no time.'

24

He watched from the van, parked across the street, as Lizzy exited the apartment block. *Emma is now alone.* His persistence had paid off. He followed Lizzy with his eyes as the strawberry-blonde crossed the street, just in front of his vehicle, and headed for the bus stop, some thirty or so metres ahead of where he was parked.

There was no way he could risk her seeing him.

He waited with growing impatience as Lizzy stood there, letting two buses pass by. He looked up at the window to Emma's flat. *Soon we'll be together.* The thought gave him a glow, a thrill, of deep satisfaction.

A bus stopped, and Lizzy was gone.

He smiled as he admired his bruised and battered face in the rear-view mirror.

It was time.

25

Emma placed Dan's wedding ring out of harm's way in a small, decorative dish that they'd bought in Cornwall, and took up where Lizzy had left off with the hoover. But the physical exertion of the vacuuming couldn't banish the anxieties about why the wedding ring had been under the sofa in the first place.

Dan hadn't mentioned anything about the ring being too big – they'd had the rings fitted properly in the shop. Normally, she wouldn't have thought anything about it, but the revelation about Dan and Stuart had shaken her confidence.

Emma's anxieties were interrupted by the door buzzer. She felt unnerved by the insistence of its sound and, for a moment, she waited, frozen to the spot in the living room. She was briefly surrounded by silence, and then it buzzed again. And again. And *again* – this time for longer, more intrusively, more menacingly.

'Please, just go away,' she whispered.

And her wish seemed to have been answered. The buzzing stopped. She moved over to the window and peered through the rain-spotted glass at the street below. It was busy with people, many with umbrellas up. Her pulse was racing. She focused on the people, scrutinising each person who passed by.

She couldn't see anyone who resembled Peter Myers.

And then the landline rang. It shocked her much more than it should have done, sending her moving for the protection of the wall, unconsciously seeking shelter.

But as the phone continued to ring, she re-gathered her composure. It could be anyone. There was no reason to assume it was something sinister. Steeling herself, she reached out and snatched up the receiver, her breathing heavy against the mouthpiece. 'Hello?'

An automated voice responded. 'This is the SMS messaging service. Press one to hear your message.'

She relaxed. This had happened before, a few months ago. Instead of texting her mobile, Lizzy had texted their home phone by mistake. She had probably done the same thing again.

She pressed one. A computerised voice told her again that she had a message, and then gave the number of the mobile it was sent from. It wasn't Lizzy's number, or any other that she recognised. Then, 'Hello, Emma,' the computerised voice said. 'I'm your number one fan. I know you're alone. You shouldn't be alone.'

Emma slammed the phone down. 'Oh my God!'

She spun around, as if someone was just hovering behind her back. Of course there was no one – yet, someone had been downstairs, pressing on the buzzer.

She ran to the door and checked that the internal lock was across. Then she returned to the phone. First she would call Dan, then Gasnier.

But before she could dial, there was a knock on the door.

She thought about making a phone call first but instead, unable to stop herself, she crept over to the door and slowly placed an eye up to the spyhole.

26

Will got the call shortly after ten thirty that morning. He'd been totally unproductive in the first hour and a half of the day, his attention wandering between the work he should have been doing, the blackmailer and Peter Myers.

He moved into the stairwell when he realised it was Sally that was phoning. The office was busy, and he didn't want any of his colleagues listening. 'Hi, Sally, how are you?'

'I'm fine,' she said. But her tone struck Will as curt and rather cold.

He waited a beat to see if she'd add anything else, but she didn't, so he filled the void. 'Aren't you at work?'

'It's first break,' she explained. In the background he could hear children shouting. 'I'm out on playground duty.'

'So it's not raining there, then? It's just started again here.'

'No, dry here for the moment.' A girl's excitable screams cut into the conversation. 'Look, Will,' Sally continued, 'the reason I called is because, well, I think it would be for the best if we didn't see each other again.'

The statement, said in such a matter-of-fact way, hit Will hard. 'What? I don't understand. Why?'

'I just think it would be for the best.'

Will tried to hide his anguish as two workers descended the stairs, deep in conversation. He waited for them to pass through the double doors into the main office. 'Is it because of what I said, about being in love with you?' He smacked his hand silently against the wall in frustration. 'What I said about just being friends, I meant it. If you don't want a relationship, and just want to be friends, that's fine. I'll never pressure you, I promise.'

'It's not that Will – sorry, hang on a minute . . . Boys, get back from over there right now! You know that it's out of bounds! . . . Sorry, Will, I had to deal with that.'

'Don't worry, I understand. You've got your job to do.'

'Will, I just think that we'd both benefit from a clean break. I'm sorry. Look, I've got to hang up now – the bell is about to go and I need to be back over in the school block. I'm sorry, Will, take care.'

Will let his arm, along with his phone, drop down to his side. He leant against the wall, feeling sick. He knew it was pathetic, mourning the death of a relationship that never really was, but he couldn't help it. *The trouble with love is that the more you try to contain it, bottle it inside, deny its existence, the more self-destructive it becomes.*

After a minute or so of wondering whether to call her back, Will returned to his desk and desperately tried to lose himself in his work. When his phone rang a few minutes later, he snatched it up, longing to hear her say that she had changed her mind. But one look at the caller ID disappointed him: it was his father. He rejected the call. He didn't want to talk to anyone at that moment, least of all his father. He would call him back later.

***

It was approaching lunchtime when Will decided on his bold, and probably foolish, course of action. His line manager gave him permission for an extended lunch break and, armed with a print-out of directions, he caught a bus towards the Angel interchange, where he switched onto the tube and headed south of the river.

All through the journey he questioned his actions and, at one point, nearly turned back. But he held his nerve, and eventually arrived at Brownstone Academy, the former comprehensive school where Sally worked.

He knew from the school website that the lunch-time break ended in half an hour, so it would give him plenty of time to talk to Sally before her classes resumed. He had no idea what he was going to say, or whether it would make any difference, but he didn't want their relationship to end on a phone call. Even if the outcome didn't change, to say goodbye in person would feel so much better. *At least, I hope it does.*

Will made his way through the entrance gate and headed for Reception. 'Hello. I'm looking for Sally Thompson. I need to speak to her, quite urgently.' He didn't know what the protocol was for allowing visitors, but the receptionist, a lady in her late sixties with a kindly face and glasses perched on the end of her nose, nodded without question and picked up a phone. 'And your name is——?'

'Will. Will Holden.'

She spoke to someone on the other end of the line. 'Sally is out on the training pitch at the moment, with the girls' hockey team. But her colleague said she'll be finished in the next ten minutes. You're welcome to wait in the sports centre office.'

The directions were easy to follow, and within a couple of minutes he reached the sports centre. Dodging his way across a crowded playground, he'd noticed some glances from pupils, distracted from their play by his presence – possibly wondering whether he was a new member of staff.

Will had once flirted with the idea of a career in teaching, maybe in business studies or English, but had been put off by his aunt, who had retired from the profession and warned him to steer clear: 'If you want a lifetime of stress, by all means go for it. But otherwise, I'd go for a nice office job,' she had said.

But the office job he had was dull and undemanding. Teaching would have been difficult, but it might have challenged and improved him as a person. There were days, especially recently, when he wondered why he had been swayed by the opinion of one, world-weary person.

Will looked out across the training pitch. He could see Sally in the middle of the girls, as they twisted and turned, hacking and lunging at the ball. She was in a dark tracksuit, her blonde hair tied back in a ponytail. He could see a whistle bouncing around her neck. She looked really good.

Instead of waiting inside the sports centre, he decided to stay where he was and watch the rest of the game. In fact, they finished after only five minutes or so, and the girls trooped off to get changed while Sally hung back with a couple of the players, chatting, as they left the playing area. She was still talking to them when she spotted Will.

Her reaction was immediate. She let the two girls go and jogged towards him; she didn't look happy. 'Will, what are you doing here?'

Will reddened. 'I . . . I wanted to come and see you.' He knew it sounded pathetic, but it was the truth.

'But I'm at work, Will. Couldn't this have waited?'

Will hung his head, his previous conviction of certainty disintegrating in the face of her disapproval. 'You're right. I'm sorry, I'll just go.' He turned, reluctantly, and started to head back the way he'd come, across the now deserted playground.

'Wait!' Sally called. 'Come back.'

Will turned around, and Sally closed the gap between them. 'It's my fault,' she said, her face softening. 'I called you from work, so I shouldn't be angry about you coming here now.'

'It's okay,' Will said. 'I can go, really. You don't want to be discussing your private life in school.'

'There's a place we can go,' she said. 'We've got an office in the sports centre. There won't be anyone there at the moment.' She turned and he followed her.

The office was indeed empty. It was a small space, with just enough room for a desk, two chairs and a filing cabinet. Shelves high up on the wall were full to bursting with ring binders, and the atmosphere was dusty. 'This isn't your staff room, is it?'

'God, no. We've got a bigger room down the corridor. This place is reserved for one-to-one meetings between staff. Although it's not the most welcoming of places, as you can see.'

Sally offered Will a seat, but he declined. He didn't want to have this conversation sitting down and, anyway, he wasn't sure it was going to last that long.

'So,' Sally said, remaining standing herself. 'What did you come here for, Will?'

'I wanted to know why you don't want to see me again.'

Sally shrugged. 'I don't know what I can add from what I said on the phone. I just think it's for the best, Will. I'm really sorry.'

'But that's not what you said before, on the London Eye. You agreed that we could be friends.'

'I know, but I've changed my mind. There's too much history' – she shrugged with exasperation – 'too much has happened between us. I thought we could get past it, but now I don't think we can. It would be too difficult to make it work.'

Will shook his head. 'There must be a reason why you've changed your mind.'

Sally's silence provided Will with his answer.

'So what is it?' he pressed.

It was Sally's turn to shake her head.

'Please, tell me. And then I'll go, and you'll never have to see me again, if that's what you want.'

'Just leave it, Will.'

But Will was in no mood to back down. He didn't want to leave the stuffy office with questions unanswered, even if he wasn't going to like the answer. 'Tell me, please.'

Sally placed her hands on the desk, staring down at them. Then, raising her head slowly, she fixed her stare on Will. 'Okay. If you really want to know, I'll tell you.'

Now that she had relented, Will almost regretted pushing her into telling the truth. Maybe he should have just left it and remained ignorant, rather than face the painful facts.

'You might like me, Will. Or even love me. But I don't think you trust me.'

'I do trust you. I said I did, and I mean it.'

'But I planned to kill you.'

'I know, but you didn't do it!' Will almost laughed. 'We've been through all of this, haven't we? We've discussed it. I thought it was all sorted out. It doesn't make sense, what you're saying.'

Sally hesitated for a couple of seconds. 'Your father came to see me last night.'

'What? My dad came to see you? Why?'

'I thought you'd know,' she said, blinking. 'After all, you gave him my address.'

'I didn't!' Will was perplexed. 'I swear I didn't.'

'Well, he said that you did.'

'Then he's lying. He didn't ask for your address from me, and I didn't give it to him.'

'Well, he must have got it from someone,' Sally replied.

Will sought an explanation. Nothing came to mind, apart from the unpalatable possibility that his father had been through his address book. But when? *Could he have used the spare key to get into my flat while I was out?* It was certainly plausible. 'Why did he come to see you?'

'He wanted to warn me off from blackmailing you.'

Will felt nauseous. He didn't know what to say. Would his father ever learn to stop trying to control everything about their lives? He hadn't changed at all.

'Well, don't you want to ask me yourself?' Sally said, remaining calm, her arms now crossed. 'Don't you want to ask me whether I'm a blackmailer?'

Will kept quiet, still struggling for a reply.

'You *do* think that, don't you? You think that I'm blackmailing you.' She shook her head. 'You see, Will, you *don't* trust me. And, to be honest, if I were you, I would probably think the same. That's why we can't be friends.'

'We did think it might be you,' he admitted.

'We?'

'Yes, Emma and the others.'

Sally seemed to find that amusing. 'You see, Will, even if you did trust me, your friends and family never will.'

'That doesn't matter.'

'It does matter. I don't want you to have to choose between me and them. It just wouldn't be fair.'

Will put his arms up and gripped the back of his neck. 'Did he tell you what I'm being blackmailed about?'

'No.'

Well, at least that was something. The way his father was behaving, throwing wild accusations around, he risked letting the truth out in the most damaging way.

'And I don't want to know,' Sally continued. 'Unless you want to tell me. But whether you tell me or not, it sounds like you should go to the police, rather than let your family and friends try to sort things out.'

Now Will did sit down. 'I can't go to the police.' He looked up. 'That's the whole problem. Years ago I did something terrible. It wasn't planned, and I've regretted it ever since. But if the police find out, then I will go to jail, I'm sure I will.'

Sally sat down too. 'You don't have to tell me, Will, really.'

Will took a few deep breaths, cupping his hands over his face. *Am I really going to tell her the truth?* He remembered how the woman on the plane coming back from Canada had reacted, those few months ago, when he had bared his soul. She had been repulsed, her

139

desperation to move seats underlining the strength of her reaction. To that woman Will was a murderer, with blood on his hands. And not just that, but a danger from whom she had to escape. *What's to say that Sally won't react in the same way?*

But, despite his misgivings, the words were already making their way out: 'I helped Stuart to dispose of a body.'

The statement hung in the air like a spectre.

Sally's face twisted in disbelief. '*What?*'

It was too late to go back now. Will closed his eyes and continued along the path rolling out before him. 'I helped Stuart to dispose of Stephen Myers' body, after he killed him.'

'You're lying,' Sally said, shaking her head numbly. 'You're a liar. Stuart wouldn't have done something like that.'

'I'm really sorry,' Will said, 'but I'm telling you the truth.'

Sally was still shaking her head. 'I think you'd better leave now, don't you?'

'I wanted to tell you the truth,' Will said. 'I didn't want to upset you.'

Her face was contorted in anguish. 'Didn't want to *upset* me?' she spat, her voice rising. 'You've just told me that my fiancé was a murderer, and you *didn't* want to upset me?'

'I'd better go.' He made to stand.

'Why are you doing this, Will? Do you think that by saying these things, it will make me just run into your arms and forget about Stuart?' She was crying now. 'Or are you just trying to get revenge, by destroying the good memories I have left of my time with Stuart?'

'I'm so sorry.' Will reached out to place a hand on her shoulder, but she shrugged him off.

'Get off me!'

Too late Will remembered what Sally had said about her vulnerability after Stuart's death, and how she had wanted to take her own life. His actions had now surely put her at risk once again. He should never had said anything. 'I'm really sorry.'

Her head was now on the desk, her voice muffled. 'Just go, please. Leave me alone.'

Will didn't want to leave her like this. He would never forgive himself if she did something terrible as a result of what he had said. 'You shouldn't be on your own.'

'Just go!' she shouted.

Will nodded and reluctantly rose from his chair. But before he could turn to the door, there was a knock on it from outside.

'Sally, are you okay in there?' A man's voice. And he was coming in.

27

Lizzy emerged from the meeting with the producer, along with her fellow cast members and the crew. The news had been important, unexpected and disappointing. It had been announced that the show, although still drawing in the crowds and receiving critical acclaim, would not continue beyond May of next year.

Although no one had expected the sixties musical, *Like We Did Last Summer*, to last for ever, there had been high hopes that this one might last longer than some: making it past the first few weeks had been an immense achievement, as bigger and much most costly shows had floundered within a month of opening. Lizzy had assumed that this initial success would drive it forward for at least a year or so, but it wasn't to be.

'I'm really sorry to have to break this news,' the producer, Jason Conway, had said. He had evidently been keen to soften the blow. 'But there is a bright spot to lift the gloom. We all know how great this show is, and how you are the people who make it so great. So we will be taking it on tour around the UK, to all the major cities. We'll have to scale things down, of course, but we'd like as many of you as possible to join us.'

If the producer had expected moods to brighten when presented with this opportunity, he was mistaken. Yes, it was better than nothing, but most of the performers had spent years, sometimes over a decade, touring around the country, with the single goal of making it to the West End. They were already where they wanted to be. The thought of performing in Bristol, Newcastle, Birmingham – an endless blur of cities – wasn't really that appealing. It would certainly feel like a step back for most of the cast, including Lizzy.

The producer had sensed the deflation among his troops. 'There is always the possibility that we might return to London. It's happened before.'

But again that hadn't cut much ice. It had happened before, but with established shows that had merely been 'rested' from West End production for a couple of years, before returning fresh for another sell-out run. Jason Conway knew this, and so did the experienced cast.

'So, what do you think you'll do, Lizzy?' Sophie asked, as they made their way out of the meeting. Sophie was in her early twenties, and had got her big break quite early in her career. She was a real talent. And, importantly, while some people in the business would step on your head to climb the ladder, Lizzy didn't think Sophie was like that at all. For that reason, she was more than happy to give her advice.

'I think I'll be looking for another job,' she replied.

'You wouldn't consider touring?'

'No, and to be honest, Sophie, I don't think it would be a good career move for you.'

'But I need to pay the bills.'

'You'll get into another show, no problem.'

'Maybe,' Sophie replied, not sounding convinced.

'There's no maybe about it, Sophie. You're a fantastic vocalist, and a great actor. You could turn your hand to a number of things – singing, television, maybe even film if given the opportunity.'

'You think so?'

'I know so.'

'Thanks.' Sophie smiled. 'I know you'll be all right, Lizzy, because you're the best.'

'Hey' – Carly, another one of the girls broke in – 'you both up for a drink across the road? You know, drown our sorrows?'

Lizzy thought of Emma, alone in the flat. 'Sorry, I've got to be somewhere else. Have a drink or three on me.'

***

Lizzy exited the theatre and headed for the tube, en route back to Emma. She was just about to descend the steps to the underground station when her phone rang.

'Lizzy, Adrian Spencer here.'

She grimaced, standing aside for a businessman as he strode past into the station. The last thing she needed right then was another conversation with Adrian Spencer. But, at the same time, she was

143

intrigued about the reason the TV researcher would have to ring her. 'Adrian, hello.'

'Whereabouts are you?'

'I'm just outside a tube station, in the West End. Why?'

'Because I want to see you,' he said.

'And what makes you think that I want to see you?'

Lizzy's response elicited a laugh. 'You would if you knew what I was going to say.'

Lizzy nearly cut the call there and then. The guy was talking in riddles again, and she really didn't have the patience for it. 'Look, I'm busy right now. I can't just drop everything.'

'I know about Peter Myers,' he said.

Lizzy's interest sharpened, but she wanted to test that he wasn't just bluffing. 'Know what about Peter Myers?'

'That he escaped from custody and is still on the loose as we speak.'

Lizzy traced her tongue across her bottom lip. He obviously had his contacts. 'That isn't public knowledge,' she said. 'Who told you?'

'I have my sources.' She could hear him smiling. 'To be successful in my job, you have to cultivate your contacts.'

'In the police.' Lizzy made the connection. She had been reading all about those sorts of goings-on in the newspapers.

'I don't reveal any of my sources, Lizzy, so I'm afraid you'll just have to speculate as to how I know what I know.'

'It must be someone in the police, because no one else knows,' she said. 'But I don't particularly care. As you'll appreciate, we've all got more important things to think about at the moment.'

'That's why I'm calling.'

'I don't understand.'

'Meet me,' he said. 'Where exactly are you?'

Lizzy shook her head as she relented. She was allowing herself to be played by him. 'Covent Garden.'

'Meet me in Trafalgar Square, under Nelson's Column - the side facing the National Gallery. I'll be there in half an hour.'

***

144

'What's going on?' the man said, looking anxiously at Sally, who was sobbing.

He was athletic in appearance: toned and well over six feet tall, dressed in a tracksuit. He closed the door behind himself.

'It's okay,' Sally said, trying hard to stifle her sobs. 'I'm fine.'

The man looked at her for a few moments, his brow furrowed. He then turned his attention to Will, who was wishing he could be anywhere else. 'Why is Sally so upset?'

'I'm sorry,' was all that Will could think of saying. 'I'm really sorry. I didn't mean to upset her.'

Sally had started to calm down, dabbing at her eyes with a tissue. 'Can you please just leave, Will.'

Will nodded, glad to have the excuse to go. 'Of course. I am really sorry, Sally.' Thankfully, the other man let him pass without another word, although Will got the impression that he was holding himself back.

Once outside, Will strode across the playground, back towards the exit. By the time he had left the school grounds, he had started to really worry. *What if, right now, Sally is telling that man my confession?* He would still be seeking an explanation for her upset, and she might just tell him.

As Will crossed the road, he wished that he had just let their relationship end at that earlier phone call. *It's all Dad's fault!* What the hell had he been thinking, getting involved in that way, throwing accusations around and revealing the blackmail attempt? His interfering had just made things worse.

Will looked at his watch. He could make up the extra time at work. Instead of heading back to the office, he made for his father's house. He needed to stop him from causing any more damage.

***

'Will. Hi!'

Will was taken by surprise to see a heavily pregnant Miranda open the door. He had assumed she would be at work. 'Hi, Miranda. Is Dad at home?'

'Yes, yes, he's up in his study. Come in, I'll call him down.'

'It's okay,' Will said. 'I'll go up to him.'

'Has something happened? Have they found Peter Myers?'

'Not that I know of. Everything's fine,' he lied. 'I'm on an extended lunch break. I just needed to chat to Dad about something.'

He left Miranda downstairs and knocked on the study door.

'Yes?' Edward must have heard him talking to Miranda, as he didn't seem surprised to see his son. He simply looked up from his desk, pen in hand. 'William. You're not working today?'

'I am. But I needed to speak to you.' He clenched his fists, trying to stop the trembling in his hands. 'You went to speak to Sally.'

Edward placed his pen on the desk. 'Just close the door.' Will did as requested and Edward continued. 'How do you know about that?'

'Because she told me.'

'You're still in touch with her?'

'Yes. We got back in touch recently.'

'Why?'

'Because I wanted to.'

Edward laughed in disbelief. 'What, you wanted to reconnect with the woman who plotted to murder you?'

'Sally isn't a bad person, Dad.'

Another laugh. 'William, I'm not sure that you're the best judge of personality.'

Will swallowed his rising anger. 'I didn't come to discuss that. I came to ask why you went round to Sally's place, accusing her of being the blackmailer.'

'Because it all points towards her,' his father replied. 'She has the past form, and she had the means of finding out about what you did, because of her close connection to Stuart Harris.'

'So you just went storming over there, without any evidence.'

'It all points towards her,' his father repeated.

'How did you even know where she lives?'

Edward stayed silent.

'You got her address from my flat, didn't you?'

'Yes.' Edward heaved a sigh from deep within himself. 'I had to do something, William. I wasn't prepared to let it carry on, and just sit by.'

'God, Dad, do you know what trouble you've caused?' Will stared at his dad, uncomprehendingly. 'Sally knows all about it now! She knows the truth, and she might have told other people.'

Edward stood up. 'What? I didn't tell her.'

'No, but I did.'

'*What?* Why the hell would you do that?' Now it was Edward's turn to look on in disbelief.

'Because it just happened. It wasn't planned.' Will was sullen.

Edward shook his head. 'Sometimes, Will, you are your own worst enemy. It's almost like you want something bad to happen – you bring it on yourself.'

'Thanks for that, Dad. Thanks for your support.'

'Oh, grow up, William.'

'Maybe I am finally growing up, Dad. And I'm sick of being controlled by you.'

'Fine,' Edward said, throwing his hands up in the air. 'If you don't want my help, then that's up to you.' He turned back to his desk and started blindly sorting through the papers there. 'But good luck finding the money to pay the blackmailer.'

Will shook his head. 'Typical cheap shot.'

Edward was about to fire back a response when they heard a sudden groan from the other side of the door.

Will flung it open to see Miranda outside, bent double against the wall, breathing hard. 'It's the baby,' she said, from between gritted teeth. 'I think it's coming.'

Edward looked horrified. 'But it's not due for another month and a half!'

Miranda glared at him. 'You'd better get my bag ready. And then you can tell me the truth about what the hell's going on.'

28

'Lizzy, hello.'

Lizzy was standing beneath the statue of Admiral Nelson. She had been admiring the twenty-foot high Norway Spruce Christmas tree nearby, a tradition of the festive season in London. She had turned as Adrian Spencer approached, his hands buried in the pockets of his trench coat. The sky was dark and threatening rain, the wind whipping up litter around her feet. 'Adrian.'

'We must stop making a habit of this,' he said.

Lizzy smiled a tight smile. 'Don't worry, I intend to.'

Adrian laughed. 'Oh, Lizzy, I do love your feistiness.'

Lizzy shuddered at the thought that he might be trying to flirt with her. 'You've got something to tell me?'

'Yes.'

'So, what are you waiting for?'

Lizzy thought she saw a smile flicker across his lips. 'I wanted to reiterate what I said about Peter Myers. He's extremely dangerous. You all need to be very careful of that man.'

Lizzy couldn't believe it. 'Is that it? Is that why you brought me here, to tell me that Peter Myers is a dangerous man?'

'I—'

'Don't you think we know full well how dangerous he is? I mean, he nearly killed Richard, and he kidnapped Dan and me! We don't need you to tell us to be careful.'

'I know you don't,' he said.

'Are you enjoying this?'

'I don't know what you mean.' He looked taken aback.

'How did you feel when you were told that Peter Myers had escaped? I bet you were glad.'

'No, I wasn't.'

'Really? Don't you like watching us suffer, and living in fear?'

'You've got me wrong, Lizzy! I'm not the one who's pleased about this.'

Lizzy stopped. 'Who *would* be pleased about it?'

'Firework Films,' he replied.

'What do you mean?'

'Well, they're the ones who will benefit from everything that is happening. I've got nothing to gain, but they certainly have.'

'I don't understand.'

'Lizzy, you can't have forgotten about the docudrama.'

Lizzy blinked. 'Of course I haven't.'

'Well, what do you think Firework Films' reaction will be when they hear the news that Peter Myers has escaped?'

'I have absolutely no idea.'

'I can tell you exactly what their reaction will be. Elation. It's more drama for their programme. They won't be able to believe their luck, because for them, the plot is just getting better and better. And one thing's for certain – they won't be thinking about the welfare of you and your friends.'

'Surely they're not that mercenary?'

He smiled. 'Firework Films is single-minded when it comes to achieving its goals. They don't care who they hurt, as long as it makes good television.'

'They're really that bad?'

'I worked for them, Lizzy, remember? I know what they're like. The participants in some of their programmes were exploited, made to look like fools.'

'But don't people complain, if they're being exploited as you say?'

'No. Most of the people who feature in their programmes are, by definition, vulnerable. They can't stand up for themselves. And in the instances where they have raised concerns, Firework Films has a very effective response strategy.'

'Which is?'

'Bribery. They pay to shut them up. Usually it doesn't take much money to appease them.'

'Has that happened a lot?' Lizzy was shocked.

'Yes. It's just part of their normal working practice. That way, the programmes get made and, to some extent, everyone is happy.'

'But it's totally unethical!'

'Yes, but that's just how it works.'

'And no one has taken things further?'

'Apart from you, no.'

'And we complained about you, rather than the company.'

His was a tight smile. 'Exactly. So they just got rid of me, and hey presto, the problem was solved.'

'When, in fact, you were just carrying out their orders,' Lizzy said slowly. '*They* were the ones who were coordinating things.'

'I think you're finally starting to understand. Don't underestimate them,' he warned.

'You make it sound like we should be afraid of them.'

'Not afraid, but wary. Lizzy, I know you're a savvy person, and from my time trying to get information out of you, it's clear to me that you care about your friends deeply, and that you want to protect their well-being. You should just be wary about anybody who threatens that, including Firework Films.'

'But what are we supposed to do? Complain to the regulator?'

'I wouldn't waste my time – it won't get you anywhere. Just be on your guard.'

Lizzy looked at him. 'But that's not really helpful. Don't you think we aren't already?'

'I'm sure you are. Just make sure that you keep your eye on all the threats.'

Lizzy let out an exasperated sigh. 'There you go again, being cryptic. If you really want to help us, then just talk straight, please!'

'Okay, okay,' Adrian said. 'I will.' He gathered his thoughts. 'Now that I'm not working for them, don't you think that they might have other people, taking up from where I left off?'

'Following us, you mean?'

'Exactly. And now with what's happened with Peter Myers, expect their interest to intensify.'

Without really thinking, Lizzy looked around the large square. There were only a handful of people in the vicinity, and they were on the move. No one appeared to be loitering.

'They're smarter than that,' Adrian said. 'They won't be that obvious. Not after what happened with me. They know that you'll be wise to people following you, so they'll more than likely adopt different tactics.'

'Like what?'

'Longer-range surveillance maybe, using telescopic lenses. Phone tapping, possibly.'

Lizzy reacted with incredulity. 'Phone tapping? You can't be serious?'

'They've done it before. It doesn't have to be fitting something to a phone – I'm sure you've read the stories about the press listening to mobile-phone voice messages of celebrities and crime victims?'

Lizzy nodded.

'So, they've done it before. How secure is your mobile messaging service, Lizzy? Have you set your own password?'

'Er, no, I haven't.'

'So it'll still be set as the factory default number, which is probably four zeros – it almost invariably is. That means, as long as someone knows your mobile phone number, which Firework Films do, they can dial in and listen to your messages.'

'Did you do that?'

'No, not with you. But I know it's been done in the past.'

'By Firework Films?'

He nodded. 'By Firework Films, indeed.'

'I need to change my password,' she said.

'Yes, you do. And so does Emma and the others. The sooner the better.'

This was great advice. But there was one thing still bugging Lizzy. 'Why are you helping us?'

'Because I want to make things as difficult as possible for them. They thought that I'd go quietly, but I'm really not that kind of person.'

'So you're not doing this out of the goodness of your heart.'

He smiled. 'No, I suppose I'm not. But does it matter?'

'No,' Lizzy replied, 'I guess it doesn't.'

'There's one other piece of information that I want to give you.'

'Go on—?'

'You've not asked me yet who Firework Films are. Aren't you interested?'

Stupidly, Lizzy hadn't really thought about the people behind the company. Adrian Spencer had always personified Firework and, beyond that, she hadn't considered who else was involved. 'Yes, I do want to know.'

'A search on the Companies House website will reveal who the directors are,' he said. 'I think you'll be surprised.'

'You're not going to tell me?'

'Just do the search,' he said, walking away as rain began to fall.

***

Lizzy sheltered across the road from Trafalgar Square, in the entrance to the National Portrait Gallery, as the rain intensified. Buses and taxis splashed past, their windscreen wipers desperately trying to push the water away. A fresh and strengthening wind whipped into the sheltered area where Lizzy stood as she pulled out her phone and searched online for the Companies House website.

It came up as the first result, and offered a full listing of all limited companies in the UK. For more detailed trading data, she would have to pay a small fee, but there was free access to basic information – including the address of the company and a list of directors. She found the 'Search for company' section and typed in 'Firework Films'.

The result came straight back. Lizzy clicked on the company name and its information page loaded. It was registered to an address in London. And there, on the right-hand side of the page, were the names of the three company directors. She didn't know two of the names. But the name of the third director certainly stood out.

Mr Guy Roberts.

'Son of a . . .'

Guy Roberts is one of the men behind Firework Films? The man who had contributed to the stress and anxiety they had all suffered over the summer, thanks to his commission of David Sherborn to pursue and photograph Emma – for nothing more than a calculated, cold-blooded PR stunt for his film – was now intending to profit from a television programme about it all? And, what was more, for that purpose he had employed Adrian Spencer to hound them *as well?*

Lizzy was seething. Now she could place the comments from Adrian Spencer in a better context. Guy Roberts was a man who apparently had no morals, and was prepared to do whatever it took to get what he wanted. Maybe it was partly about revenge – Emma had, after all, rejected his offer of a movie role, so perhaps he wanted to punish her. Or maybe it was just about money – finding another way to exploit her story for commercial gain? Whatever the reasoning, it was reprehensible.

But now the truth was out, and he could be exposed.

She dialled Emma's home number. It rang and rang. With each ring, her rage was replaced by worry. *Why isn't she picking up?* She dialled her mobile. 'C'mon, Em, where are you?' No answer there either. *Maybe she went for that run after all. But then wouldn't she have taken her mobile with her?*

She called Dan, trying to steady her nerves as the call went through. She didn't want to worry him unnecessarily.

'Dan, have you spoken to Emma in the last hour or so?'

'No. I was about to call her. I've been in meetings all day. You're not with her?'

'I got called to work,' she explained. 'Emma stayed at the flat. I've just tried to call her, but there's no answer on either your home phone or her mobile.'

'My God.'

'It might be nothing,' Lizzy said, trying to reassure herself as much as Dan. 'She mentioned wanting to go for a run, so maybe she's done that and forgotten her phone, or just hasn't heard it.'

'Maybe.' But he sounded worried.

'I'm going back there now,' Lizzy said, moving out onto the pavement and into the onslaught of rain. 'I'll call you as soon as I get there. It's probably nothing, Dan.'

'I hope to God you're right, Lizzy. I'll leave now, and keep trying her phone.'

29

Miranda might have wanted an explanation, but she didn't raise the issue during the panicked drive to the hospital – she was in too much pain to care about anything other than the there and then.

'It'll be okay,' Edward repeated, for what must have been the fiftieth time, as he accelerated along the road. He glanced in the rear-view mirror. 'We're nearly there, we're almost there.'

Miranda was in the back alongside Will. She was focusing on her breathing, gripping Will's hand. Every so often she would grimace in pain, squeezing it yet tighter.

'It's okay, we'll be there before you know it,' Will said. Then, 'Look, we're here.'

They pulled to a stop right outside the main entrance, and hurried up to the maternity ward reception.

'I think my wife's in the latter stages of labour,' Edward said to the nurse on duty. 'It came on suddenly. She's in a lot of pain. She's a doctor at this hospital.'

'I know,' the nurse said, catching sight of Miranda, who was hunched over, holding on to Will for support. She was concentrating so much on her own body that she didn't seem to even see her colleague. 'We've worked together many a time. Don't worry, Miranda, we'll get you checked out right away.'

The nurse guided Miranda over to a nearby bay and helped her onto the bed. Within seconds she was wired up to monitoring equipment, and a doctor had arrived.

Will and Edward looked on from the side of the bed as the doctor and nurse scrutinised the various readings. They exchanged a glance and the doctor nodded. He then turned to Miranda. 'Your baby is in some distress. We need to get it out as soon as possible.'

'What, now?' Edward said, blankly.

'It's okay,' Miranda said, speaking through the pain.

Edward looked at the doctor for confirmation.

'We'll perform a C-section,' the doctor said. 'Of course, you're welcome to be present.'

Edward looked at Miranda and nodded. 'Yes, of course I want to be there.'

Within minutes, Miranda was whisked off to the theatre, with Edward following behind.

Will waited in the corridor, walking up and down, on tenterhooks for news. After a while of pacing, sitting, then pacing some more, he tried to call Emma. In all the drama of the past hour or so, he hadn't thought to let her know what was happening. But there was no answer on her mobile or her landline. He then called Lizzy, but her phone cut straight through to her answer service. An uncomfortable thought rippled through him. *Has something happened to Emma?* But the thought was banished by the reappearance of Edward.

As his father approached, still wearing a theatre gown, his face didn't give anything away, but he looked drained.

Will rose from the chair. 'How is she?'

Edward broke out into a broad smile. 'They're both fine.'

The relief was total. 'Really? And it's a—?'

'Boy,' his father said. 'A little boy. We're calling him Jack.'

Will beamed. 'After Granddad.'

Edward nodded and they embraced. It felt strange, but wonderful. Will had never hugged his father before, not even in those dark days after his mother's death. The closest he had come was an uncomfortable back-pat at the funeral.

'I'm really sorry, Will,' Edward said, softly, as they held the embrace. 'I've let you down too many times. Things are going to change.'

Will pulled back. 'I'm sorry too, Dad.'

Edward sat down, and gestured for Will to do the same. 'I know I've said the same thing before, but this time it *is* going to be different. You and Emma, you mean the world to me, and I just want to do the right thing.'

'I know you do.'

'Sometimes I behave stupidly, I know that. Like yesterday, challenging Sally . . . but I did it with the best of intentions. I did it to try and help you.'

155

'I know you did, Dad . . .' Will took a breath, steeling himself, 'but you've got to understand that sometimes we just need you to be there for us – not running around taking action, doing things, trying to sort everything out single-handed, but support us just by being there. You nearly ended up in jail last time you tried to sort things out for me.'

'I know, I know.' Edward looked deep into Will's eyes. 'I just want to make things better.'

'You need to let go of your guilt, Dad, about not helping us when Mum was dying. You need to stop blaming yourself. I know I've been angry about it for a long time, but it's no good living in the past.' Will shrugged. 'We've all got to move on.'

Edward looked puzzled for a moment – the comment had pierced his armour. He cracked, and began to sob into his hands.

Will had never seen his father cry. It was disturbing yet strangely reassuring – he'd always suspected that his hard exterior was just a carefully constructed mask, one that ultimately stopped him from dealing with his issues. He placed an arm around his father's shaking shoulders. 'I'm sorry, Dad. I didn't want to upset you. This should be one of the happiest moments of your life. You have another son. You have a wonderful partner.'

Edward recovered quickly, checking to see if any passers-by had noticed what had just happened, looking embarrassed by his lapse. 'Thanks, Will. It means so much to me that you're here. I don't want you to think that this means I'll forget about you and Emma, because I won't.'

'Don't worry, Dad, we've never thought that. We just want you to be happy.'

'I don't deserve you two,' Edward said. And then he smiled, wistfully. 'I've never told you this, Will, but you really remind me of your mum. Your expressions, your mannerisms, they remind me of her so much. And I still miss her deeply.' A single tear trickled down his cheek, which he stopped with his thumb.

Will nodded. 'I miss her too. But she'd want you to be happy, and to move on. She would hate to think that, years later, you're still racked with guilt about anything you did or didn't do.'

'I know she would. Your mum always wanted the best for us.'

'Exactly. So, you've got to move on. Seize the wonderful opportunity that you've got.'

His father sighed deeply. He was obviously still shaken by his outburst. 'I just don't think I deserve it. I messed up with you and Emma, I was a terrible father. And now I've been given another chance. Why?'

Will shrugged. 'I don't think life works like that. For too long I've tried to work out explanations for why things happen – was it because I did this or said that . . .? As if life is so logical! But I've realised that life *isn't* logical. It's chaotic, filled with chance happenings and events. Some of them are bad, some are good. Mum was a wonderful person. She didn't do anything to deserve to die of cancer, and there's no point thinking of why it happened. It just did. The important thing is how you deal with the good and bad things. You can't spend your life looking back, because then you affect the present, and that is the one thing you do have more control of.'

'I always knew you were a thinker, Will.'

'That's half my problem, generally.' Will gave a dry laugh. 'But in terms of the here and now, you've got to focus on what matters most – Miranda and Jack. And Emma and I will be here to help.'

Edward smiled. 'Thank you. You don't know how much it means to me, to hear you say that. I really want you and Emma to be part of our lives. I would hate it if you thought that Miranda was trying to take your mother's place, because it's not like that at all.'

'We know. We've known that for a long time. I know we had reservations, about the age gap and the timing after mum. But we both think Miranda is great, and she's really good for you. So you've got nothing to worry about, honestly. We're right behind you.'

'I was worried that the baby would cause problems,' Edward said, with the look of someone having a deep secret wrenched from them. 'I was really worried about how you would feel. I thought it might push us away from one another.'

'Don't be silly. Emma and I love babies!'

'I'm stupid, aren't I?' Edward said. 'I shouldn't have underestimated you two. I should have given you more credit from the beginning.'

'As I said, there's no point looking back. Just do the right thing now.'

Edward nodded.

'I tried to call Emma,' Will said. 'I can't get hold of her.'

Edward seemed to be thinking. 'Oh, right . . .'

Just then a nurse approached. 'Mr Holden? Your wife was wondering if your son would like to come in and see the baby.'

'Yes, I'd love to,' Will said.

They followed the nurse into a small ward, partitioned into four with light blue curtains. Miranda was in a bed at the far left-hand corner, with baby Jack next to her in a plastic crib on wheels. He was asleep, wrapped in sheets.

Will could see dark hair peeking from underneath a tea-cosy-style hat that the baby was wearing. 'He's absolutely beautiful.'

Miranda smiled. 'He is, isn't he?'

Will edged towards the crib.

Miranda noted his nervousness. 'It's okay, you can touch him. The doctors have done all their checks, and he's absolutely fine. He's a bit smaller than normal, but that's just because he decided to put in an early appearance.'

'He's amazing,' Will said, moving his finger slowly over Jack's skin. 'He's just so soft and perfect.'

'You can hold him when he wakes up,' she said.

Will looked hesitant.

'Holding him, it's just amazing' Edward said.

Miranda smiled. 'He'll want to meet Uncle Will.'

Will grinned. 'Uncle Will, I like that.' It sounded more appropriate than half-brother. Then he collected himself – he was so caught up in the moment, he hadn't asked Miranda how she was. 'I totally forgot to ask. How are you?'

'I'm fine,' she replied. 'A bit sore but, otherwise, I feel good. Still a bit shocked by how quickly all this has happened.'

Will reached out again to Jack. His appeal was magnetic. 'Yeah, I bet.'

'Your dad was great, though,' Miranda added, reaching out to hold Edward's hand. 'He was so calm, and just kept talking to me, so I didn't really think about everything else that was happening.'

Edward grinned, then grimaced slightly. 'I wasn't present for you or your sister, Will,' he said. 'Back in those days, it wasn't as common for the father to be there in the room. And I've got to admit, I didn't really fancy it. But I regretted it afterwards. So I wanted to do the right thing this time.'

'I'm proud of you, Dad,' Will said.

Edward seemed to really appreciate that. 'Thanks.'

'Does Emma know what's happened?' Miranda asked. 'It would be great for her to be here and see Jack – have all the family together.'

'I couldn't get through,' Will said. He looked across at Edward. 'I'll give her a quick call now, and let her know the good news.'

Edward nodded, suddenly looking serious again.

Will headed back to the corridor and called Emma's landline first. Once again, it just rang and rang. When he tried her mobile, it didn't even ring at all, instead just diverting straight through to the message service. He decided to leave an unworried message, as if by doing so it would increase the likelihood that everything was all right. 'Em, it's Will. I've got some really great news. Dad and Miranda have had their baby. It's a boy and they've called him Jack, after Granddad. Everything is fine. We're at St Thomas' Hospital. Give me a call as soon as you get this.'

He waited for a few seconds after he had ended the call, in the hope that she would ring back immediately. But when there was no response, he called Lizzy. This time, she answered. 'Lizzy, it's Will. Are you with Em?'

Lizzy's response sent him reeling.

30

Lizzy decided it would be quicker to walk, so she set off at a pace through the drenched London streets. The sky was a dark, lowering grey, and there was no sign of the rain abating. She didn't have an umbrella with her and while her winter coat was warm, it was not waterproof, but she kept going, ignoring how soaked she was. Her hair was sticking to her forehead, and water tickled her nose as it dripped off the end.

Lizzy made her way through the back streets of Soho, to the junction of Oxford Street. Buses coasted past, splashing oily rainwater up from the road's edge. She managed to avoid catching any of the large waves. Crossing Oxford Street, she continued northwards, towards Emma and Dan's flat.

Please let everything be all right.

Lizzy pulled out her phone again, in case she had missed a call. She hadn't. But, just as she was about to slide it back into her coat pocket, a call came through.

Her hopes were dashed when she saw from the caller ID that it was Will.

'Lizzy, it's Will. Are you with Em?'

'No,' she replied, narrowly avoiding a deep puddle by the side of the road. 'I had to go to a meeting at work. She stayed at the flat. I'm just on my way back there now.'

'I've been trying to get in touch with her,' Will continued, 'but I can't get any answer, either from their home phone or her mobile. Have you spoken to her recently?'

Lizzy hadn't wanted to involve Will yet, as she didn't want to worry him unnecessarily. But now she had no choice. 'I can't reach her, either. That's why I'm going there now.'

'You don't think—?'

'I'm sure it's okay, Will,' Lizzy cut in quickly. 'There's probably a good explanation as to why she's not answering.'

'I don't like this. It just seems so reminiscent of . . . what happened last time, with Dan.'

'I know, I know. But we shouldn't assume the worst. I'll call you as soon as I get there. It should only be ten minutes or so.'

'Okay,' he said. 'But I might not be able to answer straight away. I'm at the hospital.'

'Hospital, why?'

'Miranda's had her baby. A boy, called Jack.'

Lizzy stopped at a busy junction, waiting to cross. 'That's amazing. Are they all okay?'

'Yes, they're fine. I'm with them. I just popped out to call you.'

Lizzy went for a gap between two taxis. There wasn't much space, but she was quick enough to make it. 'Don't say anything to them, Will. They shouldn't be worrying at such a special time.'

'My dad already knows I can't get in contact, so I'll have to update him. But we won't tell Miranda. I agree. It wouldn't be fair.'

Lizzy ended the call with another promise to call as soon as she knew anything.

As she closed in on the apartment block her nerves grew, and by the time she reached the front entrance her heart was going like a jackhammer. She stood at the base of the steps, looking up to Emma's window. Will had been right: it was too reminiscent of all those weeks ago, the night of the hen party, when they had arrived in the taxi, hoping to find Dan safe. Instead, they had discovered Richard, beaten to within an inch of his life, Dan gone, and the nightmare had begun. It seemed such a long time ago, but it really wasn't.

Lizzy closed her eyes, and mouthed a silent prayer for her friend. Then she keyed in the security code, pulled open the door and stepped into the hallway.

Emma's neighbour, Mr Henderson, was inching his way down the stairs, his hands gripping the banisters tightly and his eyes focused on the floor. He looked so fragile.

Despite her concern for Emma, Lizzy knew she couldn't just ignore him. 'Can I help you?' she asked, moving towards him.

She couldn't help but think of the parallels with last time, when Mr Henderson had intercepted them on the way up to the flat.

161

He looked up, evidently surprised to see her. 'Oh, it's okay, dear, I can manage.' He conquered the last two steps and, looking relieved, made to go past her.

'Mr Henderson, have you seen Emma?'

He turned around slowly. 'No, but I heard her, moving around upstairs.'

Lizzy had never felt so relieved. She climbed the staircase with renewed optimism, convincing herself that everything was indeed all right. It wasn't until she reached the top that the dread returned.

The door to the flat was ajar.

Lizzy froze. 'Please, no,' she whispered. 'Please, not again.'

She considered turning around and calling for help, but then she heard a noise coming from inside the flat. It sounded like a door opening. 'Em? Is that you?' She moved towards the outer door. 'Em?' Her voice was still no more than a whisper.

She pushed open the door as quietly as possible and poked her head around the doorframe. She was sweating as she inched along the passageway towards the kitchen. The door there was half-open, and she could see the light on. 'Emma?' There was no response, but she heard a noise from inside the room. A clatter.

Lizzy didn't like this at all, but it felt too late to turn around. Gathering her courage, she reached out to the door and it swung open.

A black shape bounded towards her.

Lizzy shrunk back. 'No, no, NO!'

The shape skirted past her and sprinted for the open door.

It was a cat. She recognised it. It was often hanging around outside the apartment building. *It must have somehow got in the building and then come in through the open door.* It disappeared down the stairs.

Lizzy put a hand to her head, and looked back at the kitchen. Blowing out a breath of relief, she began to half laugh to herself.

And then another noise came from behind her. She swung around, and caught her breath.

A man was standing in the doorway to the flat.

'It's okay,' he said, holding up his hands. 'It's DI Gasnier.'

Lizzy put a hand up to her mouth. 'You frightened me to death. I thought you were . . .'

162

'I'm really sorry,' he said, seeming uncomfortable in coming any closer and risking putting Lizzy more on edge. 'I saw the open door, and heard your shouts. I really didn't mean to sneak up on you like that.'

'It's okay, really.'

He seemed to relax. 'I came to speak to Emma. Is she around?'

'We've been trying to ring her. I came here looking for her.' Then the realisation dawned. 'My God, something's happened to her. He must have her, he must have taken her!' She covered her mouth with her hands, staring desperately at Gasnier.

Gasnier stepped towards her. 'Please, try not to jump to any conclusions.' He maintained a respectable distance. 'And try not to panic. Can you tell me everything that's happened?'

Lizzy nodded. She felt sick as he shepherded her to the kitchen table and made her sit down. 'I shouldn't have left her alone, I should have said that I couldn't make the meeting. Or I should've insisted that she come with me. And now that monster Peter Myers has got her. Despite all the warnings, I let it happen!' She realised she was beginning to panic and took a deep breath to try and calm herself.

'What makes you think that he's taken her?'

She looked at him as if he had just said the most ludicrous thing imaginable. 'Well, of course he's got her.'

'Lizzy, we work on evidence. Do you have any evidence?'

'Well . . . no,' she admitted. 'But I know that's what has happened.'

'So you tried to call her and there's no answer?'

Lizzy nodded.

'I tried to call too,' Gasnier said. 'I got the same response. Could she have gone out, and maybe her phone is out of battery, or she just can't hear it?'

Lizzy shook her head. 'She said she wanted to go for a run, but I don't think she did.'

'But it's a possibility?'

'Maybe. But I just don't think so. Oh my God, what are we going to do?'

Gasnier held her stare for a couple of moments. 'Are any of her possessions missing? Phone, purse, coat, trainers? Anything you might expect Emma to have on her person.'

'I don't know. I haven't had chance to look.'

'Take a look now,' he said.

Lizzy nodded and searched hurriedly through the flat, while Gasnier watched on.

'I can't find her purse or phone,' she said, looking at Gasnier expectantly. 'I think her winter coat is missing too.'

Gasnier didn't give away any reaction. 'There have been some developments,' he said finally.

'Developments?'

'With Peter Myers. That's why I came here, to tell Emma.'

Lizzy's hopes rose. 'You've recaptured him?'

'I'm afraid not.'

'Then what?'

He seemed to be thinking about how much to tell her. 'We now believe that Peter Myers planned his escape.'

'But you said you thought it was probably just a spur of the moment decision!' Lizzy looked at him, wide-eyed.

'These things often are. But we've got evidence that this isn't the case here.'

'What evidence?'

'Peter Myers was admitted to hospital after being attacked by a fellow inmate. We've now had information that it was planned. Peter Myers asked the prisoner to do it, so that he would be transferred to hospital.'

'So he let himself be attacked?'

'It appears so. And it was a pretty nasty assault. Which it had to be really, to require a hospital transfer. Otherwise it could have just been dealt with by the prison's medical team.'

'He'd go to those lengths?' Lizzy asked, disbelievingly.

'It appears so. Although the attack may have been more severe than he'd planned. It's often the case that when this sort of thing is set up.'

Lizzy was thinking of Emma. *Where is she? Is she okay?* 'You've got to help Emma. You've got to do something! Can't you call your colleagues, let them know what has happened? They could start looking for her.'

'There's something else first.'

'But every minute you wait, something could happen to her!'

164

'It's not as simple as that.'

Just then Dan burst into the flat. 'Emma, Lizzy?'

'We're in the kitchen,' Lizzy shouted, before realising that Dan would interpret the 'we' as being Emma and she.

Dan pushed through the door. 'Thank goodness you're —' He stopped dead at the sight of Gasnier. He looked at Lizzy, his voice cracking. 'Oh my God, no.'

'She wasn't here when I got back,' Lizzy explained. 'And the front door was open.'

'It can't be,' he said, shaking his head. He turned and strode towards the other rooms. 'Em! Emma?'

Lizzy glanced at Gasnier. They could hear doors opening and closing.

'Dan, can you please come back in here?' Gasnier sounded a little as though he was ordering him.

Dan staggered back in. He was crying. He looked over to Lizzy. 'He's got her, hasn't he?'

'I hope not,' she said. 'I really hope not.'

Dan let out a wild, swinging kick at the kitchen bin, shouting, 'I shouldn't have left her!'

It toppled over and crashed to the floor, spilling its contents.

'Dan, you've got to calm down,' Lizzy said. *He's in danger of doing himself, or someone else, harm.* She'd never seen him in such a state before, although in the circumstances it was totally understandable.

Gasnier stood up and took him by both shoulders. Dan fought against looking at him, but eventually fixed his eyes on the officer's. Only then did Gasnier speak. 'Dan, please, just breathe deeply, and take a seat,' he said in a calming, steady voice.

Dan nodded, and did as requested. But although he was now quiet, Lizzy could see that he was only just keeping a lid on his raging emotions.

'Right,' Gasnier said. He recapped the first piece of news, for Dan's benefit. Dan didn't react, but as he listened he appeared to be calming down. And then Gasnier moved on to the next revelation. 'Peter Myers had someone on the outside, helping with the escape.'

'It was all so well planned,' Lizzy said.

165

'Yes, it was. The CCTV from the hospital revealed that there was another person involved – they were driving the car that Peter Myers used to escape from the hospital.'

'Could you see what they looked like?' Lizzy asked.

'Not particularly well,' he admitted. 'The camera was at a distance, and the driver was wearing a baseball cap, so their face was shielded. They knew what they were doing.'

Lizzy caught her breath. *A baseball cap? Could it be—?* 'Do you know what colour it was?'

Gasnier seemed surprised by the detail of the questioning. 'What, the cap or the car?'

'The cap.'

'Dark. Possibly blue, but difficult to say.' He appeared suspicious. 'Why do you ask?'

Lizzy looked across at Dan. He nodded. 'Because there's something we haven't told you.'

31

Gasnier's eyes narrowed. 'I'm listening.'

Lizzy hesitated. Was it really possible that the person who helped Peter Myers escape was the same individual who had been sending the messages? *After all, the fact that they both wear a dark-coloured baseball cap could just be a coincidence.* It certainly wasn't anything like proof.

Gasnier didn't hide his impatience. 'Please, Lizzy.'

She nodded. She wasn't sure that this was all connected, but he needed to know, in case. Emma's life might depend on it, and for the police to do their job properly, they had to have the facts. 'Someone has been following us, and leaving us messages. It started while Emma and Dan were on honeymoon, just over two weeks ago.'

'And how is this relevant to Peter Myers?'

'It might not be,' Lizzy replied. 'But this person, I've seen them – they were in the downstairs entrance of the apartment building, hand-delivering a letter. They were wearing a dark baseball cap. Just like the person in the car.'

'You didn't see their face?'

'No. I ran after them, but they were too fast, so I didn't get a proper look.'

Gasnier didn't give away whether he thought that this was relevant or not, but his continued questioning did signal that he was taking Lizzy seriously. 'What was the nature of the messages? Were they threatening?'

'Not particularly,' she replied. 'They were warnings, telling me not to trust anyone.'

'Anyone in particular?'

'My friends.'

'By which you mean Emma, Dan . . .' His trailed off, letting his expression ask the question.

'Yes.'

'And have you kept the messages?'

'They're back at my flat.'

'I'd like to see them,' he said. 'Did anything else happen with this person?'

'They posted a photograph to me. It was an old photo, showing Dan with Stuart Harris. It must have been designed to cause trouble between Emma and Dan. An attempt to destabilise their relationship.'

'I knew Stuart Harris before I met Emma,' Dan explained. 'But I never told her about it.'

Gasnier nodded his understanding. 'You said the photograph was old?'

'Yes,' Lizzy said.

'Several years old,' Dan confirmed. 'Before Emma and I got together.'

'And whose photo was it?'

'Stuart's,' Dan said. 'It was taken with his camera.'

'So he would have had the image in his possession?'

Dan nodded. 'I assume so.'

'So this person, who sent the photograph, must have had access to Stuart Harris's possessions, either before or after his death.'

'That's what we thought,' Dan said.

'Did you?' The question dripped with sarcasm as Gasnier fixed Dan with a stare. 'Tell me more about your thoughts.'

Dan looked a little intimidated by the tone of questioning. 'Well, we thought it might be Sally Thompson. She was Stuart's fiancée, so she would have had access to his things, especially after he died. And she has the motive and the recent history of trying to hurt us.'

Gasnier listened. Lizzy could see him thinking it over. 'Did you do anything about your suspicions?'

'No,' Dan said.

'Good. We can question her. I agree that it sounds logical, but I'd caution against jumping to any conclusions. And I don't want you getting involved. You know what happened the last time you took things into your own hands – Edward Holden was extremely lucky to escape a jail sentence for shooting and wounding Peter Myers. And both your lives were put at risk by the actions taken by him and William. It could easily have turned out very differently.'

Dan nodded, but Lizzy bristled. She fought the urge to say something, but couldn't hold it in. 'We took action because you refused to believe that Dan had been kidnapped! You didn't take our concerns seriously. You thought Dan was the villain.'

'That's not the case at all, Lizzy,' Gasnier replied, looking at her. 'We have to work with the evidence, and keep an open mind. There were many angles to the case, and we had to consider all possibilities. A man had been brutally attacked, Dan was missing and we had sufficient concern to believe that he may have been responsible.'

Lizzy shook her head. 'It was more than that. You dismissed our concerns. You made us feel as if we had something to hide.'

'Lizzy . . .' Dan said, trying to rein her in, but she was undeterred.

'Your indifference pushed us into taking action.'

'I understand that you have strong feelings, Lizzy, about what happened. But—'

'And now,' she interrupted, 'you're doing it again. Emma has been taken, by *that* man, and instead of getting out there and looking for her, you're telling us that we shouldn't take action. Well, how about a little action from you and your colleagues by getting out there and finding my friend, instead of lecturing us?'

'Lizzy, it's clear that you're upset—'

'Every minute that goes by is a minute lost.'

'Look,' Gasnier said, seeming to lose patience, 'every minute you argue with me is a minute lost too. I assure you, our concern is to get to the truth, and to solve each crime that we are presented with. That's what we do. But when you've been in this job for as long as I have, you learn that sometimes the best thing to do is to just pause, and challenge your instinct.'

'He *has* got her,' Lizzy said, calming. 'I know he has. Do you think that?'

'I'd like to take a look around the flat,' he said, evading the question, much to Lizzy's disgust. 'You don't mind, do you?' Gasnier asked Dan.

'Go ahead,' he replied.

As Gasnier moved into the passageway, Dan flashed Lizzy a warning look and spoke to her in a low voice. 'You've got to stop attacking him, Lizzy. We need their support. I know you're upset. So am I. But we don't want to turn them against us. You're going to have to put up with him.'

Lizzy just shook her head.

'There are no signs of a struggle,' Gasnier said, re-entering the room. 'Lizzy, you said that the door was open when you got to the flat?'

'Yes. It was ajar.'

'I might be wrong, but if Emma did leave with someone else, then it looks likely that she went willingly. The fact that her purse and phone are missing points to that. Do you have any idea whom that might be? Was she due any visitors?'

'No,' Dan said. 'There weren't any pre-planned visits.'

'And I don't think Emma would have gone off with someone else,' Lizzy added. 'I mean, she knew the situation, and she wouldn't have risked that.'

Gasnier raised an eyebrow. 'Unless it was someone she trusted.'

Lizzy was far from convinced. 'Like who?'

'I don't know – you tell me.'

'Well, I can't think of anyone she trusts that would want to do her harm,' Lizzy said.

'Dan?'

'I can't think of anyone, either.'

'Okay,' Gasnier said. 'If you do think of anyone, then let me know. In the meantime, be vigilant. I suggest you consider staying together, maybe not here. And please, do report anything you feel is suspicious. You have my number.'

He moved out into the passageway, heading for the door. But before he could reach it, Lizzy caught up with him. 'Are you going?'

'I am.'

'But what are you going to do? What are you going to do to find Emma?'

He turned at the threshold. 'Don't worry, we'll be doing whatever it takes to find out what has happened to Emma. And there are still a lot of us out there looking for Peter Myers. Everyone is doing their best to bring this situation to a swift conclusion.'

This didn't sound enough to Lizzy. 'Aren't you going to search the flat more? You know, dust for fingerprints, and do forensics? It might confirm that Peter Myers has taken her.' Her frustration was evident.

Gasnier looked at her sympathetically. 'Lizzy, you have to trust us. We need to prioritise our actions. As soon as I leave this building, the first thing I'm going to do is ask my officers to obtain access to the CCTV from the street outside. I've noticed that there are new cameras just down from here.'

'They put them up a few weeks ago,' Lizzy replied, nodding. 'Emma told me there's been some vandalism on the shops.'

'Well, the cameras might show Emma, and anyone else that may have been with her. So we'll pursue that line of enquiry first.'

Lizzy acquiesced. But she felt as if she was on the verge of collapsing, reaching out to the doorframe to steady herself. 'Please, just find her.'

Lizzy closed the door behind the departing DI. She turned to Dan, who was standing there, his back against the wall, his eyes closed. 'What are we going to do?'

'I don't know, Lizzy, I really don't know.'

'*He's* got her,' she said. 'We've got to face it. I know he's got her.'

'Don't,' he said. 'I can't bear it.'

'I'm going to see if anything else is missing,' she said, heading for the living room. Dan watched from the doorway as she scoured the room – she didn't know what she was looking for. She brushed past Dan, back into the hallway, and headed for the bedroom. He followed her, unspeaking. Finally, Lizzy stopped, realising the futility of her actions. She moved back out into the corridor with Dan. 'We need to do something,' she said. 'We can't just stay here, waiting for news.'

'Lizzy, we're powerless. We can't do anything.'

'We can go out, search the streets,' Lizzy said.

Dan shook his head. 'London is a huge place – even if Emma is still somewhere in the city. It might make us feel better, give us the sense that we are doing something, but where would we start? Gasnier is right. As frustrating as it is, we need to let the police get on with it and put our faith in them.'

'If Emma had given up on you, then you might not be alive today,' she shot back.

The comment stung. 'I'm *not* giving up on Emma, okay?' Dan stormed into the kitchen and slammed the door.

Lizzy stared at the closed door for a few seconds. *What the hell are we going to do?* If she thought about it too much, she would go mad. She considered following Dan and making peace. After all, they were all on the same side, and they all wanted the same thing; for Emma to be back with them, safe and unharmed. They needed each other. But maybe a bit of time to reflect would do both of them some good. She retreated to the living room.

As she stood in the centre of the room, not wanting to sit down and add to her sense of inaction, she spotted Dan's wedding ring, on top of the television, in a little red and white dish. She moved across and picked it up, turning it over in her hand. Lizzy turned to look towards the kitchen. A surprising and disturbing thought flashed through her mind. She would have to have this out with Dan.

32

Lizzy sat there, wondering whether she would be wise to raise the issue of the ring with Dan at such a moment. But she realised she needed to hear his explanation, otherwise there would be the element of doubt, and that would be no good at all.

She suddenly realised that she hadn't called Will back. He would be waiting for her. Picking up her phone and ringing his number from her contacts list, she let him know the worrying news. He promised to come straight round.

Just as the call was ending, Dan appeared at the entrance to the room.

'I'm sorry,' he said, as Lizzy said goodbye to Will.

'Me, too,' Lizzy said. 'We need to stick together.'

'We do,' he agreed, moving a couple of steps closer. 'Has something happened with Will?'

'I'm sorry, I meant to tell you – Miranda's had her baby. A boy called Jack. They're at St Thomas' Hospital.'

'But it wasn't due for another four weeks or so . . .'

'I know. She went into labour and they had to do an emergency C-section. But everything is okay.'

Dan snorted, digging at the carpet with his foot. 'I wish everything *was* okay. More than anything.'

'I know.'

Lizzy had the ring in her left hand. She decided to get it over with, especially now that things had calmed down between them. 'Dan. This morning we found this.' She opened her palm and watched for Dan's reaction.

'My ring.' He reached for it and screwed it back onto his finger.

'Did you not realise you weren't wearing it?'

'No, I guess not. I suppose that with everything that's been going on, I just forgot about it.' The admission seemed to sadden him. 'Where did you find it?'

'It was under the sofa.'

He nodded.

'Did you take it off?'

'Yes,' he said.

'Why?' Lizzy tried to keep her tone light.

'Because it's too tight. I know it sounds silly, but it makes me feel claustrophobic. It's like when you were little and you got your finger stuck in a bottle. You start to panic, and you have to get it off.'

'You didn't tell Emma?'

'No. I thought it might have just been the hot climate when we were in Mauritius – you know, making my fingers swell. So I waited until we got back home, but it's still the same. I've been taking the ring off at night; otherwise I can't get to sleep.'

'Why didn't you tell Emma when you got home, then?'

Dan shrugged, looking at her with exasperation. 'I don't know. I guess I didn't want her to think that there was any problem. I thought she might have worried that there was some greater meaning to it – some symbolism – but, really, there isn't.'

'It's just that Emma wondered why it was under there.'

His expression darkened. 'Look. I slept in this room last night. Right next to the sofa. I took the ring off, and placed it underneath, because that's where it was safest. And this morning I forgot about it. Why all the questions, Lizzy?'

'It's okay,' she said. 'It makes sense now.'

'Don't you trust me? Didn't Emma trust me?'

Lizzy stood up. 'Of course she does.'

Dan went to respond, but stopped himself. 'This person, they want to drive us apart, and they're winning.' His tone had softened considerably. 'We're attacking one another, and we really shouldn't be.'

'I know, Dan, I know. You're right.'

Dan looked close to tears again. 'What are we going to do, Lizzy?'

'I don't know.'

Dan moved over to the window and took out his phone. 'I'm going to try Em again.' As Lizzy watched hopefully, he shook his head, grimacing. 'The phone's turned off.' His shoulders slumped and he cupped his hands over his face. 'I shouldn't have gone to work today. I left her on her own.'

174

'But you didn't,' Lizzy replied. 'You left her with me. I'm the one who shouldn't have left her.'

His hands still covering his face, Dan didn't appear to be listening. 'I left her to the mercy of Peter Myers. I went to work, as if everything was normal.' He brought his hands down. 'It's all my fault, Lizzy,' he repeated, his face pained. 'It's all my fault. We shouldn't have stayed around here. We should have left this morning, either gone to up to Salford Quays, or anywhere else. But instead I just made it easy for him.' He shuddered. 'If anything has happened to her, I'll never forgive myself.'

Lizzy moved across to him. She knew that they had to haul themselves out of this mire, despite the horrific reality of their situation, for Emma's sake. She needed them.

She placed a hand on his arm. 'We have to think positively, Dan. We'll be no good to Emma if we just assume the worst.'

'I know,' he said, 'but I can't help thinking about where she is, and what's happened. It's killing me.'

'I'm the same. But we've got to fight those thoughts, Dan, because if we don't, then it *will* be all too much, and he'll win.'

Dan nodded. 'I just wish he would take me instead. I've never been as scared as I was when he was holding me in that house, but I'm more scared now. I'd gladly swap places if it'd bring Emma back safety.'

'I know you would.'

'You should stay somewhere else tonight,' Dan said. He put his chin up and took a deep breath. 'In a hotel. You and Will. I'll pay. I didn't protect Emma, but I can protect you.'

'What about you?'

'I'm staying here,' he said.

'But why?'

'Because Myers might come back. And I want to be here if he does.'

Lizzy stepped back and looked at him. 'What, you're going to use yourself as *bait*?'

'I wouldn't put it like that, but I suppose so, yes.'

Lizzy nodded, once. 'Then I'm staying too, and I'm sure that will also go for Will. We're in this together, so I'm not letting you do that on your own.'

Dan seemed to deflate a little, and didn't argue. 'Thanks, Lizzy. I know how much being taken by Myers affected you. You're very brave.'

Lizzy shrugged, deflecting the praise. 'So, what do we do now?' she asked.

'Will's on his way, isn't he?'

'Yes.'

'Then we'll wait for him, and take things from there.'

Will arrived some thirty minutes later. They updated him on what Gasnier had said, and their plans to stay in the flat, rather than hide out somewhere else.

'Count me in,' he said. 'We have to stick together.'

'That's great, Will,' Dan said. 'Really great.'

'Thanks,' Will replied, but he still looked perturbed.

'What is it?' Lizzy asked.

'Well, you didn't tell Gasnier the full story. You didn't tell him about the blackmail.'

'No,' Lizzy said.

'You don't need to worry about protecting me,' Will insisted. 'If we think that telling the police that this person knows about my involvement in Stephen Myers' death will help to identify them, then we tell them.'

Dan looked across at Lizzy, then at Will. 'Emma wouldn't want that.'

'I know she wouldn't,' Will said, 'but that's not the point. The point is doing whatever we can to help her.'

'I agree that we need to do whatever it takes,' Lizzy said, 'but I just don't think that would help.'

'Well, I'm just saying that if either of you believe that it would help, then I will gladly do it.'

'Thanks, Will,' Dan said.

For a few minutes they sat in the living room in silence, waiting for the phone to ring. Then Lizzy remembered her conversation with Adrian Spencer. 'There's something else I need to tell you both,' she said.

Both Will and Dan looked sick at the thought of another revelation, and she hurried to reassure them. 'I met up with Adrian Spencer today. He told me all about Firework Films. Apparently

176

they're ruthless in what they do. They take advantage of the people in the programmes they make, and they bribe or threaten those that complain.'

'It doesn't surprise me,' Dan said, only really half listening. 'Some of those programmes, you can see there's no ethical values.'

'That's not the revelation,' Lizzy continued. 'He told me to look up the directors of the company on the Companies House website. Well, I did, and we know one of them.'

'Go on,' Dan said, his attention now fully on her.

'Guy Roberts.'

'You're joking,' he said, getting to his feet, his face flushing in anger. 'As if that man hasn't already done enough damage.' Dan began to pace the room, as Lizzy and Will looked on. 'He tried to ruin Emma's life to promote *that* film, and now he's behind the company who's making a TV programme about us all?'

'I can't believe it,' Will said, slowly. 'What a low-life. He's profiting out of our suffering. *Again.*'

'I know,' Lizzy said. 'And, now that I know the truth, I'm not going to let him get away with it.' Lizzy nodded to herself. She felt completely useless just sitting in Emma's flat, knowing all the while that her best friend was out there somewhere, in all probability being held by that madman Peter Myers. It felt like there was nothing she could do – it was in the hands of Gasnier and his colleagues now. But then she realised: there was something she could do – something that would help make her feel very much better, and sort things out for Emma when she was back. *Because she is coming back,* Lizzy told herself firmly. She could stop the docudrama once and for all, by going to see Guy Roberts.

Dan stopped pacing. 'What are you going to do?'

'I'm going to pay Guy Roberts a little visit first thing tomorrow.'

Will looked uncomfortable. 'Do you think that's wise?'

'Possibly not. But I'm not going to sit back and take this. I feel like that at this moment, it's the one thing I can do for Emma.'

'I'll come too,' Dan said. 'I want to look that piece of dirt in the face and tell him some home truths.'

33

Will wandered aimlessly around Regent's Park, early the next morning. There was something about that green oasis in the heart of the city that kept pulling him back. It now held so many memories: some good, some bad. There was the time, in late summer, when he had struggled to decide whether to tell Emma about his fear over the real reason for Dan's disappearance. Then, just a few weeks ago, the girl whom he knew then as Amy had bounded over to him, all smiles and full of positive energy. He had fallen in love with her that day. But it seemed like a lifetime away now.

He made his way up to the far end of the park, squinting in the bright, wintry sunshine. A break in the wet and windy weather appeared to be holding, and it was a clear, if blustery and chilly morning outing.

Will sat down on a bench and scanned the area. He knew it wasn't realistic, but part of him hoped that he might suddenly see Emma walking in the distance. He would call her over, and everything would be all right. He closed his eyes, feeling so tired. He hadn't slept much at all in the night, his head was so crammed full of worries.

Will stayed like that for a few minutes, before opening his eyes again and pulling out his mobile. He had to call his dad – he had asked for an early morning update.

Edward was already at the hospital, at Miranda's bedside.

Will was amazed. *Maybe baby Jack really will be Dad's new start in life.* He waited as his father moved out of the ward, to be able to talk properly. But in hushed tones.

'Any news?'

'I'm afraid not. We've not heard from the police since they left last night. Did you decide whether to tell Miranda?'

'I haven't said anything yet, but I'm going to have to tell her something. She's wondering where Emma is, and is expecting her to come today. I can't lie to her about this – it would be the final straw.'

'And she hasn't asked about what our argument was about?'

'No, but she probably will at some point.'

'And are you going to tell her the truth?'

'Not for that, no.'

Will looked around the park again. Suddenly he saw a figure off in the middle distance, jogging parallel to where he was sitting. From here, it looked spookily like Emma – the dark jogging attire, the peaked cap with dark hair tied back into a short ponytail – even the running style was reminiscent.

'William, are you still there?'

'Yes, yes, I'm still here,' Will replied, transfixed by the jogger. He tried to turn his attention back to the call. 'I'll let you know as soon as I hear anything.'

'I'm sure she'll be okay,' Edward said.

'I wish I felt so positive.'

The call now over, Will got to his feet. He traced his eyes across the horizon, but the figure had gone. His level of disappointment surprised him: it wasn't likely that the person really was Emma.

And then, suddenly, emerging from the tree line, there they were again.

Will began to run towards them.

***

Lizzy entered the kitchen in her pyjamas. Dan was already up and dressed, making breakfast. She noted that he was wearing his wedding ring.

He looked up and smiled tiredly. 'Morning.'

'Morning.' The absence of the word 'good' was obvious to them both.

Dan handed her a coffee. 'How did you sleep?'

'Not good,' she replied. 'I must have been awake more than half the night. Every time I woke up, I'd remember about Emma. And then I just couldn't stop thinking about what's happened to her.' She sipped at the hot, strong drink: Dan knew that she liked a coffee that packed a punch. 'How about you?' she asked, leaning against the breakfast bar.

'I feel really guilty,' he said, 'but I didn't wake up once. I think I must have been so tired from the stress that my body just shut down.'

'That's good. I wish I could have had the rest.' The thought brought out a yawn. 'We're going to need all the energy we've got.'

'I did dream of her, though,' Dan continued. 'It was a nice dream. We were walking along the sand in St Ives. We stopped and kissed. The sky was an amazing, vivid blue. And the sea was sparkling like crystal. She looked so beautiful. It felt so real.' Dan stared off, lost in the image.

'Everything will be all right,' Lizzy found herself saying.

Dan went back to buttering the toast. 'You don't know that, Lizzy.'

Lizzy struggled for a justification of her statement. 'You and Emma, you've got a future. You'll have children. You'll grow old together.'

'Please, Lizzy,' Dan said, suddenly dropping the knife with a clatter onto the plate, and desperately pinching his tears back. 'I know you're trying to make me feel better, but I can't think about things like that. It hurts too much.'

'Sorry, I didn't mean to upset you.'

'I know you didn't,' he said, recovering. 'You know, Lizzy, I'm so glad you're here. I really need the support.'

'Don't mention it.' Lizzy reached over and picked up a piece of toast, pulling the corner off it. Chewing was laborious. She didn't have much of an appetite, but knew that she had to eat. 'Is Will still asleep?'

'He's gone out. Said he needed a walk to clear his head. I think he's heading up to Regent's Park.'

'How was he?'

Dan shrugged. 'He was pretty quiet. But from what he said, I don't think he slept very well, either. He's taken it pretty hard – like us all.' He gulped back some coffee. 'Oh, Lizzy, I just feel so *helpless*. I know now what you all went through when I was missing. It's the worst feeling in the world, when someone you love is gone and you don't know what's happened to them!'

'I know,' she agreed. 'It's like parents whose children go missing without any explanation. I don't know how they cope.'

'I guess there's always the chance of a happy ending.'

'Yes, there is. And we've got to hold on to that. We need to fight for that happy ending. Because I feel that if we don't, and we just give up, then . . . then we might get an ending that we don't want.'

'You're right,' Dan said. He thought for a few seconds. 'Are you still planning on going to speak to Guy Roberts?' he asked.

'Definitely. I know it's not going to help us to get Emma back, but it's something that I feel like I need to do. That man has to know that he can't get away with treating people the way he does. He might be able to bribe or threaten other people, but I'm going to get him to stop this docudrama if it's the last thing I do.'

'But what are you going to do?'

'I don't know exactly. Just tell him that we know what he's doing. Maybe that will be enough to sink the programme idea.'

Dan looked sceptical. 'Do you really think so?'

'Maybe, maybe not. But at the least, he'll know his secret's out. Are you still coming along?'

'Of course,' he said.

Lizzy had a thought. 'What about if Emma or the police call here? We need someone to be here, in case, don't we?'

'I'll ask Will.' Will, like Dan, had taken time off work because of what was going on.

'Good idea.'

'So are you just going to turn up, and hope that he's at home?'

'I don't have his phone number so, yes, I'm just going to take a chance. And if he isn't there, then I'll come back again and again until he is in.'

'You're extremely tenacious, aren't you?'

Lizzy managed her first smile of the day. 'You could say that, yes.'

***

Will returned half an hour later. 'Hi,' he said, entering the living room, where Dan and Lizzy were now sitting. In his absence, Lizzy had taken a shower, and Dan cleaned up after breakfast. They'd also decided that as soon as Will got back, they were leaving for Guy's house.

'Where did you go?' Lizzy asked.

Will looked bad. Heavy, dark lines under both eyes revealed his lack of sleep, and his skin was ashen. 'I did a circuit of the park. And something really strange happened – it's completely freaked me out.'

Lizzy sat up. 'What?'

'I saw someone jogging in the distance, and they looked like Emma. Same kind of clothes, same hairstyle, same running action. I went to speak to them, thinking how stupid it was of me to even consider it might be Em. But when I got close, the likeness was uncanny. The girl's face, it was so like Emma's.'

'What did she say?' Lizzy said.

'Well, I was a bit stunned, really. I just said how much she reminded me of my sister. She seemed a little embarrassed, and then just jogged off. I think maybe she thought I was trying to chat her up.' He sank down onto the sofa and exhaled. 'I think I'm starting to go mad. I can't take this, I really can't. The thought of never seeing Emma again . . . I've been thinking. The person with the cap, they're the key to this, aren't they? If the police could find out who they are, then they have a much better chance of finding Emma. And they'd have a much better chance of finding out who they are if they had all the information.'

Lizzy knew where he was going with all this. 'Will, I don't think giving yourself up to the police would do any good. They know that whoever this person is has insider information that could only have come from Stuart Harris. Knowing about your role in disposing of Stephen Myers' body probably also came from Stuart – he either told this person, or they found something. So I don't think it would give the police any more clues.'

Will seemed unconvinced.

'Lizzy's right,' Dan said. '*We* know that information, and it hasn't helped us to identify the person. We still have only one suspect.'

'But we haven't given it much thought, have we?' Lizzy said. 'Who else do we know was close to Stuart? Someone who might have that information?'

'What about Guy Roberts?' Will offered. 'Maybe Stuart told him about what he had done, and also that I'd been involved.'

'But what about the photo of you and Stuart?' Lizzy asked. 'Do you think Roberts would have had access to that?'

'I don't know.' Will clamped his hands around the back of his head, close to tears. 'I just want Emma back safe.'

Lizzy moved over to him and placed an arm around his shoulders. 'Dan and I have been talking. We need to stay positive, no matter how difficult it is.'

'Yes,' Dan said, 'and very soon we should hear back from the police about the CCTV. That might help.'

'We have to believe that it will be all right, for Emma's sake,' Lizzy said. 'She wouldn't want us to give up and assume the worst, would she?'

Lizzy's comment seemed to resonate with Will. 'You're right,' he said. They could see him steeling himself. 'It's going to be okay.'

***

The girl kept on running. She'd made a big mistake, letting him get so close. But, amazingly, he hadn't recognised her. The hair extensions – a different colour from her natural shade – and the years between their last encounter probably accounted for that. She ran all the way down to the entrance of Paddington Station before stopping to make a call. It was a good ten-minute run, alongside busy traffic, and it gave her time to think how she was going to explain this turn of events to him.

He picked up after a few rings.

'Something bad just happened . . . I've just been approached by Will . . . I was jogging in Regent's Park . . . I didn't see him! . . . No, I don't think he recognised me . . . I can't be sure, no . . . Okay, I'll be there as soon as I can.'

She entered the station and paid to enter the public lavatory with what little small change she had on her. She took advantage of the deserted washroom to admire herself in the mirror. The sight lifted her spirits. She smiled and straightened her cap. 'You're looking good, Emma Holden.'

PART FOUR

34

Will agreed with Dan and Lizzy that he should stay in the flat, just in case Emma or the police called, while they went to speak to Guy Roberts. Promising to check their mobile phones at regular intervals in case of missed calls, the pair headed off for Notting Hill.

On the way, they rehearsed their tactics in dealing with Guy Roberts – Lizzy favoured a more confrontational approach, while Dan counselled against it. But he knew that when Lizzy was in the sort of mood she was in, there was little that could be said to change her mind.

They reached Guy Roberts' home shortly before eleven. A brief rain-shower had cleared, and sunlight streamed through the trees that lined the secluded street. BMWs and Mercedes were parked alongside Ferraris and even a Lotus.

Lizzy now realised how Roberts could afford such a luxurious property in the most exclusive part of Notting Hill: he wasn't only a casting director. He was also a director of a successful television production company. Firework Films had several big hits under their belt, and were courted by several of the major channels.

'That's the house, if I'm not mistaken,' Lizzy said, indicating a white-painted Georgian house to their left.

'Yes, that's the one.'

'Beautiful, isn't it?'

Dan gazed up at the top windows. 'From what I remember, it's even more amazing inside.'

'Pity the person who lives there is such a low-life.'

It was just under two months since Dan and Lizzy had accompanied Emma to Guy Roberts' house to ask him about the unidentified stalker pretending to be Stephen Myers, to whom David Sherborn had photographed him talking. The subsequent information provided by Guy Roberts had led to the solving of that mystery, but Lizzy didn't feel any particular sense of gratitude towards him. He had completely manipulated and controlled them for all that time.

They entered through the gate and rang the doorbell. There was no answer, so Lizzy pressed the button again. She had just given up on Guy Roberts being at home when they heard a noise from within the house. Then they heard the sound of a latch being turned, and the door swung open.

Guy Roberts – his white hair now streaked with blond highlights, Lizzy noticed, and still trendily short and dishevelled – stared at them for a couple of seconds. He was dressed impeccably, in a designer, open-collar white shirt, and a pair of dark trousers. His single silver ear stud glinted in the morning sunlight. 'Lizzy, Dan,' he said, finally. 'To what do I owe the pleasure?'

'We'd like to speak to you,' Lizzy said.

'Well, I guessed as much,' he replied. 'What about, exactly?'

Lizzy decided to just come out with it. In fact, she couldn't wait to see his reaction – she wanted to wipe away the smug look from his face. 'About your role with Firework Films.'

Roberts' face smoothed itself of all expression. Instead, he stood at the entrance, considering his next move. 'You can come in,' he said eventually, to Lizzy. 'But just you. Not Dan.'

Dan and Lizzy looked at one another. 'Why?' Lizzy asked.

'Because,' he said, 'my house, my rules.' He flashed a cold smile at them. 'If you want to come in, then you follow them.'

'We could have the conversation out here,' Lizzy said. 'I'm sure the neighbours will be very interested to hear about what you get up to.'

'Don't threaten me, Lizzy.' His voice was like ice.

'It's okay, Lizzy,' Dan said. 'I'll wait right outside. If that's what he wants.' He didn't look at Guy. 'But if you need me, come straight out.'

Lizzy followed Roberts into the lounge. The framed movie posters still decorated the walls, the piano still stood in the corner. She noticed some arty, silver-framed photographs now stood on it – Guy Roberts meeting famous actors and actresses; Guy Roberts striking party-like poses with pouting girls. *Some of them young enough to be his daughters*, Lizzy noted with an eye-roll.

188

'I've just been having brunch,' he said expansively. 'Can I get you anything to eat, or drink? I have some pastries left over.'

'No, thanks,' Lizzy said. 'I'm not here for the hospitality.'

'You'll at least take a seat?' Guy said. 'Do we really want to have this conversation standing up?'

'Yes, I do,' Lizzy replied. 'I wasn't intending on staying here long.'

Guy shrugged, his palms towards her. 'Whatever makes you happy, Lizzy.' His eyes travelled over her. 'You know, I think you'd make a great leading lady. You've got a real fire inside, haven't you? That's just the kind of thing that works with the public. I'd love to cast you in one of our up-coming productions.'

'I've already said no to being in one of your productions,' Lizzy retorted. 'As have the rest of my friends.'

'Touché,' he said, his smile not quite reaching his eyes. 'Indeed you have. And, I must say, I was very disappointed that none of you wanted to take part in what I am sure will be a highly interesting and informative docudrama.'

Lizzy struggled to control her anger. 'And profitable. For you and your fellow directors.'

'Of course,' he said. 'I'm part of the entertainment business, as are you, and a business is about making money, and being profitable. Don't pretend the money doesn't matter to you, Lizzy.' He smiled, a chess player who had just called checkmate.

'The money is important, but it's not the most important thing,' she said. 'And I have morals. Unlike you and your company.'

'Steady, Lizzy.'

Lizzy was undeterred. In fact she felt emboldened, knowing that she had more weapons in her arsenal. 'I know what kind of company Firework Films is.'

'A television production company,' he replied. 'And a very successful one at that. In the few years since we established Firework, we've become major players. We're highly respected in the field.'

Lizzy decided to hold back for the moment. 'Why are you making the docudrama?'

He seemed surprised that she felt the need to ask the question. 'Because it's an amazing story. Full of drama, suspense, mystery, emotion . . . the TV viewers are going to love it, Lizzy. You really should be part of it. It's still not too late to change your mind. We'd really value your input.'

Lizzy was amazed by his brass neck. He seemed serious. She scoffed. 'Not a hope in hell! And I take it your docudrama isn't going to detail the role you had in contributing to Emma's ordeal?'

There was a short pause. 'I don't know what you mean,' he replied, in a way that made it clear he knew full well what Lizzy was getting at.

'I mean the way you used David Sherborn to take advantage of the media attention that Dan's kidnap offered you. The way you made Emma feel so scared, getting him to follow her around.'

'Well, it's a docudrama,' he said lightly. 'Not everything will be included.'

Lizzy smiled thinly. 'I bet it won't.' She paused – it was time. 'But maybe if you do go ahead with this programme, then the press might be interested in hearing about all the details.'

Guy Roberts gave her a level look for a moment. 'I don't care,' he said, eventually. 'I'd welcome the media coverage. And, anyway, I'd deny whatever you are planning to say about me. My friends in the media can spin a story in many ways, Lizzy.'

'They can't all be your friends.'

'No, but I have some powerful allies. If I were you, I'd be wary about going to them. You may find that you and your friends will make the headlines for all the wrong reasons.'

'Threats,' Lizzy said. 'I'm disappointed that you didn't start with the bribes.'

At this, Guy affected not to hear her, instead glancing at a clock on the mantelpiece. 'I've got an important call coming through from New York in a few minutes.'

It was the moment Lizzy had been waiting for – now she knew she had him under pressure. 'Feeling uncomfortable at the line of questioning?'

'Not at all.'

But his expression told the true story. It was time to go for the jugular. 'Why does Firework Films exploit the people who take part in its programmes?'

'We don't exploit anyone.'

'So you don't try to bribe people who complain about how you have treated them?'

'I think you should get your facts straight before you start making such wild accusations.'

'Oh, I have. How many people have you threatened to keep quiet?'

'Who have you been talking to?'

'That really doesn't matter,' she said. 'Your company, it's criminal in the way it works. I'm sure the police would be very interested in hearing about it all.'

'Adrian Spencer,' he said. 'He's been telling you all this, hasn't he?'

Lizzy didn't answer.

Guy smiled, seeming to have regained some of his bounce. 'Your silence is your answer, Lizzy. Let me guess, Adrian Spencer made contact with you a few days ago. Am I right?'

Again Lizzy stayed quiet. She hadn't wanted to bring Adrian Spencer into this, although it now seemed impossible to avoid.

'Adrian Spencer was, we had thought, a hard-working and loyal member of the Firework Films team. That was until last week, when we discovered that he had been intimidating an old lady into taking part in an up-coming programme. Given how he had behaved with you, coupled with this new complaint, we had no choice but to let him go.'

'You're lying.'

'Believe what you want to believe. We sacked him, and he's obviously now aggrieved. So he takes his revenge by going to you and saying what he said. It's all lies, Lizzy, the man can't be trusted. He's bitter and out for revenge.'

'Are you sure you're not talking about yourself?'

Guy frowned. 'How so?'

'Well, aren't you still bitter about Emma rejecting the part in the movie? And isn't the docudrama about you taking revenge?

'Absolutely not. I've already told you, it's purely a commercial decision.' His face was stony. *But was that a twitch?*

'It's going to cause us a lot of hurt and pain.'

He shrugged. 'Don't watch it if you feel it will negatively affect you.'

191

'Thank you for your very helpful advice. I take it you've heard that Peter Myers has escaped from prison?'

'I had heard that, yes.' He still didn't show any emotion.

'I bet you're happy. It's more drama for your programme.' Lizzy had decided not to tell him about Emma's disappearance. She didn't think she could cope with his feigned concern.

'Maybe it's time you left. My transatlantic call will be coming through any minute.'

On cue, the phone in the corner started to ring. He looked relieved to be able to end their conversation. 'Lizzy, you don't mind seeing yourself out, do you?'

'Don't worry. I'd be more than happy to.'

As Lizzy left the room she heard Guy Roberts pick up and say hello. He was gushing to someone called Brad, talking loudly enough that Lizzy believed it was for her benefit: 'Oh, yes, glad to hear the film is going so well, Brad, my man. I have a strong feeling about the Oscars.'

Lizzy paused at the bottom of the staircase near the front door, now out of earshot, and shook her head in frustration. She felt as though she hadn't played that very well. She had got off some shots, yes, done a little bit of damage – at one point he had been definitely struggling. But she hadn't inflicted the significant blow that she had sought. Indeed, he seemed to have ended the conversation in the ascendancy. And for that, Lizzy felt that she had let herself, and, more upsetting for her, Emma down.

She stood there for a moment, tempted to wait until his phone conversation was over before going back in for a second attempt. Then she heard a noise coming from upstairs. She listened carefully. There was another noise. It was definitely another person. Guy Roberts lived alone, she knew that.

It seemed ridiculous, but her first thought was: *Could it be Emma?*

35

'Tell me what you think,' Mark Gasnier said to DS Davies, as they sat in the stiflingly hot station office that Thursday morning. Davies pulled at his shirt collar, to relieve the pressure on his wide neck - there was a time when he had no trouble fitting into a size seventeen. *Maybe he should try to lose some of that excess weight he'd put on a few years ago.* The heating was on full blast, and they were waiting impatiently and uncomfortably for the CCTV recording to be delivered. A couple of uniformed officers were currently en route from the private contractor who operated the cameras for the local council. 'What's your gut feeling about Emma Holden?'

'I'm not sure,' Davies replied.

Gasnier raised an eyebrow. 'All those years of police training, thousands of hours of case experience, and that's all you can come up with?'

Davies shrugged. 'Something doesn't make sense to me.'

Gasnier seemed more satisfied with that response. 'Feel free to expand . . .'

'Well, I know I didn't see the flat but, from what you said, there were no signs of a struggle. If she'd been abducted, then you would expect there to be some signs of violence. Unless the person came to the front door, pulled out a gun or knife and led her outside without needing to use any force. What do you think?'

Gasnier picked up a pen from the desk and twirled it around his fingers. He wasn't ready yet to reveal his own opinion. 'Have you got any other theories about what's happened to her?'

'Well, the most obvious explanation is that she left of her own accord. Either on her own, or with someone she knows.'

'Exactly,' Gasnier said, placing the pen carefully and deliberately back on the desk so that it lay parallel to the grain in the wood. He sat back. 'So, what about the first option. How likely do you think it is that she just walked out and left?'

'Hopefully the CCTV will answer these questions in the next few minutes.'

Gasnier smiled. 'But it's fun to hypothesise. It keeps the brain active. And we're passing time. So, do you think she could have just walked out?' He sipped from his plastic cup of water. Coffee would have been his drink of choice, but the machine was playing up again, spouting sludge that resembled something that might be found on a beach after an oil spillage.

'Possibly, although if that's the case, she would have known that she would be causing a lot of hurt to her friends and family. And from our dealings with her, my instinct is that Emma isn't the kind of person who would be comfortable doing something like that.'

'You might have got her wrong.'

'I might. But I don't think so. She seems like a genuine person to me.'

'Are there circumstances in which you might think she would consider doing it, despite the hurt it would cause?'

Davies thought. 'Well, if she thought that the benefits of leaving would outweigh the negatives.'

'Such as?'

'She might have done it to protect them. She might believe that she's the one placing them at harm, that Peter Myers is out of prison and after her, so if she leaves, her friends and family are in less danger.'

'Possibly. Do you think that's likely?' Gasnier looked hard at the younger man.

'No, not really. I don't think she would do it – just walk out without any explanation. She didn't *need* to do that. She could have left a note, called them or sent a text, and still achieved the same outcome. That would have avoided the suffering. So I think that, if she wasn't taken by force, it's more likely that she left the flat with someone she knew and trusted.'

'So who could that be?'

'Any of her friends and family.'

'No one specific in mind?'

'No, not really. It could be anyone – maybe someone we don't know about.'

'And what about a motive?'

194

'No idea.'

'We can speak to them all, see where they were yesterday morning. That's if the CCTV doesn't answer the questions for us.'

'Should be here any minute,' Davies said, referring to his watch.

Gasnier exhaled and glared at the door. 'You said the same ten minutes ago. They should blue light it over here.'

Davies nodded. 'You haven't given your opinion yet. What do you think is the most likely scenario?'

'I'm of the same mind as you. Something doesn't feel right about all this – not right at all. I agree that the lack of any struggle in the flat is very suspicious. And when I was talking to Lizzy and Dan, I got a sense that there was something they were holding back on.'

'Like what?'

'I don't know. But I just had a feeling there's more going on than they're telling me. I had the distinct impression that I was getting half the story, which wouldn't surprise me in the slightest when it comes to that group of people.'

'You suspect one of them might be involved in Emma's disappearance?'

'Possibly. But probably not Lizzy.'

'You're still not sure about Dan, are you?'

'You know my suspicions about what happened. I know there's no evidence that Dan wasn't the innocent victim he claims to be, but I still have concerns. It's as if the jigsaw was put together, but there were a few pieces out of place.'

'So do you think Dan is a greater suspect here than Peter Myers?' Davies started making little doodles on the jotter that was on the desk. He found it helped him link ideas, and his boss was throwing out some good ones.

'I'm not saying that. And I'm not saying categorically that there was something else about his disappearance. After all, Peter Myers did confess. But I'm keeping an open mind. We both know that sometimes danger lies much closer to home than most people would ever want to believe.'

'We certainly do.' They'd investigated many murder and disappearance cases where the perpetrator was found to be the grieving spouse or loving family member. Sometimes the level of deception – and performances given by those individuals – was astounding.

There was a knock on the door.

'At last,' Gasnier said to himself. 'Come in.'

A young, uniformed constable entered with a padded envelope in hand. 'Sir, the CCTV recording. Sorry we were so long. Got stuck in an accident on Hammersmith Bridge.'

'Thanks,' Gasnier said, taking the package. He looked over at DS Davies. 'Time to see whether any of our theories are correct.'

36

Without really thinking through the consequences, Lizzy decided that she had to find out who it was in Guy Robert's house.

She began to climb the first few stairs, hoping that they didn't creak. But she didn't need to worry – the thick pile of the carpet muffled any sound of her ascent. She reached halfway and stopped to listen. The stairs curved around to the right towards the top, and she could only see up another few steps before the bend. No noise from above. But below, she could hear Guy Roberts again. He was still on the phone. That was good.

As she went to move, she caught sight of the picture – one of a series – hanging nearest to her in the stairwell. It had been shot using soft focus, but that was the only gentle thing about the image. Raw and savage, Lizzy could only hope that the clearly underage girl in the photograph had been happy to pose like that.

Shaking her head to clear it of the image, as she moved on up the stairs Lizzy realised that her heart rate was fast, her breathing shallow. *What am I thinking, going further into Guy Roberts' house?*

She continued, and turned the corner; four more stairs and she was on the landing. A noise came from her left. It sounded like someone moving around behind the door at the end of the landing.

Only then did Lizzy really consider the potential ramifications of what she was doing. She was snooping around someone else's house. How would she explain it? Roberts might call the police. She looked back towards the staircase. But before she had had the time to really consider whether to abort her actions, she heard a lock click open on a door in front of her, and it swung open.

A pretty girl emerged from a mist-filled bathroom. She was wrapped in a towel, with another towel twisted around her hair. 'Oh, oh my god!' she said, jumping back at the sight of Lizzy standing there.

Lizzy felt the warmth of the steam against her hands as she held up her palms. 'It's okay, don't be scared.' The girl took another step back. She looked panicked, as if at any second she might shout out for help. Lizzy thought quickly. 'I was just looking for the bathroom. I didn't realise there was anyone else up here.'

The girl nodded, but she still looked spooked and avoided eye contact, maybe out of embarrassment at being caught unawares.

Feeling uncomfortable for the girl, Lizzy averted her eyes. But not before she had got one last look at her. She looked vaguely familiar. 'Sorry for scaring you. I'll go now.'

'You don't want to use the bathroom?'

'I'm okay. Thanks, anyway.'

Lizzy retreated back downstairs. Guy was still deep in conversation. She let herself out and was relieved to breathe in the fresh air and feel the sun and breeze on her face.

Dan was waiting on the pavement, and turned around on hearing the door close. 'Hey, you okay?' he said, as Lizzy approached.

'Not really. Have you heard anything from anyone?'

'I phoned Will. There haven't been any calls.'

'Come on,' she said. 'Let's get back to him.'

'So, how did it go?' Dan asked, as they crossed the road.

'I let myself down in there. I should have made more of the information we had.'

They turned right and headed towards the tube.

'What did he say?'

'He didn't deny being part of Firework Films. In fact, he was proud of it. He taunted me about not wanting to be involved in the docudrama.'

Dan shook his head. 'He really is a low-life.'

'Absolutely. I thought I had him, though, when I brought up the issue of the threats and bribery.'

Dan stopped. 'You didn't say that?'

'Of course I did. I couldn't resist. But he just denied it. He said Adrian Spencer was lying because he'd been sacked.'

'So he guessed who'd told you?'

'He knew, really. I suppose it's obvious.'

'How did the conversation end?'

'With a phone call from New York. He told me to let myself out. Except that I didn't, not at first. I heard a noise from upstairs, so I went to investigate. I know it sounds silly, but I thought it might be Emma. Of course, it wasn't.'

'So who was it?'

'A girl. Just stepped out of the shower. Younger than us by a few years, I reckon. She seemed familiar, but I can't quite put my finger on it. I'm thinking that maybe she's an actress who I've seen somewhere. Maybe at a party, or an audition. I don't think I've spoken to her, otherwise I'd remember more clearly.' She blew out a puff of air in exasperation. 'It's really annoying me that I can't remember where I know her from!'

Dan snorted. 'I can imagine Guy Roberts using his position to seduce younger girls. I wouldn't be at all surprised if he makes a regular thing of it.'

'He probably offered her a part in his next project, just to get her into his bed.' Lizzy shuddered. 'No role would be worth that.'

'Not for you, maybe. But for someone just starting out, desperate to get their big break, they just might do it.'

'I don't doubt it. I've heard lots of stories of girls doing similar, or worse, to get the role that they wanted. One of my friends slept with a producer, on the promise that he would find a role for her in a new West End play.' Lizzy broke into a jog to cross the road in front of a taxi, which hooted at her. 'Of course, it was just a load of rubbish. She never really got over it – she quit acting the next year.'

'Yes, it's terrible.' But Lizzy could see that Dan was thinking about something else. 'Did you tell Guy about Emma?'

'No. I didn't want to see his reaction. But I did mention Peter Myers, and he knew about it.'

'I wonder how he knows, seeing as it's not been made public yet.'

'No idea. But it shows he's got good contacts.'

'I bet he's loving all this.'

'Oh, he admitted as much,' she said. 'I wanted to punch his lights out, but it would only have given him more material.'

'True. Come on,' Dan said. 'Enough of that man. Let's get back to the flat.'

***

DI Gasnier rubbed his eyes. This had to be the most mind-numbingly boring thing he had done in a long time: reviewing CCTV footage of a street. Their time frame was more than an hour and a half, so there was a lot of material to go through, and then there was still the chance that they wouldn't find an answer to their questions: the purpose of the CCTV's introduction to deter vandalism along the row of shops meant that the direction of focus was not the best for assessing passers-by.

'We've seen that woman before,' Davies stated, pointing to a figure carrying a shopping bag. 'A few minutes ago, she walked the other way.'

'Just been to the shops,' Gasnier replied.

'Yes, probably.'

Gasnier looked at the time. 'Almost an hour in. Feels like longer.' In that time, they'd seen quite a number of people walking past, but no one that resembled either Emma Holden or any of the other individuals known to her. He stifled a yawn.

'At least we'll soon be able to escape this broom-cupboard of a room. It's so hot in here,' Davies said.

'Not soon enough,' Gasnier replied. 'If I'd wanted to watch CCTV, I would have got a job as an operative. I don't know how those guys do it, staring at a screen for hours at a time, just in case something happens.'

Davies glanced over at him, grinning. 'Lots of coffee.'

'They've obviously got a more reliable machine than we—there!' Gasnier suddenly said, clicking his fingers at a point on the screen.

Davies looked back around. 'You saw her?'

Gasnier smiled, satisfied and surprised by what he was sure he had just seen. 'Just rewind it.'

Davies moved forward and played with the controls. The recording started up again. 'This okay?'

Gasnier nodded. 'Perfect. Keep your eyes on the right. They'll appear in five or so seconds . . . there!' He sat back, satisfied.

'Wow,' Davies said. 'That was who I think it was, wasn't it?'

'Yes, it certainly was. Time for us to pay him a visit.'

37

Will was almost asleep when the call came, just after lunch. He'd been lounging on the sofa, listening to the radio, hoping and praying that Emma would get in touch. He'd been determined to stay alert, but the lack of sleep in the previous night was taking its toll, and he had found himself slipping into a slumber that only the shrill of his phone pulled him out of. He scrambled for the mobile, which was wedged in his trouser pocket. There was no way on earth that he wanted to miss the call: it might be Lizzy and Dan again, or his father, but it might also be Emma.

The number wasn't one he recognised. 'Hello?'

Silence.

'Emma, is that you?'

Still no answer.

He got to his feet, his feelings a mixture of excitement and trepidation. 'Emma? Emma, if it's you, just say something.'

'It's not Emma,' a girl's voice said. 'It's Sally.'

Will didn't really know how to respond. He looked around the room, as if he was going to find inspiration there somewhere.

'Will, are you still there?' Her voice was weak, but she seemed to have recovered from yesterday.

'Yes, yes,' he said. 'I am. I just don't know what . . . you know, after yesterday.'

'Has something happened with Emma?'

Will thought of denying it, but he was tired of the lies. 'Yes. She's missing. We think she's been taken.'

'Is this connected with what you told me? About what you said about Stuart, and Stephen Myers?'

Will closed his eyes briefly. 'I think so, yes.' He thumped back down onto the sofa and put a hand to his head.

'Can we get together and talk?' she said.

Will took a breath. 'I don't think now's the right time, Sally. There's so much going on, with Emma being . . .'

'Please. I really need to talk to you.'

'Okay,' Will said. 'But I'm at Emma and Dan's flat, in case Emma or the police call. And I need to wait here until Dan and Lizzy get back, before I can go anywhere.'

'I can come there.'

'Do you think that's a good idea? Dan and Lizzy will be back soon. Don't you want to discuss things in private?'

'No. In fact, it would be best if they are there. There's something I need to tell you all.'

Lizzy and Dan got back a few minutes later. 'Still nothing?' Lizzy asked, as she met Will on his way out from the living room.

'Nothing from Emma or the police, but I got a call from Sally. She's coming over here.'

Lizzy froze in the act of taking off her coat. 'Sally Thompson? Whatever for?'

'I don't know. She said there's something that she needs to tell us all.'

Lizzy turned to Dan, who was listening intently, having just double-checked that there were no answer phone messages. 'Do you think it's something to do with Emma?'

'What do you think?' Dan asked, batting the question to Will.

'I don't know. Maybe. But when I told her that Emma was missing, she didn't say that she knew anything about it.'

'But why else would she want to meet with us all?' Lizzy said.

Will shrugged. 'I think maybe she wants to talk about what I told her about Stuart. She probably wants answers.'

Lizzy looked unconvinced. 'But you said that she told you she's got something she needs to tell us all.'

'I know. I guess we'll find out soon enough. She should be here in the next half-hour.'

In the kitchen, Lizzy filled Will in on the rest of the information from the meeting with Guy Roberts. 'I keep trying to think of where I know that girl from,' she said. 'I'm just so sure that I've never actually spoken to her, but still, I feel like I should know her. It's so frustrating.' She tapped the side of her head. 'I feel like if I can just think hard enough, it's there somewhere, in the depths of my memories.'

'Maybe once you stop actively thinking about it, it'll come to you,' Will said.

'You're probably right,' she agreed. '*If* I can stop thinking about it.'

Dan came in, blowing out his cheeks in frustration. 'The police should have updated us by now. They're just leaving us to stew, not knowing what the hell is going on.'

'Shall we call them?' Lizzy said. 'To see if anything's happened?'

Dan shook his head. 'I know it means that there haven't been any developments – they'd call us otherwise. But it's just the principle of the thing. They must realise how terrible this is for us. I know they deal with this type of thing day in and day out, but they must still be able to empathise.'

'Maybe they're just busy investigating,' Will suggested. 'For us, time has slowed down, because we're sitting here and waiting. But it's not the same for them. They might be following multiple leads.'

'I guess,' Dan said.

'I know how you feel' – Lizzy took Dan's arm – 'we're just powerless. But we've got no choice but to hope and pray that the police are making progress, and they'll bring Emma back to us.'

'I'm going to try her phone again,' Dan said. 'I'm not giving up on her answering.' Seconds later, he was again left dejected. 'Straight through to voicemail again.' It looked to Lizzy as if Dan was about to launch his phone at the wall, but he lowered the device and slipped it back into his trouser pocket. He looked skyward. 'Dear God, please, *please*, let her be okay.'

The other two nodded in agreement.

***

Sally arrived within the half-hour. Will buzzed her up and waited nervously at the open door as she appeared at the top of the stairs.

'Hi,' she said. Her smile was genuine, but clearly uncomfortable, which wasn't surprising given all that had happened.

'Hi,' Will replied. For a couple of seconds they stood there, watching one another. 'Are you sure you want to talk about this with everyone? If you've changed your mind, we can go elsewhere. There's a coffee shop a few doors down. It's usually quite quiet.'

'No, I haven't changed my mind,' she said. 'But thanks, anyway, Will. It's very kind of you to give me the option.'

Will nodded. 'You'd better come on in, then.' He led her through to the kitchen, where Dan and Lizzy were waiting, sitting around the table. They smiled a polite hello.

'Hello,' Sally said. She addressed Dan. 'Thanks for letting me come over here, to your place. I know you'd probably rather not have ever seen me again, after what happened.'

'It's no problem,' Dan said. 'Please, take a seat.'

She sat down, taking a few seconds to compose herself. Then she looked at Will. 'There's something that I should have told you yesterday,' she said, 'when you told me about what happened between you, Stuart and Stephen Myers.'

'What is it?'

She looked away briefly, then back at Will. 'You weren't the first person to tell me that Stuart had killed Stephen Myers. I already knew.'

38

'They first contacted me two weeks ago,' she said. 'They called me at work and left a message. I don't know how they knew where I worked, but I later discovered that they knew a lot more about me than that. They told me that they wanted to speak to me about taking part in the television programme.'

'Firework Films,' Dan stated.

Sally nodded. 'Yes, Firework Films.'

'Who exactly?' Lizzy asked.

'The man called himself John, although I don't know if that's his real name.' She gave a dry little laugh. 'I call him Ginger John, becau—'

'The man in the park?' Will interrupted. 'Tall, ginger hair?'

Sally turned to him. 'I *thought* you were following me that day.'

Will reddened. 'Sorry. I didn't intend to spy.'

'It's okay. You're right, that was him. Anyway, I just ignored the message, and hoped that would be the end of it. But, a couple of days later, he came to my flat after work and offered me money to take part in the docudrama. All I had to do was to give my side of the story, my insight into what happened. They wanted me to appear in the programme.' She shook her head. 'I wasn't interested. It was only just after what had happened with you, Will, and I just wanted to move on. The idea of reliving everything – it seemed too much. I also didn't particularly want the world to know about what I had done. He didn't get past the door.'

'How much money did they offer you?' Lizzy asked, curiosity getting the better of her.

Sally smiled tiredly. 'Half of what they offered me the following day.'

'Which was?'

'The day after they came back with an offer of five thousand pounds.'

'Wow,' Dan said. 'They really wanted you.'

'I still refused,' she said. 'I told him that I wasn't interested at any price. And that's when they changed their tactics.'

'Let me guess,' Lizzy said. 'Threats?'

'You obviously know them well,' Sally replied.

'I'm starting to understand them much better, after what I've found out about them in the past few days.'

'A week ago he called at my flat again. He said that if I didn't take part, they would paint a particularly bad picture of what I had done, and, you know, what I had planned to do, with Will. But I still told him to go away. Then he said there was something they knew about Stuart that I should know.' She swallowed. 'That's when I found out about what Stuart had done to Stephen Myers.'

'So Firework Films do know,' Lizzy said. *Stuart must have confided in Guy Roberts, a man whom he had considered a trusted friend.*

Sally nodded. 'They told me everything. About how Stuart had killed Stephen Myers and disposed of his body.' She was having trouble getting her words out. 'They said that even if the police had concluded it was suicide, if I didn't take part in the programme, they would expose what Stuart had done.'

'So you went along with it,' Dan said.

'Yes. At first I said that I didn't believe them, that they were just making it up to scare me into taking part. But to be honest, I did believe it. Because everything fitted together – cryptic things that Stuart had said sometimes. Once he made a comment that everyone had a dark secret, and that he was no exception. And another time I think he nearly told me. He told me about dreams he had, where he died and was made to face up to what he had done during his life.'

'Did they mention me?' Will asked. 'Did you already know that I was involved?'

'No. They didn't say anything about you. Of course, when you told me about the blackmailing, and why, it all fell into place. I guess that's why I got so upset – a small part of me had still hoped that it wasn't true. But when you said that, I knew it was real.'

'So what about now?' Lizzy said. 'Are you still helping Firework?'

'As far as they're aware, yes. But I really want to pull out. I just don't know what to do – I'm scared that if I back out, they'll go ahead and tell the world about what Stuart did.'

Lizzy was thinking. 'Is that why you came here to tell us about this, for help?'

'Not really.' Sally turned to Will. 'I came here to tell you that I think Firework Films are the people who are blackmailing you.'

'You don't know who's behind Firework Films, do you?' Lizzy asked.

'No, should I?'

'It's Guy Roberts.'

Sally was stunned. 'What?' She shook her head. 'No.'

'It's true,' Will said. 'We've got the evidence. And this morning he admitted to Lizzy that it was true.'

Sally was having trouble taking everything in. 'But, he was Stuart's friend! They were so close. And he was so supportive after Stuart died. Nothing was too much trouble. He even offered that I could stay at his place, until I felt better.' She looked around the group. 'Are you sure?'

They nodded. 'There's no doubt,' Lizzy confirmed. 'Guy Roberts is registered as a director of Firework Films.'

'I can't believe it . . . He's *exploiting* me! He doesn't care about me at all.' Her face hardened into anger. 'I didn't think things could get any worse after what happened to Stuart, but for the past two weeks, it has. And *he*'s the cause. The man who was supposed to be helping me! He's been putting the screws on us all just to make his precious little programme more ratings-worthy!'

Will bit his lip. 'I'm so sorry, Sally, for thinking that it was you doing the blackmailing.'

'When it seems it was Firework Films all along,' Lizzy added.

'It's okay,' Sally replied, taking a breath to calm herself. 'If I was you, I would have thought the same.'

Dan leant forward. 'So, how does Guy Roberts know about what Stuart did to Stephen Myers?' He answered his own question: 'Stuart could have told Guy,' he said. 'If they were that close, then it's definitely a possibility that he could have admitted it to Guy.'

'But why would he tell Guy?' Will said.

'Maybe he needed to tell someone. Or maybe he didn't intend to. I know how he got when he was drunk. So maybe, one night, it just came out.'

'Maybe,' Sally said. 'He trusted Guy. He would never have thought that he would use that sort of information for something like this.'

'Guy Roberts is a nasty piece of work,' Lizzy stated. 'Nothing I hear about him surprises me any more.'

'So, let's just say that Firework Films is behind the letter-sending and the blackmailing,' Dan continued. 'Maybe that means they're also involved with Peter Myers' escape. Because we suspect that person in the cap who has been sending the letters was also the one who drove Myers away from the hospital.'

'It's a bit of a leap, though,' Will said. 'Why would they want to help Peter Myers?'

'To increase the drama,' Lizzy replied.

Will frowned. 'Really?'

'As I said, nothing would surprise me.'

'It does sound unlikely,' Dan said, slowly, 'but if you think of things from their perspective, then it might just make sense.' He warmed to his theme: 'They bring the villain right back into the story—'

'So they're creating the story, not just reporting on it,' Sally finished for him.

Dan nodded. 'Exactly. It happens all the time now with television. Reality TV, for example. The producers manipulate the people, who are in effect the actors, and the story is created not just by the people, but by the makers of the programme.'

'Guy Roberts has certainly got a history of manipulative behaviour,' Lizzy said.

'But it still sounds crazy,' Will said, 'to think that we're all being manipulated by someone just for a television programme.'

'I didn't say it was just for a programme,' Dan replied. 'There is another motive for Guy Roberts.'

'Which is?'

'Revenge.'

'Revenge for what?' Will said.

'Revenge on Emma for pulling out of the film. We know the sort of controlling person he is. He likes to get his own way, and he's got an extremely high opinion of himself. Emma rejecting his offer, it would have hurt. Maybe the whole idea of the docudrama is about revenge, and about maintaining control of Emma and her story.'

'I'm just not sure how plausible that is,' Will said.

Lizzy was more convinced. 'I said as much to Guy himself. He denied it, of course.'

The group considered Dan's theory in silence.

'Do you think they've got Emma?' Will said.

'I hope so,' Dan replied. 'Because it's much better than the alternative.'

Will dropped his head into his hands. 'I hope to God that Peter Myers doesn't have her. I don't really care if the police catch him or not, as long as he stays away from Emma.'

Again the group fell silent.

'Oh my God!' Lizzy said, suddenly. 'The girl in the house! I've worked it out. I think I know who it is!'

39

She sat on the edge of the bed, alone and scared, as she listened for the sound of him downstairs. He had been out of the house a number of times since he had snatched her – was it only one day ago? – but his leaving had offered no chance of escape.

Each time he went out, the door to the box room that was her prison was bolted shut.

The lone, small window in the corner of the room was barred – she couldn't even reach the glass to knock for help. Not that anyone would be passing by to hear her – the brief look she had had out of the window whilst balancing precariously on the foot of the bed had told her that it looked out onto a back garden, strewn with household rubbish, interspersed with thick weeds.

But now, after a night and day in which she had despaired, there was at last some hope.

Fifteen minutes ago, he had visited her. When he left, he had forgotten to lock the door. And then the sound that she had been waiting for – the sound of the front door closing.

He had gone out.

She waited another few minutes, still listening intently, before raising herself from the bed.

Can I risk it?

She had to. She moved across to the door and paused with a hand on the knob. Again she listened. No sound. Opening the door as silently as she could, she moved out onto the landing.

Please, let the front door be open, please . . .

As she crept towards the staircase however, she suddenly heard a noise, and he was on her, grabbing her hair, yanking her back with brutal force.

'Don't think . . . you're . . . getting away,' he said, as they struggled on the landing.

She managed to lash out with an elbow and connected with his ribs, shaking him off and running for the stairs. But as she went to descend, he pushed her hard from behind and she careered downwards, crashing down the stairs and tumbling head over heels to the bottom.

Peter Myers stared impassively from the top of the staircase at her lifeless body.

If she hadn't tried to leave me, this would never have happened.

He moved slowly down the stairs and knelt down next to her. He brushed back the strands of brown hair that had fallen forwards over her face. Her eyes were closed and it didn't look as if she was breathing. 'So beautiful.'

He pressed two fingers into her neck, and waited for several seconds. 'You shouldn't have tried to run.' He stroked her cheek. 'Rest in peace.'

40

Gasnier rapped at the door for a second time, then peered through the downstairs window, cupping his hands against the cool glass. No sign of movement. He cursed the fact that they didn't have a mobile telephone number for him.

'What now?' Davies said. 'Try the others?'

Gasnier nodded. 'Yes, let's go.'

They walked back down the path but, just as they got to the car, a voice called out behind them. 'Excuse me?'

It was the next-door neighbour. A middle aged woman, who must have been watching them from inside as she did the dishes – she was still wearing yellow rubber gloves, soap suds dangling from the fingers like stalactites. 'Are you looking for Edward?'

'Yes, we are.' Gasnier smiled, but inside he wasn't happy with himself – why hadn't he tried the neighbours? It was a pretty basic thing. Maybe he was losing his touch. Or maybe he was just tired – his wife had reminded him that morning that it was over a year since he'd taken any significant holiday. 'Do you know where he's likely to be?'

'I do.' She beamed. 'He'll be at the hospital, with his new baby.'

'Really?' Gasnier sensed Davies look over at him. 'So, congratulations are in order?'

'Oh, yes,' she said. 'He's had a little boy called Jack. He showed me a photograph. He's such a lovely baby. I think this baby will do him the world of good. Even though he's quite old to be a new dad.'

'Do you know which hospital they're at?'

'Oh, yes, St Thomas'. It's where my daughter went, too.'

'Great,' Gasnier said, already turning back towards the car. He nodded to Davies. 'You've been a great help, Mrs—?'

'Blackmore,' the woman said. 'Elizabeth Blackmore.' Her face creased slightly. 'There's nothing wrong, is there? I mean, at such a happy time . . . nothing's happened, has it?'

Gasnier paused at the open car door. 'Just some routine questions. Nothing to worry about.'

'Because, of course, I know all about what happened to his daughter, Emma, and her boyfriend. I mean, that really was an awful thing.' She shook her head at the thought. 'Such a dreadful thing. I've known Emma since she was a small child. She always was such a wonderful little girl. I hope she's happy now.'

'So do I,' Gasnier replied, getting in the car. 'So do I.'

***

'So, how do we play this? Davies asked, as Gasnier parked outside the hospital entrance.

'Well, we don't want to create a scene. We need to deal with this away from the mother and child. I don't want to be held responsible for any upset – I know from experience how protective of new mothers the nursing staff on maternity wards can be. And if I remember correctly, Edward's partner, Miranda, works here, so it will be even more the case, I'm sure. We just go in there, ask for him to be brought to us, and then deal with things in a private room.'

'Sounds sensible. And if he's not there?'

'Then we may have to involve Miranda. But let's hope that isn't the case.'

They swept through the sliding doors of the hospital's main entrance and headed for the lift.

The maternity ward was on the second floor, its reception straight in front of them. It was staffed by two nurses, one of whom had spotted their arrival. 'Can I help you?'

'Detective Inspector Mark Gasnier, Metropolitan Police, and my colleague, Detective Sergeant Christian Davies. We're hoping to find a Mr Edward Holden. We've been led to believe that his partner, Miranda, is here.' He showed his badge, which the young nurse studied. The sound of new-born cries drifted in from adjoining rooms, and a young girl in a blue hospital gown shuffled gingerly past them.

'Just one moment,' the nurse said, turning to her colleague. 'Yvonne?'

The other nurse – the older of the two by some margin – was already looking up from her paperwork. 'I know who you mean. He's in with Miranda and the baby now. I'll go and fetch him. I'd prefer it if you didn't go onto the ward.'

'Of course,' Gasnier replied. *Great, he's here.* 'Is there somewhere where we can talk?'

She nodded. 'You can use the tea room.'

Edward Holden entered the room looking like a man bracing himself for very bad news. Gasnier and Davies had remained standing during their minute's wait, but they had arranged three chairs in preparedness for his arrival.

Gasnier smiled. 'Mr Holden, hello. If you wouldn't mind closing the door behind you.'

He nodded and pushed the door shut.

Gasnier gestured. 'Please, take a seat.'

They all sat down, the two officers facing Edward Holden.

'Has something happened to Emma?' Edward asked.

Gasnier studied his face. It was a passable act, but he had seen much better. 'Do you have something to tell us, Edward?'

The cracks were already opening up. 'I . . . I don't know what you mean. How would I have something—?'

'Edward. You were extremely lucky to escape without charge for what you did, back in September. And you only escaped on a technicality, not because you didn't deserve to be punished. So, if I were you, I would be very grateful for your good fortune. And I would also ensure that I didn't place myself in a similar situation in the future. Because, believe me, things don't always work out so well. Individuals do often get what they deserve.'

'I understand,' Edward said, softly. 'I am grateful.'

'Good. So I'll ask you again. Do you have something to tell us?'

Edward closed his eyes.

'Mr Holden. Last chance. It would be much better if it came from you.'

Edward nodded, his eyes still closed tightly. 'I know where Emma is.'

Gasnier waited for him to elaborate, but he didn't. 'How do you know?'

214

Edward's eyes opened, tears pooling in them. 'Because I took her.'

41

'Do you have the photograph?' Lizzy said, excitedly.

'What photograph?' Dan replied.

'The one that the person sent you. With you and Stuart.'

Dan looked puzzled. 'Yes, it's in my coat pocket, I think – inside pocket.'

Without explanation, Lizzy rushed out into the hallway and came back clutching the photograph. 'I knew it!' she said, slapping the photograph onto the table. 'The girl who I saw at Guy Roberts' house, I didn't recognise her. I recognised her *brother*.'

Dan looked up. 'It was Stuart Harris's sister?'

'I'm as sure as I can be,' Lizzy replied. 'The resemblance is clear, now I've seen this.'

'Charlotte does know Guy,' Sally said, 'but not very well. Just through Stuart. They've never socialised together, as far as I know. Are you saying that she was there *with* him?'

'She was half-naked in his house,' Lizzy said. 'My first reaction was that they were together.'

Sally seemed unwilling to contemplate that idea. 'Are you sure it was Charlotte?'

'I'd place money on it.'

'I saw them talking at Stuart's funeral,' Sally said, almost to herself, her thoughts churning. 'Afterwards, at the wake, they were talking for quite a while. He had his arm around her. I thought he was just offering her support and comfort.'

'Do you think there's more to this than just a friendship or relationship?' Will said to Lizzy.

'Yes, I do.'

'I know what you're thinking,' Dan said. 'Charlotte Harris is another person of use to Guy. Another person from whom he can obtain information for the docudrama.'

'That's exactly what I'm thinking.'

'But what's in it for her?' Will said.

'Maybe she believes in the relationship,' Lizzy replied. She turned to Sally. 'Do you think Guy could have seduced Charlotte?'

'It's possible, I suppose. Guy has a reputation as a ladies' man, and he's not afraid to use his position, if you know what I mean.' She shook her head. 'I know Stuart always used to joke that he rarely saw the same woman on Guy's arm more than twice, before the next one came along. They were always quite a bit younger than him, too.'

'But you'd be surprised if Charlotte was having a relationship with him?' Dan said.

'Yes, under normal circumstances. But I know Charlotte was very low after what happened with Stuart. She likes people to think that she's strong, but she's actually quite vulnerable. She's had quite a few problems, and I can understand how she might be exploited by someone she trusts. If Guy made the first move, she might have fallen for him.'

'And there's his close connection to Stuart. Charlotte might find it comforting to be with someone who was friends with her brother,' Lizzy said.

'Yes,' Sally agreed. 'It makes sense.'

'So Guy Roberts begins a relationship with Charlotte Harris, for the purposes of getting information off her for the docudrama,' Will said.

'And the other perks,' Lizzy added. 'Charlotte is a very attractive girl. Dating her as a way of getting more information for the programme wouldn't have been a difficult option for Guy to contemplate.'

'So, what do we do now?' Will said. 'Even if you're right about this, how does it help us find Emma?'

'It doesn't, really,' Lizzy replied, looking deflated.

'No, it does help,' Dan said. 'It gives us another piece in the puzzle. And it gives us someone else who can maybe provide more information about what has been going on.'

Lizzy looked more hopeful. 'You think we should speak to Charlotte?'

'We should let the police deal with it,' Dan said, firmly. 'I think the time for us playing private detective is over. I want to see Gasnier and the rest of the Met all over Guy Roberts and Firework Films. Because I think they're the best chance we've got.'

217

'Let's call them now, then,' Lizzy said.

But before they could do anything, the intercom buzzer sounded.

They all looked at each other, for a moment not moving.

'I'll go,' Dan said, going out into the passageway. He returned a few moments later. 'You won't believe who's on her way upstairs. Charlotte Harris.'

42

'It's not what you're thinking,' Edward said, glancing between the two officers. 'You're looking at me as if I've done something to harm her.'

Gasnier bit back his anger and frustration. 'Just tell us what's going on, Mr Holden. Before I'm forced to arrest you, and we continue this down at the station.'

'Okay,' Edward said, hurriedly. 'There won't be any need for that, please. I don't want Miranda to find out what's going on. She's only just had a baby—'

'That much we do know,' Gasnier said, dryly. 'If we'd wanted to make a scene, then we would have already done so by now. Why do you think we are speaking in here, instead of approaching you at the bedside?'

Edward understood. 'Thank you. I appreciate that you've been discreet. And I am really grateful for that.'

Now it was Gasnier's time to nod his understanding. 'As I said, we don't wish to make a scene. But we have a job to do, just like the nurses in here. We want to find Emma, and bring her home safely. So, Edward, what's going on?'

Edward gathered himself. 'She's safe. She's staying at a house I own.'

'She was reported as missing. I take it her husband doesn't know about this?'

Edward shook his head slowly.

'So what's this all about?'

'I was warned not to trust anyone,' Edward said. 'Not Dan, or Lizzy, or even Will.'

'By whom?'

'I don't know. They called me on the phone, and warned me that Peter Myers was coming for her, and that I shouldn't trust anyone. I decided I couldn't take any chances, so I took Emma to the house. I reckoned she would be safe there, until Myers is recaptured or I decided what to do next.'

'And Emma agreed to this?'

'She wasn't that happy, but yes, she did agree to it.'

Gasnier raised a disbelieving eyebrow. 'Even though she knew the worry it would cause to her family and friends?'

Edward looked uncomfortable. 'She thinks that they know where she is. I told her that I'd let them know.'

'So as far as Emma knows, everyone is in on the plan?'

'Yes.'

'Except for us,' Gasnier added. 'Mr Holden, you are aware that wasting police time is a criminal offence?'

He looked as if the thought had never occurred to him. 'I . . . I didn't ever mean for it to waste police time.'

'Leaving the door to Emma's flat ajar – was that an attempt to throw us off the scent?'

'Ajar?' He looked confused. 'No, I meant to close it. But we were hurrying, so maybe I didn't put it to. It certainly wasn't deliberate.' Edward's voice was growing wild. 'I didn't want to hurt or mislead anyone. I just want to protect my daughter. I would do anything to protect my children. Anything.'

'I understand that,' Gasnier said. 'But didn't you think that, maybe, we could help protect Emma? And that by misleading us, or shutting us out, you risked making things a lot worse?'

'I see what you're saying.'

'Do you? Sometimes, Mr Holden, I do wonder whether you understand anything that I say.' Gasnier let that comment hang in the air for a few seconds. 'Your behaviour throughout all of this, well, to me, it's mind-boggling.' Another pause. 'So, where is this property?'

'It's just south of the river,' Edward replied. 'In Croydon. It's a small property we bought recently for rental, and we're still getting it ready to let out. I thought it was the ideal place for Emma to hide.'

'So Emma will be there now?'

'Yes, yes she will be there. She hasn't been outside since she arrived. I got supplies in for her. I didn't want to risk her being seen.'

'Is she contactable? Dan and the others have been calling her, without success.'

'I took Emma's mobile phone off her, but the house has got an active landline.'

'Then call her now,' Gasnier said. 'Tell her that we'll be along shortly.'

'Me, too?'

'Yes, of course.'

Edward nodded. 'What should I tell Miranda?'

'Anything you like.'

He dialled the number, and waited. 'There's no answer,' he said.

'Keep on the line,' Gasnier said. 'She might be in the bathroom.'

Edward waited for a few more seconds. 'She's not answering.' He looked up at the two police officers, suddenly aghast. 'What if something's happened?'

Gasnier's question was swift. 'When did you see her last?'

'This morning. Just before I came over to the hospital. I delivered some milk, and checked to see that she was okay.'

'Let's go,' Gasnier said, getting to his feet. 'What's the address? We'll get a patrol car over there right now.'

43

Guy Roberts sat back on the sofa, holding a glass of chilled champagne lightly in his fingers. He finished it in one, and had just poured himself another when the doorbell rang.

It would be her, begging for his forgiveness.

He smiled thinly as he stood up, and waited for a few seconds.

By the time he reached the door, the bell had sounded again. 'Take it easy, my dear. Don't come across as too desperate.'

He would sleep with her one more time. But then that was it.

He swung open the door with a theatrical flourish. 'I knew you wou—'

The slide of the knife blade into his chest was as cold as the glass that slipped from his fingers.

44

'Hi,' Charlotte said, as Dan led her into the kitchen. Still sporting her brown bob, her pretty face looked puffy, as if she had been crying recently and had not yet recovered fully. She averted her eyes on catching sight of Will, but she was caught by surprise at the presence of Sally, who just nodded a greeting.

The room was by now pretty full, and there were just enough chairs to go around. But Charlotte didn't move to sit down. 'Is Emma not here?'

'No,' Dan said. 'We don't know where she is. We hoped that you might be able to help.'

'It was you!' Will said, suddenly. 'The girl at the park, jogging! It was you!'

She looked away.

'You were pretending to be Emma, weren't you?'

She didn't answer that.

'What's going on, Charlotte?' Lizzy asked. 'Why were you at Guy Roberts' house?'

'I feel so stupid,' she said. 'I've been a fool.'

Lizzy pressed. 'How do you mean?'

Charlotte shook her head at some thought, looking up towards the ceiling. 'I mean, I *really* thought that he liked me. He was so supportive after Stuart . . . you know, and so kind. I don't think I could have got through the funeral without him, I really don't.'

'You're talking about Guy?' Lizzy said.

Now Charlotte did take a seat. 'Yes. He was just so good to me. I didn't intend for it to happen, but we met up a couple of times for a drink . . . well, a few drinks. He was such a good listener and, I thought he really understood what I was going through. Then things went from there.'

'You started a relationship?'

'Yes. For the past few weeks. It all happened so quickly, but I really felt like it was genuine. Things were going so well. But I know now that it was all just an act.'

'What makes you think that?' Lizzy asked.

Charlotte smiled, ruefully. 'Because of what he said to me after I told him what happened today.'

'You mean, seeing me?'

'Yes. I told him that I'd seen you upstairs, and he really lost it. He was so angry. He started throwing stuff at the walls, and he was really shouting. If I'd known how he would react, I wouldn't have said anything. It was horrible.' She shuddered.

'What did he say?' Dan asked.

'I can't remember everything, but he was just shouting about how I'd risked everything by not being careful – I'd told him about seeing you in the park, Will.'

'You were pretending to be Emma, weren't you?' he said.

'Yes.'

'Why?'

'Because I wanted to convince Guy that I could play her,' she said. 'I wanted to show him that I was good enough.'

Lizzy laughed in disbelief. 'You wanted to play the part of Emma in the docudrama?'

Charlotte looked embarrassed and hurt, like a scolded teenager. 'I know, I've been really stupid.'

'Is that how it worked?' Lizzy continued. 'Guy made promises in return for information?'

'Well, no, not—'

'You gave him the photograph of Dan and Stuart, didn't you?'

'What?'

'This photograph,' Lizzy said, producing it.

Charlotte paused, open-mouthed, then looked at Dan. 'I did, yes. I'm sorry. It was in the parcel that Stuart posted to me, before he killed himself. It contained personal photos and letters he wanted me to have. How did you get that?'

'Someone sent it to us,' Dan said. 'Why did you give it to Guy?'

She shrugged. 'I figured that Stuart had sent it to me for a reason. And' – she paused, then sat up a little straighter, looking defiant – 'and I wanted to hurt Emma, I guess.'

'Because you blamed her for Stuart's death?' Lizzy asked.

'Yes.'

'And you still believe it was Emma's fault?'

There was a pause. 'I don't know what to believe any more.'

'What else did you give Guy?' Lizzy asked, more gently this time.

'Nothing else. I told him how it had affected me.'

'Do you know whether Guy Roberts was involved in helping Peter Myers to escape from prison?' Dan asked now.

'No!' Charlotte looked appalled. 'I didn't even know that he had escaped.' Her face suddenly flashed with horror. 'Is that who you think has Emma?'

'We don't know,' Dan said. He looked across at Lizzy and Will, then back at her. 'Are you sure that you don't know anything about where Emma might be?'

'I don't. I'm really sorry. I'm sorry for everything I've done.'

'And you don't know anything about the messages we've been getting?'

'No, I swear.' She hesitated. 'I don't.'

'What is it?' Lizzy said. 'Charlotte, if you know anything else that might be able to help, then just tell us, please.'

'Okay, okay,' she said. She paused again for a few moments, then: 'I think Guy might be infatuated with Emma.'

Dan leaned forward. 'What makes you think that?'

'He talks in his sleep,' she said. 'It wakes me up. He often talks about Emma. On Monday night, he was talking a *lot* about her.'

'What does he say?' Lizzy said.

'That he loves her, wants to be with her. A lot of what he says doesn't make much sense. One night he just kept repeating "You're my star" over and over again.'

Lizzy's jaw dropped. 'That would explain why he might feel so bitter about Emma turning down the film role . . .'

'Maybe,' Dan said. 'Did you not challenge him about it?'

'No. I guess I didn't want it to be true. If he is infatuated with Emma, I didn't want to hear him admit it.'

Lizzy looked at Dan. 'So, what's our next step?'

'We call Gasnier.'

45

Emma stood at the bay window, looking out at the tree-lined street outside. It was quite a busy residential area, so was good for people-watching. A young Asian couple strolled past, pushing a toddler in a pushchair. She watched as they passed the window and turned the corner at the top of the street. It had started to feel claustrophobic in the house, and she longed to just walk out of the front door. But her father had been insistent: she should stay inside.

She thought of the others, and how they might have reacted to the news that she had gone into hiding. *Will they understand?* Emma still felt very uncomfortable with the decision. It felt as if she had abandoned them, particularly Dan.

She moved away from her vantage point and slumped onto the sofa, channel-hopping on the TV for something to watch.

It was after a minute or so of gazing at the TV screen that she thought she heard a noise coming from the kitchen. Reaching for the remote control, she muted the volume. She listened, her breathing shallow, as the television show played on in silence. She couldn't hear anything else.

Probably just my imagination.

But she left the volume down as she rose from the sofa and moved across towards the door. She turned the corner, and froze.

The back door that led into the small garden was open.

Instinctively, she stepped back into the lounge and slammed the door shut, remaining there, both hands pressed up against the wood. *If anyone's there, they can't get in.*

But in her panic she had forgotten that there were two doors into the living room.

'Emma. I've waited so long for this moment.'

She spun around. Peter Myers had entered the room silently, the door on the other side already closed behind him.

He smiled, as if greeting a long-lost friend. He had nasty bruising around his eyes, and his left cheek was still swollen.

Emma backed into the door behind her, and reached down for the handle, wondering if she could get through in the time it would take Myers to reach her.

She wouldn't have a chance.

Peter Myers took one small step closer. Not once did he avert his lingering gaze. 'I've waited so long for us to be together,' he said, smiling. 'I'm your number one fan.'

Emma searched desperately for words that might rescue her from the situation, but nothing came. *How did he know where I was?* were the only words echoing in her head.

'Your father led me here,' he said, as if stealing her thoughts. 'I followed him from his house, this morning. So, after completing some unfinished business, I came back for you.'

'Please, Mr Myers,' she said, her voice faltering. 'Let's sit down and talk.'

'Call me Peter,' he said. Another step forward. 'There will be plenty of time for talking. I always knew we'd be together. Ever since I saw you for the first time in the photo that Stephen brought home to me, I knew you were the one.'

His certainty was terrifying. 'Please, Peter.'

Just then the phone in the hallway began to ring. It could only be her father, calling to check whether she was all right. But there was no way she would be able to reach it in time.

'I should thank my son for bringing us together,' he said. 'And I would, if he was still alive.'

'I'm sorry about what happened to Stephen,' she found herself saying. 'I really am sorry.'

He shrugged. 'I'm not here to talk about that. You know,' he said, 'I did try to forget about you. Before the phone call, I'd tried to move on, I really had.'

'What do you mean? What phone call?'

As if on cue, the phone in the hallway stopped ringing. Maybe her lack of response would in itself raise the alarm. She could only hope and pray.

'His phone call, Emma. It reignited something inside me, and it just grew and grew, until I couldn't deny it any longer. It's such a beautiful feeling. Do you know what it's like, to live for years in a loveless marriage? To share a bed with a woman you can't stand the sight of? After Stephen died, Margaret began to lose her mind. In some ways, that made things easier. And then the phone call – well, it changed everything.'

'Who called you?'

Peter Myers smiled. 'Guy Roberts. All those years later, he brought you back into my life. He called to tell me what Stuart Harris and your brother had done to my son.'

'Guy Roberts told you?'

'Yes, he did.'

'So everything that happened, it's because of *him*.' Emma was shocked, her thoughts rushing wildly around her head. Stuart must have told him, and then Guy contacted Peter Myers. *All because he wanted to raise the profile of his stupid movie? Would he really have stooped so low?* She had so many things she wanted to say, so many unanswered questions, but she couldn't order them all in her spinning mind.

'Yes, I suppose so. It brought us back together. And my time in prison, it just made things clearer to me – I don't want to be apart from you. You know, I had a photo of you in there, and it really kept me going. I slept with it under my pillow. I'm your number one fan, Emma.'

Emma looked longingly over at the window. A middle-aged couple walked past the house, carrying shopping bags. She was so close, yet so far, from help. 'Peter, please, you have to leave.'

'But why would I go? I only want to be with *you*. I tried someone else, Emma. I took her from outside your flat, yesterday. I had come for you, but your father got there first. So I took her instead. But it didn't work out. She tried to leave me, and . . .'

'You're scaring me.' She really hadn't meant to say it, but it had burst out in her rising panic.

Strangely, Emma's comment seemed to leave him puzzled. 'You shouldn't be scared of me, Emma. I won't ever hurt you. I want to protect you, from the men in your life who cause you so much pain. Stuart Harris, Dan, Guy Roberts – even your own brother, Will. That's why I took him, Emma, to try and save you from making a terrible mistake.'

'You're talking about Dan?'

'Of course. I did my best, Emma, to stop you from marrying him. I tried to save you.'

Everything was coming together, explained by this delusional man. 'So all this, taking Dan, it wasn't about revenge for what happened with Stephen? It was about you . . . wanting me?'

'I didn't want to hurt you, Emma. I know you thought you were in love with Dan, and that's why I didn't harm him. I could easily have killed him. Just like I killed Guy Roberts.'

The last sentence hit like a hammer blow, coming from nowhere. It made her want to turn and run, but there was no escape. 'What? You—?'

He closed the gap between them. She considered tackling him physically, but he was a big man, and her martial-arts knowledge did not guarantee that she could overpower him. There was also the chance that he might be carrying a weapon.

'He thought he could use me, Emma, just like he used you. He caused you a lot of suffering. But, don't worry, he won't be able to hurt you any more.' He reached out and traced the back of his hand across her right cheek. Emma could smell stale alcohol on his breath.

For the first time, she wondered whether she would ever see her family and friends again.

46

'You think I'm reckless, don't you?'

Gasnier maintained his grip on the steering wheel and fought his instinct to answer in a way that would only be unhelpful. He slowed at a red light and came to a stop, taking a look at Edward Holden in the rear-view mirror. He actually felt sorry for him. He would have had to possess a heart of stone to not feel for the man.

DS Davies looked across from the front passenger seat, checking that Gasnier was going to reply.

'I believe you did what you thought was best,' he said, finally.

'I just wanted the best for my family,' Edward said, meeting his eyes in the mirror.

Gasnier nodded. The lights changed, and he moved off. The unmarked car didn't have any sirens, which was one of the reasons why he had called out a patrol car to lead the response. They were probably already there. Although there hadn't been a report through yet.

They were only a few minutes away.

'It's a left, just here,' Edward said. 'Then next right, and the house is a few metres from the junction, on the right-hand side of the road.'

Gasnier made the left and right turns. He stepped on the brakes as they came upon the scene.

'Oh my God!' Edward cried.

The patrol car was there, but so too was an ambulance. There was also a crowd of people huddled by the roadside, being chaperoned by one of the officers.

'Stay inside the car,' Gasnier ordered, as he swung open his door. DS Davies followed him.

Gasnier passed through the onlookers and addressed the officer. 'Detective Inspector Gasnier.'

'Sir.'

'What's happened here?'

Edward Holden came running up before the officer had a chance to reply. 'Is it Emma?' he demanded, wildly. 'I'll never forgive myself.'

Gasnier resisted the temptation to scold him for disobeying his instructions, and instead just ignored him. 'Officer . . .'

'It's not Emma Holden,' he said. 'But we think it might be linked to the collision.'

'Collision?' Now Gasnier noticed the mangled bicycle by the kerbside.

'There was a collision between a cyclist – a young lady – and a white van. We've got a couple of witnesses. The van drove off at speed from outside the house in question, and cut right across the cyclist.'

'Did anyone see who was driving?'

'A man matching the description of Peter Myers. And from what the witnesses said, it seems highly likely that Emma Holden was in the front passenger seat.'

'Have you got plates?'

'Yes. We've put out an alert.'

'Good, that's good.' Gasnier thought for a second. 'The cyclist, is she okay?'

'Just minor cuts and bruising, sir. And she's a bit shaken up. But nothing serious.'

Gasnier nodded. 'Good to hear.' His attention switched back to the task at hand. 'Is the house secure?'

'Yes.'

'Good. I don't want anyone going near the place. No doubt the press will be arriving soon.'

'He's taken her,' Edward said, 'hasn't he?'

'It looks that way,' Gasnier replied. 'But every police officer and camera operator in the capital will be looking for that vehicle. There's no escape.'

Edward didn't look reassured.

'Sir,' a second officer shouted, jogging over to them. 'The van's been located, spotted on camera. It's heading north, on the A23.'

'He's going to cross the Thames,' Gasnier announced. 'We could head him off. Pity there's so many damn bridges.'

'Can we get cars to the most likely crossing points?' Davies asked.

'We can certainly try. How many bridges are we talking about? Eight or nine?'

'Sounds about right. The most likely options, anyway.'

Gasnier turned to the officers. 'Go on, what are you waiting for? Call out the troops.'

'We'll know more about his intentions,' Davies said, 'when the van reaches the junction of the A202.'

Gasnier agreed. 'The next few minutes will tell us.'

They waited impatiently for news.

'The vehicle is continuing north,' the officer reported back. 'Cameras have confirmed it's now on the A3.' He stopped to listen again to his radio. 'We've got a patrol car following from a distance.'

Again, more waiting.

'Now right at the Elephant and Castle roundabout onto the A201.'

'Tower Bridge,' Gasnier said, crisply. 'He won't risk all the traffic to the tunnels. He'll swing up left and cross the river there. Have we got cars waiting on the other side?'

'I'm not sure, sir, I'll check. Hopefully.'

'Hopefully isn't good enough,' Gasnier replied. 'Those cars have to be there, because that's the bridge he's heading for.'

47

Emma looked out of the dirt-splattered windscreen as the van moved through the London afternoon traffic. The roads were busy, but they were moving. Again, safety was so close, but just out of reach. Peter Myers had locked the doors, and only he could reopen them with the button on his right, located on the inside door handle. He had been quick to tell her that she couldn't get out.

'Where are we going?' Emma said. It was the first thing she had said to him since he had dragged her down the path and into the van. The vehicle had taken off at speed, and they had cut right across the path of a cyclist. Emma had watched with horror in the wing mirror as the cyclist had buckled and hit the ground, unmoving. There had been no way of telling whether she was okay.

'You'll see,' he replied.

They approached the roundabout at the Elephant and Castle, turning right. Out of the corner of her eye, Emma looked first at Peter Myers, then across at the lock release button. It was in sight, but would only be within reach by lunging across Peter Myers' lap. *Could it be done?* While she thought, they reached another roundabout and Peter Myers turned second left. He was heading for Tower Bridge. *And after that, where?* Suddenly, the bridge took on a greater meaning. She had to try something before they crossed it. That meant taking action within the next minute.

She formed a plan, and waited for the moment, her adrenalin levels rising. But suddenly Peter Myers seemed to switch his attention from the road back to Emma: he threw frequent glances her way as the bridge came into view, its twin towers thrusting skywards like a medieval castle straddling the Thames. There was no way she could try anything yet.

Upon reaching the bridge, the glances stopped. The traffic was bottle-necking over the bridge, and there were cyclists flashing past both sides of the car. Tourists were also crossing in front of and behind them, taking advantage of the slow-moving traffic.

Emma decided it was her only chance. The next time Peter Myers had to move forward, following the car in front, she moved. In two swift actions, she unclipped her seatbelt and lunged across him, scrabbling for the button.

'What are you doing?' he yelled, struggling to maintain his control of the van whilst also trying to get a grip on her top to stop her moving for the passenger-side door handle. He got a hold of her shirt and wrenched her back, her head slamming against the side of the driver's seat, the van swerving a sharp right then left as Myers tried to correct himself.

It was then, halfway across the bridge, that he noticed the police car waiting at the other side. With a loud curse, he slammed on the brakes, causing a taxi to crash into the back of the vehicle. They were both thrown forward, Emma hitting the front console and only narrowly escaping injury by throwing out her hands to cushion the impact.

She recovered quickly, however, lashing out with an elbow and catching Peter Myers on the cheekbone, and threw open her door. The seatbelt caught around her ankle, sending her toppling to the ground but she fought free of it, sprang up and vaulted over the pedestrian barrier.

Only to be caught from behind by Peter Myers.

'Don't leave me,' he rasped into her ear, as he gripped her tightly.

She broke away using one of her standard karate release moves, but he ran at her again. She twisted out of his path and used his speed and weight to throw him against the low barrier that ran along the side of bridge.

His momentum sent him toppling over the side, where only a desperate grab at the railings stopped him from plummeting into the river below.

'Help me!' He flailed about like a landed fish with his other hand, struggling to grab on to the railings.

Without thinking, Emma moved to the side of the bridge and threw out her hand, grabbing his jacket collar, holding on to him as he dangled over the edge. She reached down with her other hand and tried to haul him in, but he was heavy, and she felt herself lifting off the pavement.

'Don't leave me,' he said, straining upwards to look in her face, the Thames flowing beneath him. 'I'm the one you love, not him.'

A cold, water-soaked wind whipped up from the river, blasting against Emma's face. She screwed her eyes shut as she tried to hold him, but her grip was failing. Wedging a foot underneath the bottom of the railing, Emma tried to gain more leverage, but it was no use. 'Help!' she shouted. 'Somebody help!'

She heard someone approaching, but it was too late.

Peter Myers knew it too. 'Emma!'

He slipped from her grasp, arcing backwards as he headed for the river below. But he didn't hit the water.

A container vessel passed under the bridge just as he fell, and Myers slammed onto its flat deck.

Emma watched, breathless and in shock, as Peter Myers' lifeless body was carried away down river.

48

Emma waited in the back seat of the police car, clutching the coffee that one of the officers had fetched her from a nearby café. She looked across at the bridge, which was now a sea of flashing lights from the various emergency vehicles that had descended on the area. The bridge was closed, with traffic diverted at both ends.

She processed the piece of news that Gasnier had relayed to her just a few minutes before – they'd found a girl tied up and gagged in the back of his van. She was in shock, but okay. According to the girl, she had been snatched off the street by Peter Myers the day before. Gasnier had sworn under his breath when he'd been told about the missing person report – and who that missing person resembled. Croydon was a long way from Marylebone, so no one had thought to bring it to his particular attention.

That must have been the girl he spoke about. Thank God she's okay.

Lost in thought, Emma was caught by surprise – Dan appeared at the window, smiling gently. He opened the door and they hugged tightly. 'Thank God you're okay,' he said. Emma closed her eyes tightly as she wallowed in the warmth of her husband's embrace. She pulled back and, over his shoulder, saw Lizzy and Will, looking on.

'I've never been so pleased to see someone in my whole life,' Lizzy said.

'Seconded,' Will added.

They all seemed to turn as one to look down towards the opposite side of the river, where the vessel carrying Peter Myers' body was now moored.

'He's really gone,' Lizzy said. 'Just like Guy Roberts.' She turned to Emma. 'Have they told you any more about what happened to Guy?'

'No specifics. Just that they found a body.'

Dan sensed her unease, and brought an arm around her. 'It's okay, you know, to be happy.'

Emma shook her head. 'Two people have died. I will be happy, but now's not the right time.'

The friends nodded their understanding.

'There're so many things I wanted to ask them,' Emma added. 'Those two men, they've made our lives an utter nightmare. They've put us through so much. I feel like I haven't got all the answers. And now I never will.'

'Sometimes you don't get all the answers,' Lizzy replied, gently. 'Life doesn't always provide a neat ending.'

'We will find out more,' Dan said. Emma suddenly realised someone was missing. 'Where's Dad?'

'Over there,' Will said, gesturing to the crowd behind the police cordon. 'I think he's a bit worried about how you'll react.'

Emma looked over and could see her father near DI Gasnier, looking out towards the river as if in a dream. 'What, after he lied about telling you where I was?' Gasnier had also thought to pass this tidbit on. She thought for a moment. 'Will, can you ask him to come over?'

Edward looked crestfallen. 'I'm so sorry, Emma. I put you in danger. I didn't trust your friends, or even Will.'

'It's okay, Dad,' she said, hugging him. 'It's what they wanted to happen. But they didn't win.'

'I do love you,' he said.

'Me, too.'

'This time it really is over.'

Emma looked over to Dan and they exchanged a smile. 'I know.'

49

Two weeks later

'This was a great idea, Lizzy,' Emma said. 'Cheers!' They clinked glasses. 'Just what I needed.' She looked across the room. The Irish-themed pub was filling up, but it was still relatively early in the evening. Just a few months before, the nightmare had started there, with Will's phone call. But they were there now to extinguish those unhappy memories and reclaim the territory for happier times.

'Will and I planned to do this when you and Dan got back from honeymoon – a combined and long-overdue stag and hen party. Though things didn't quite go to plan,' Lizzy explained. 'But having heard about the demise of Firework Films, I thought now was the perfect time to celebrate.'

Two days before, they'd heard via DI Gasnier that the production company had shut down operations, pending the outcome of a police investigation. The two remaining directors had denied any knowledge of Guy Roberts' behaviour, and said that they would co-operate fully. And, most importantly, the docudrama had been cancelled.

'I heard from Adrian Spencer this afternoon,' Lizzy added. 'He called me with the news too. He was very happy.'

'I bet.'

Lizzy looked over her shoulder, towards the door. 'I wonder where the others have got to?'

Emma checked the time. 'Dan said he'd be a little bit late, but they should be here by now.'

Lizzy knew what her friend was thinking. She smiled. 'It's over, remember?'

Emma nodded. 'I know, I know. I just wish the police had been able to trace the man in the baseball cap.'

'It's still over,' Lizzy reassured her. 'At least we know who it was and why - the phone message proves that Guy was paying him to do it.' The message from the mysterious "Ginger John", asking when he was going to get paid for his work, was found by the police on Guy Roberts' home phone answer machine. Firework Films had denied any knowledge of such an employee, and the police couldn't find any employment records to refute this.

Just then David Sherborn walked in and spotted them. Coming over, he said, 'Emma, Lizzy, can I get you two a drink?'

'Why not?' Lizzy replied, 'We'll have another of these.'

'Just an orange juice for me,' Emma said, earning a surprised look from her friend. 'I want to take it easy.'

'Cool.' David smiled. 'Thanks for the invite, by the way. It means a lot.' He made his way over to the bar.

Emma watched him as he ordered. 'Dad and Miranda came over with Jack this morning. It's lovely to see Dad so happy and content.'

'He decided against coming tonight?' Lizzy said.

'He said he would have liked to, but Jack's got a bit of a cold, so he's staying in.'

'He *has* changed,' Lizzy joked.

At last, the others arrived. 'Sorry we're late,' Dan said. He had Will and Sally in tow; Emma noticed that Will and Sally were holding hands. 'I was getting this.' He brought out a small, red jewellery box, and opened the top.

Inside was a necklace. Emma recognised it. She looked up at Dan, puzzled. 'Is that Mum's?'

'I had it mended and restored,' he explained. 'I know you said how much you liked it.'

Emma picked it up. The chain, which had been broken, was now complete, and the tarnished silver and diamond had been cleaned. It sparkled under the pub lights. 'It looks like new,' she said.

'I also had my wedding ring resized. I won't be taking it off any more.'

'You'd better not!' Emma joked. She undid the clasp of the necklace and placed it around her neck. 'Thank you, Dan.'

'It looks amazing,' said Lizzy. The others agreed.

Will took a drinks order and went to join David at the bar. They were served quickly and, once they were back, Dan turned to Emma.

239

'I've got a confession to make,' he said, solemnly. 'The necklace, it wasn't the reason I was late.'

'Oh?'

'It was because of this man!' He beckoned over to his brother, who had been standing out of Emma's sight, behind her.

'Richard!'

'Sorry, Emma,' he said, smiling. 'Train from Edinburgh was delayed.' They kissed a hello.

'It's amazing you're here,' she said. 'Thanks so much for coming.'

'Wouldn't miss it for the world.'

'So,' Lizzy said, having taken a sip of her drink. 'Where do we go from here?'

'Well, I thought later we could maybe go to that salsa club,' Will suggested.

Lizzy laughed. 'I didn't mean tonight. I meant in general.'

'Forward,' Emma said. 'We go forward. No more looking back. Speaking of which, Dan and I have got a very important announcement to make.' She looked around all her friends, taking in their faces, and smiled.

Epilogue

Ten months later

Emma woke suddenly. She turned to look at the clock radio next to the bedside; it was two fifteen in the morning. In the blackness of the room, she thought she heard a noise. A slight movement. She listened carefully. There it was again. Turning to her right, she discovered that Dan wasn't lying next to her. Then she noticed a chink of light coming from outside in the passageway. And there was the noise again.

She rubbed her eyes, then folded back the covers and turned up the dimmer switch on her bedside lamp, lighting the room a little more. Unsteady on her feet, still half asleep, she moved across to the Moses basket that was balanced across the wooden stand in the corner of the room.

'Hello,' she said, softly. 'I thought I could hear you snuffling around.' She smiled warmly as the baby with perfect blue eyes looked back at her. 'Are you hungry?'

'Nappy change,' Dan said, as he re-entered the room, his hair standing up at all angles and his face tired. 'I've just set up the stuff next door.' He smiled. 'You know, I thought I would hate having to get up in the middle of the night, but now Rose is here, I really don't mind at all.'

'Me, neither,' Emma said, as baby Rose toyed with one of her fingers. 'We're definitely under her spell.'

Dan put his arm around Emma. 'I don't think I've ever been this happy.'

Emma leant into him. 'I feel the same.'

They stayed like that for a few moments, watching their beautiful baby daughter.

'C'mon,' Dan said, finally. 'Mademoiselle needs a clean nappy. Enough baby worshipping for the moment.'

'Yes,' Emma agreed, unable to take her eyes off Rose. 'Just for the moment.'

THE END

Read the first chapters of Paul's suspense mystery,
Someone to Save You.

1

The teenage girl came from nowhere, running straight out into the middle of the country road from behind a line of trees.

Sam Becker slammed on the brakes and wrenched the wheel hard right, feeling the seat belt lock as he was thrown forward at speed. The car jerked before losing control, spinning on its axis while throwing up an ear-piercing screech. Everything was a blur until suddenly the spinning came to a violent stop, sending Sam's head flying back into the headrest.

Shaking off his dizziness, he twisted anxiously left then right, looking for the girl, but he couldn't see her. 'Please, no.'

He staggered out of the car and was about to look underneath the vehicle when he spotted her standing across the road, several metres down a dirt track that ran off to the left.

'Please, help us!' she shouted, crying. 'Please!'

He moved towards her as she ran in the opposite direction, heading further back down the lane. 'Wait,' Sam shouted after her. 'Are you okay?'

He followed her around the corner and found her standing by a smashed down fence. 'Down there, you've got to help us,' she pleaded. 'Please, help us, quick.'

As Sam moved closer he could see down the embankment at the railway line below.

'Oh my God.'

The car was astride the railway line and someone was sitting motionless in the driver's seat.

'Please, help us!' the girl repeated, standing there at the edge, sobbing.

Sam nodded, trying to take in the situation. His eyes traced the journey of the car, from the point where they stood, through the smashed wooden fence, and down the steep grassy embankment onto the track. 'What's your name?'

'Alison.'

'My name's Sam.' He placed a hand on the girl's shoulder while trying to think. His body was on overdrive. As a cardiothoracic surgeon he was used to dealing with emergency situations, but nothing like this. He looked left, then right down the line. No trains. But he would have to be quick. 'Is that your mum down there?'

Alison nodded, sniffling. 'She said she wants to die. I didn't know she was going to drive on there. Please, help.'

'It's going to be okay,' he promised, hurriedly picking his way through the broken fence. Alison began to follow but he gestured at her to stop. 'You'll be safer staying here.'

'Jessica's in the back,' she sobbed.

'Right,' he replied, turning back to the car. Now he looked more closely, he could see something in the back seat. 'Just wait there. Everything will be okay, I promise.'

Alison nodded, but already Sam was scrambling down the bank, his hands brushing against stinging nettles as he tried to keep his balance. He raced onto the track and up to the car. Now he, too, was in the impact zone for any approaching train. He would have to act quickly. He pulled at the door handle.

Locked.

'Open the door,' he shouted at the woman inside. She appeared slightly older than him: maybe late thirties. She looked utterly vacant, staring straight ahead at the track, not even acknowledging his presence. He banged on the glass. Without her co-operation, this could end very badly. 'Open the door, please.'

He peered through the back window. There were two young children in the rear, a boy and a girl about a year old, strapped into booster seats. The child nearest to him met his gaze. They'd both been crying; their reddened faces were tear-stained, but they seemed calm now.

Sam looked back at the woman. Then he noticed the handcuffs attached to the steering wheel. What the hell? This hadn't been a spur of the moment suicide attempt; this was well planned. It would make things so much harder. 'Christ.'

He looked down the track, which turned off at an angle a few hundred metres ahead. This was no longer just a matter of coaxing her out of the car. Blood was pulsing in his head as his heart raced.

He thrust his hand into his pocket for his mobile, but it wasn't there. It was in his jacket, on the front seat of his car.

'So stupid,' he said, chastising himself for not picking it up at the time. There was no time to go back.

He tried to push the car, straining until his body felt like it was about to explode with the effort. But the handbrake was on, and his feet slid on the stones between the tracks, denying him any grip. The vehicle just rocked back and forwards. Sam turned back to the woman. 'I know how you must be feeling,' he pleaded, 'but you don't want to kill your children, do you?'

She never flinched.

'Look,' Sam shouted, throwing another nervous glance down the track. 'Any minute a train could come, and we'll all be dead. Your daughter up there,' he said, pointing to Alison, 'you don't want her to see this, do you? What will she do without you, without her brothers and sisters?'

Nothing.

Sam looked at the two children, then at the window. There was no other way.

He searched between the rails and found a sharp-edged stone, about the size of a tennis ball. 'Close your eyes,' he ordered, already hammering on the bottom right-hand corner of the passenger front window. He increased the force, until cracks appeared. After four more hits the window shattered but, being safety glass, held itself in place. The children in the back seat began crying, shocked and scared by the drama. 'Close your eyes,' Sam shouted again, as he elbowed away the glass as gently as he could. Cubes of glass flew onto the front seat, some hitting the woman, who remained wide-eyed and motionless. Finally, the way was clear for Sam to reach the inside door handle. Undoing the lock, he ripped open the passenger door and grabbed for the handbrake. Once more, he tried to push the car, straining with the effort. 'For God's sake, please move.' This time the car did move forward a little, but the wheels were jammed in between the tracks, and there was no way it could be pushed any further.

Another glance down the line – still no train.

He needed to try something different. Stay calm, stay focussed. He reached back in the car and thrust the spare passenger seat forward, giving him access to the children.

248

'Come on,' he said, undoing the children's seat belts with shaking hands. He grabbed at the little boy. 'Come with me.' He pulled him close to his chest and placed him carefully on the grass bank, just a couple of metres away. Rushing back to the car, he brought out the little girl. Then, as carefully as possible, he scooped up the two children, one under each arm. They were heavier than he expected, weighing him down as he fought his way up the embankment. The steep incline was hard going, but this was the safest place. He passed the children to Alison, peeling them away from him as they clung onto his shirt. 'Look after your brother and sister.'

And that's when he heard the ominous hiss, reverberating across the overhead power lines.

A train was approaching.

'My mum, please help my mum!' Alison screamed.

He slid back down towards the car, burning his hands against the dry scrubland, momentum slamming him into the car's side. Still no train. But the hiss was getting louder.

His chest felt volcanic and he struggled to catch his breath. The woman was still silent, still staring dead ahead. 'The keys to the handcuffs,' he gasped. 'Where are the keys?'

No answer.

'The keys!' he shouted. 'Tell me where they are.'

He thrust his hands into her coat pockets and then the rest of her clothing, desperately searching every possible place where the keys might be. There was no reaction from her, even when he forced his hands into her tight jeans pockets. The keys were nowhere.

What was he going to do now? Maybe he should have told Alison to retrieve his mobile phone. He looked up at her, watching from the top with the children in her arms.

And then the train appeared around the top of the bend, travelling fast. A horn blared and the emergency brakes screeched. 'Please, God, no,' Sam cried, stepping back from the car as the train sped towards them. 'Look away!' he shouted to Alison, through the deafening scream of the brakes. 'Don't look!' The horn blared again, but the train didn't seem to slow. Sam tried to push the car again, in one last desperate effort.

It was still held fast.

'Please, help Jessica!' Alison screamed hysterically from the top of the embankment. 'She's in the back! Jessica's in the back!'

Sam looked up at her, then back towards the car. What did she mean? Then a sickening realisation hit him.

The boot.

He thrust his head in the car, scrambling to find the boot release lever. As with his vehicle, it was on the far side, near the accelerator pedal. He threw himself across the still motionless woman and strained to reach the lever, pulling it upwards, knowing that any second the train would hit. Hauling himself out of the car he rushed to the back. The train was bearing down on them, brakes still screeching, no more than a hundred metres away. He had only seconds before impact. He threw open the boot. A new-born baby, wrapped in a pure white shawl, looked up at him with watery blue eyes. He grabbed it as a thunderous noise enveloped him, instinctively sprinting off to his left and diving for cover, shielding the baby from the impact as he hit the ground.

And then everything went black.

2

Sam's head was pounding with the sound of sirens, shouts and screams, piercing the darkness. Then a soft Irish voice sliced through the gloom.

'Sam? Mr Becker?'

He opened his eyes, the harsh, artificial hospital light blasting him like a full-on torch beam. For that first moment he didn't know where on earth he was; his bearings were all over the place. And then, with shocking suddenness, he remembered – the train crash. His dry lips peeled apart as he tried to speak.

'Sorry to disturb you,' the sister said, smiling warmly, 'but there's someone here that I'm sure you'll want to see.'

Sam shifted in the bed, his eyes still adjusting to the conditions, seeing his wife Anna approach. For a second, watching her standing there with her face full of concern, he wondered if the blow to his head was causing him to hallucinate.

She shouldn't be here.

'I'll leave you be,' the sister said, exiting with a smile.

Anna moved anxiously towards the bed. 'Thank God you're okay.'

Sam raised himself from his pillows to meet her, trying to reassure her with the movement that things weren't as bad as they seemed. 'How did you... you should be on a plane to Bangladesh.'

As co-ordinator for Hope Springs, an emergency relief charity based in London, Anna had been called out to respond to severe flooding in the delta region of the south of the country. A water and sanitation specialist, she had spent years working abroad, mostly in India, where Sam had first met her six years ago during his placement in the paediatric department at the Christian Medical Hospital in Vellore. And although she now spent most of her time working out of the London offices, occasionally her technical and organisational skills would be required on site.

'The hospital called me just as I was about to leave for the airport,' Anna explained, taking his hand. Her skin was warm and smooth and as she kissed his cheek Sam breathed in her familiar, comforting perfume. She'd bought the scent on a romantic break in Rome three years ago, and it always reminded him of that magical weekend in the Eternal City. 'Louisa and I drove up here as quickly as we could,' said Anna.

'But what about the trip? The emergency.'

'Don't worry about that,' she replied, examining his face with concern. 'Anyway, I'm pretty sure this classes as an emergency. Let me deal with one at a time, eh?'

She placed a comforting hand on his head, gently brushing away some stray hair.

'It only comes in black and blue,' Sam noted, referring to the nasty-looking bruising around his left eye that was throbbing to its own pulse.

'Looks sore. Are you sure you're okay?'

'I'm fine, honestly. Just minor bruising – nothing broken, no lasting damage. They've done all the obs. Said they might let me go in a couple of hours. Feel like I could sleep forever, though.'

He twisted to read his wrist-watch on the bedside, wincing at the short stab of pain from his side. He'd been asleep for just over an hour, and it was now three hours since the crash. He'd slept most of the time since that horrific event, and everything was a bit of a blur. There were snippets of memories – the acrid smell of burning, the shouts and the moans, the wail of sirens and flash of blue lights, the squawk of radios, the young female paramedic talking him back to consciousness and then struggling to keep him awake, the first few minutes in the ambulance as it rocked and rolled away from the scene over the uneven ground.

He slumped back onto his pillow. 'Did they tell you what happened?'

'Not much,' Anna said, perching on the edge of the bed. 'There was a crash involving a train, a car, and you. I was so scared when they called,' she added, squeezing his hand as her green eyes glistened with tears. 'What the hell happened?'

Sam shook his head, thinking back to the events. 'I was driving home and a girl ran straight out in front of the car. Somehow, I really don't know how, I managed to avoid hitting her, and then she led me to her mother. She'd driven her car onto the railway track, with her kids strapped in the back. Her baby was in the boot.'

'My God,' Anna said, aghast. 'You think it was a suicide attempt?'

'Her daughter told me she drove the car straight onto the track, and that she wanted to kill herself,' Sam replied. 'I tried to talk to her, convince her to move, but it was like she was in a trance, just staring straight ahead. I tried to move the car, but it wouldn't budge. I got the children out, but I couldn't get her before the train came.' He thought of the woman in the driving seat, the emotional shutdown that he'd seen too many times before in the eyes of mothers and fathers, brothers and sisters, who had just lost a loved one on the operating table. 'Did they say anything about the children and the mother? They wouldn't tell me anything.'

Anna shook her head.

'The people on the train?'

'They didn't tell me anything else.'

'Who spoke to you? The hospital?'

'The police. They're waiting outside to see you. I think the nurses have been holding them back until they think you're ready.'

'I should speak to them.'

'Only if you're ready,' Anna replied. 'If you're not, I'll tell them to wait.'

Sam smiled – Anna was always ready to defend people in their hour of need, and now it was his turn. 'I'm okay. Where's Louisa?'

'Getting some coffee – it was a busy, stressful drive. It took us two hours to travel the twenty miles from home. Louisa said she's never going to travel through London at rush hour ever again.'

Louisa was a childhood friend of Sam and now a good friend to Anna also. She was considered more like family. Probably the only aspect with which Sam didn't trust her completely was her driving skills – her car, a rusting old-style mini, had had more bumps and scrapes than a dodgem.

'You didn't have to ruin your trip for me you know,' he said. 'The people in Bangladesh need you more.'

Anna kissed his forehead tenderly.

Sam smiled. 'But I'm glad you're here. That's all the treatment I need.'

***

The two plain clothes officers strode in, led by the Irish sister. As the sister left them, she exchanged a glance with the officers that Sam could tell was a warning to take it slowly with her patient. After twelve years on hospital wards, he was adept at interpreting the body language and expressions of staff.

'Mr Becker,' the taller of the two began, as Anna reluctantly stepped back from the bed and took up a place a few feet away, her arms folded across her chest. The policeman was pushing six foot four, and built like a rugby front row forward. His dark hair was shaved short, and his face was strong and sculpted. Sam placed him in his late thirties. His partner, the scribe, was round-faced, noticeably shorter and older, maybe in his fifties. He sported a greying moustache. 'How are you?'

'I'm okay,' Sam replied, sitting up straighter. He could smell diesel and smoke, and noted that their white shirts were holding black dust.

'That's good,' the officer said. His accent wasn't too dissimilar from Sam's own: somewhere around Manchester. 'I hear you're a doctor yourself.'

Sam nodded.

'What speciality?'

'Paediatric heart surgery.'

The officer unfurled a lip, impressed. 'Must be strange to be on the other side, being the patient rather than the one doing the looking after.'

'It is,' Sam agreed. And it was. Sam, like most doctors, was a terrible patient, as Anna had commented on the previous year during a dose of heavy flu. It felt completely wrong to be in the bed rather than the one standing over it. Maybe it had something to do with the loss of control: placing yourself in someone else's care. When it came to it, most doctors were control freaks. 'I don't intend to be a patient for much longer,' he added.

254

The officer suppressed a smile, getting back to the task at hand. 'Mr Becker...' He hesitated. 'It is Mr, isn't it?'

Sam nodded. He had successfully completed his training and Royal College of Surgery exams six months ago, and in the ironic world of medicine, the seventy-hour weeks, the nights sleeping on the ward whilst on-call, the years of study, all those personal sacrifices, had resulted in the dropping of the Doctor title he'd worked so hard for in the first place.

'Well, Mr Becker – Sam – I'm Detective Inspector Paul Cullen, of the British Transport Police, and this is my partner, Detective Sergeant Tony Beswick. We're part of the accident investigation team examining this afternoon's crash. We have a few questions, if that's okay with you.'

'Sure,' Sam replied. 'But can I ask a question first?'

Cullen nodded.

'How are the children, and their mother?'

'The children are all fine.'

'Even the baby?'

'Yes.'

'And the mother?'

'I'm sorry,' said Cullen.

Sam wasn't surprised but it still saddened him greatly. He nodded his understanding.

DI Cullen continued. 'No one could have survived a head-on impact at that speed. The train was travelling at fifty miles an hour when it hit. She would have died instantly.'

Sam took in the news. The woman had got part of what she wanted, but she hadn't taken the children with her. Had she really wanted them to die too? And what about the other people who were affected? Did she think about them when she'd made the decision to crash through the fence and drive onto the track?

'The passengers on the train?'

'All okay,' said Cullen. 'A few walking wounded – half a dozen or so cases of whiplash, minor injuries to arms and legs, and some people with shock. The driver is being counselled. As you can imagine, he's pretty shook up about the whole thing. Thankfully, the train stayed on the tracks. If the thing had derailed, the situation would have been very different.'

Sam pondered on that thought. It was still hard to believe that he'd been a matter of metres from a head-on high-speed train collision, yet had survived with nothing more than a black eye and slight bruising. And for the baby to have been unharmed too – it was nothing short of miraculous.

'Are you okay to answer some of our questions now, Mr Becker?' the officer asked, his voice revealing a touch of impatience. 'We'll be as quick as we can.'

'Fire away,' Sam said.

'Great. We need to piece together what happened. How you became involved, what you did, what you saw, right up until the impact.'

Just then Sam heard a commotion outside and saw a flash of light up against the window of his private room.

Cullen spun round and pointed at the door. 'Get that photographer ejected from the premises,' he barked at his colleague. 'And if they resist, arrest them. I told them, no one is allowed up here.'

His colleague nodded and exited the room.

'Sorry about that,' said Cullen, regaining his composure. 'We tried to keep the media away from this, but there's a swarm of them down at reception. Somehow they must have found out which ward you were on.'

'It's okay.' Sam exchanged glances with Anna, who was looking out towards the melee. DS Beswick could be heard directing the photographer back downstairs in no uncertain terms.

'Right,' Cullen said. 'First of all, what brought you to the location of the crash?'

'I was driving back home from a family event in the North West,' Sam explained.

'Family event?'

'My sister's birthday.'

'So you were with your sister over the weekend?'

'Not exactly,' Sam replied.

'I don't understand.'

Sam hesitated and Anna, who had been listening intently, picked up the baton. 'Cathy, Sam's sister, died when she was young. Yesterday would have been her thirtieth birthday.'

'Oh, right,' Cullen said, his brow creasing. 'Sorry to hear that. So, it was a commemoration...'

'Celebration,' Sam corrected, 'at least that was the plan.'

'Okay.' Cullen made some more notes. 'So can you just talk me through what happened as you were driving back home?'

'I was driving back, it was about five o'clock, when something ran straight out in front of me. It came from my left, and my first thought was that it was a deer or something. But I realised it was a girl, a teenage girl. I swerved to miss her, and then I followed her down to the...'

'You were led to the scene by a teenage girl?' interrupted Cullen, his face expressing surprise, and possibly disbelief.

'Yes, Alison,' Sam confirmed, noting Cullen's reaction. 'The woman's daughter. What's the matter?'

Cullen didn't answer, simply raising a hand as he brought a police radio receiver up to his mouth. 'Hi. DI Cullen here. We've got a problem.'

3

The morning following the train crash, Sam prepared the breakfast, handling the knife with a surgeon's skill as he buttered the toast and skimmed off the top of the boiled eggs. He'd been up for three hours now, since just before five, unable to stop his mind from racing and his body aching. For a time he'd just sat up in bed, staring at the wall while Anna slept, before tuning in to the early morning news. The main news items that had been replayed several times in the ensuing hours – a hurricane slamming into the Caribbean, and yet more killing in the Middle East – weren't a recipe for sound sleeping.

Anna appeared, and Sam smiled as she approached. Her slender, almost fragile frame belied an inner toughness, and her youthful face disguised a wealth of life experience. She was wearing her pyjamas, with her hair tied back away from her lightly tanned skin in a loose ponytail – a style that always reminded him of the first time they had met, when a feisty, determined twenty-four year old Anna had burst into his sweltering corrugated-iron outreach theatre room in the tiny rural Indian village, cradling a young girl whom she had found lying by the side of the road having been hit by a motorcycle. Bypassing the security on the door, who had told her to wait, Anna had taken it upon herself to bring the child, Grace, to Sam's attention. And for good reason – ten minutes later and the girl might not have survived her internal injuries. That meeting had sparked an instant and lasting mutual attraction between Sam and Anna. They grew closer throughout Sam's year elective at the Vellore Christian University Medical School; and for the next two years, when Sam returned home, inspired to train in paediatric surgery following his experiences in India, and Anna continued her work abroad, they stayed in contact by email and phone. Then one day Anna turned up at his flat. She'd been promoted, and her time would now be split between co-ordinating projects in countries around the world from the London offices, with occasional travel abroad to oversee the work. A year later they were engaged, and eighteen months after that married. It was only then Anna admitted that, with her father being a successful but work-addicted consultant neurologist who always put medicine before family, she had initially been extremely hesitant about getting into a relationship with a doctor.

'Couldn't sleep?' asked Anna, rubbing her eyes as she watched Sam pour the tea.

'Not much,' he admitted, turning to face her.

'Bad dreams?'

Sam shook his head, stirring the tea. 'I just keep seeing the look in the eyes of that woman. And I keep thinking – how can you do that to your children?'

Anna shrugged.

'I mean, what could be so bad that you'd lock your baby up in the boot of your car, strap your children in the back seats, and drive straight onto a railway track?'

'She can't have known what she was doing.' Anna took the tea that Sam proffered.

'Probably not,' Sam agreed, looking off towards the left.

'What are you thinking?'

'I'm thinking that she must have locked the doors after driving down the embankment. She watched one of her children get away and run for help, and her reaction was to lock the doors, knowing that the other three would probably die as a result.'

'It's impossible for us to understand,' Anna said.

Sam exhaled, taking a sip of tea and grimacing at the singeing heat. 'If only I could have got the car off the tracks. I was nearly there; I could feel the car moving...'

'You're bound to think things like that.' Anna cradled her drink. 'But you couldn't have done anything more. You saved three people's lives.'

But he hadn't saved one person's life. And that thought gnawed at him, the same as it did whenever a patient was lost. Yes, you pushed it to the back of your mind – you had to, in order to focus on the next person – but the regret was still there. It was what drove him to improve: he didn't ever want to find such failure acceptable.

'I should have called someone to stop the trains. I should have gone back to get my phone.'

'It's easy to say that now,' Anna countered. 'Hindsight is a wonderful thing. And who's to say the outcome would have been any different?'

Sam nodded. 'You're right – as usual.'

'Come here,' she said, putting down her tea and embracing him. They hugged tightly, and Sam wallowed in the comfort of Anna's body as it moulded to his. He buried his head into her hair, smelling her shampoo.

'I do love you, Sam Becker.'

'I love you too,' he replied over her shoulder, kissing her hair. He pulled back to see Anna with watery eyes. 'You okay?'

Anna nodded. 'Just a bit emotional after everything that's happened. I don't like the thought of losing you.'

'You won't,' he reassured her, hugging her again. 'I promise. I'll take you to the airport. Seeing as I've now got the day off.'

This time it was Anna who pulled back. 'Are you sure you don't want me to stick around?' she said, searching his eyes for the answer. 'I can call Bob now and that will be that. They'll just have to make do without me this time.'

Sam shook his head. He had persuaded Anna on the drive home from the hospital that she should make the trip to Bangladesh – they desperately needed her expertise – so she had somewhat reluctantly booked a replacement flight when they got home. 'They need you, Anna. Honestly, I'll be okay. The hospital wouldn't have let me go so soon if they hadn't been satisfied. I just need some rest. Anyway, it's only four days.'

'Okay,' Anna replied, not sounding convinced. 'But on one condition.'

'Go on.'

'That you'll think about seeing that counsellor.'

The hospital had offered Sam an appointment with a counsellor, which was now standard procedure for anyone involved in a traumatic event. It was meant to reduce the likelihood of developing post-traumatic stress disorder, although there were some who believed that it actually increased the chances of suffering after-effects. Sam had politely declined, although Anna had thought it could be a good idea.

'Okay,' he conceded. 'I'll think about it.'

***

One hour and a hearty breakfast later, Doug McAllister, a consultant anaesthetist who was a good friend and colleague of Sam's, rang to let them know that there was a short piece in the Telegraph about the train crash. Anna set off immediately to the local newsagents, returning ten minutes later.

'I checked all the papers, and the story is in five of them.'

She handed Sam the pile of papers as he sat by the large bay window of their ground floor flat. It offered a lovely view across to a small but beautiful area of parkland in Clerkenwell, North London. The place, the bottom half of a Georgian property, wasn't the largest, but it was more than adequate for two people, and they were lucky in having the garden. It had also been fortunate that they'd bought when they did – just before the London house price boom. Their long-term upstairs neighbours, a young couple with whom they had become good friends, had recently sold the top floor apartment for just over three hundred thousand. It was no wonder that the new guy to move in was a city banker — you had to be to afford those kinds of prices. Sam had been meaning to return the spare front door key, which they'd recently found buried in a kitchen drawer.

Sam surveyed the papers on his lap with horror, hardly daring to open them for fear of what was written inside.

'They don't mention you by name,' Anna said, flicking through the top newspaper and pointing at the story on page ten. The headline read, "Good Samaritan saves train crash family". Sam skimmed the article. There was indeed no mention of his name, although the piece documented the identity of the dead woman, Jane Ainsley, from Islington, North London, and her children Alison, Simon, Charlotte and baby Jessica.

'They only live just down the road.' Anna settled down next to Sam, perching on the wide ledge.

Sam nodded. 'It doesn't mention that Alison is missing,' he noted, reading on.

'None of the papers do,' Anna confirmed. 'They're all a little sketchy. I guess they had to go to print before they could get many details. What do you think's happened to her?'

261

'Who knows? Maybe like Louisa said, she's traumatised and just wanted to get away. I just hope that she's safe, wherever she is. I guess we'll just have to wait to hear from the police.'

Anna nodded. 'They'll probably want to speak with you again.'

'I'd say definitely, especially if Alison isn't found soon,' said Sam, moving on to the next paper. The story was essentially the same. He placed all the papers on the side and looked out across the street outside, watching the people pass by. He watched a stocky man as he crouched down, stroking his dog in front of the flat, before moving on. 'I hope that's the end of the press. I don't want any publicity.'

'You're afraid they'll pick up Cathy's story?'

'They did last time.'

Twelve months ago, in the middle of a transatlantic flight to a conference in Washington DC, Sam saved a baby's life. The baby, who was suffering from a collapsed lung, was saved by using a straw and a needle, which enabled Sam to reopen the airways. The saving of the baby, who happened to be the child of a high-profile American senator and expected future presidential candidate, made headlines around the world. It brought press attention that Sam found difficult to handle – especially when they picked up on the story of his sister Cathy's death, who, over a decade ago, had been brutally raped and murdered by Sam's then best friend, Marcus Johnson. The coverage had reopened wounds that even a surgeon of Sam's talent couldn't easily mend.

'Maybe today's stories will be it,' Anna said.

'Hopefully.'

Anna reached for his hand. 'I'm really sorry. With all that's happened we haven't even spoken about what it was like at the weekend. Was it okay?'

'Better than I expected,' Sam replied. 'Mum and Dad seem to be finally moving on with their lives. It's only taken fifteen years.'

'Did anyone mention Marcus Johnson's release?'

Marcus Johnson, the person who had so brutally cut short his little sister's life, was now able to walk the streets and make a new start. Sam was shocked by the strength of hatred he still felt towards the man he used to be so close to. It remained unfathomable to him how Marcus could have betrayed such trust. And during his fifteen years in jail, Marcus had offered no explanation. In fact, he had always protested his innocence, despite the overwhelming evidence against him. It had happened on a camping trip in North Wales. Sam and Marcus, Louisa and Cathy. On the second morning Louisa had woken Sam and Marcus. Cathy had gone. After twenty minutes of frantic searching, her body was found on the nearby sand dunes. Tests revealed later that Cathy's body had been covered with Marcus's DNA. There was hair, skin, semen – it all matched. They had never found the murder weapon, thought to have been a glass bottle, but they hadn't needed to. In the immediate aftermath Marcus had denied being with Cathy that night. But when it became clear that the evidence was so stacked against him, he changed his story. He claimed they had been dating in secret for months, and that they had crept out of the tents and walked down to the beach, before drinking vodka under the stars and making love. He had written to Sam, protesting his innocence. He said his last memory was lying down next to Cathy, and although he was unable to remember anything after that, he would never have hurt her.

Sam shook his head. 'No one said a word about it, including me.'

His parents hadn't spoken about Marcus's release, and instead it had hung over the remembrance day like a ghost.

'So you don't know how they feel about it – your parents?'

'I can guess,' Sam replied. 'I think they just want to pretend that he's still locked up.'

'And you?'

Sam shrugged his shoulders. 'Pretty much the same, really. I think he should have spent the rest of his life inside. But he's out, and that's it.'

***

Sam glanced across at Anna in the front passenger seat, as they crawled through the traffic on the outskirts of Heathrow later that afternoon. She'd been uncharacteristically quiet throughout the journey to the airport, and had spent most of the time staring out of the window. 'You're sure you're okay?' he asked.

She shook herself out of her daydream. 'What? Sorry?'

'Just wondering if you're okay,' Sam explained. 'You've been really quiet. If it's about going away, I'll be okay, honestly. And if it's

263

about me risking my life like an idiot, I promise I won't do that again.'

He glanced over at his wife.

'It's something else?' he tried. She was biting on her lip – a sure sign that something was bothering her.

But Anna kept quiet.

Sam brought his attention back to the road as the traffic thinned slightly. He followed the signs for Terminal 3, edging around coaches and cars that were busy unloading luggage irrespective of traffic laws. One car was parked across half a lane, the boot jammed full of cases. Heathrow was always a nightmare to negotiate. Once they were finally parked in a drop-off zone, Sam looked across at Anna, whose eyes were now glistening with tears. She very rarely cried.

Sam placed a hand on her shoulder. 'What's the matter, A?'

Anna surprised him by smiling as she pinched the tears away. 'I've got something to tell you,' she began. 'I was going to tell you last night, but it didn't seem like the right time. And I wanted to be sure, so I did another test just before we left the house.'

Suddenly Sam knew, breaking out into a smile of his own. 'You're...?'

Anna took his hand in hers and smiled broadly. 'We're having a baby.'

4

Sam Becker watched little Sophie Jackson. She looked so fragile while asleep, like a doll, eyes closed with alabaster skin. Born with a congenital heart defect, Sophie, now two years old, was clinging onto life as her heart failed. But now she had a chance, thanks to the Berlin Heart, a miniature heart pump that acted as a bridge between her own failing heart and a donor one. Five days ago Sam had led the procedure to fit the device. It had all gone to plan, yet it would all come to nothing unless she could get that transplant.

'Your mum and dad love you very much, Sophie. Keep fighting.'

Sam had known Sophie and her parents Tom and Sarah since her birth, and they had been in contact ever since. The adorable little girl had been a fighter since her first breath, and she was still fighting, but time was running out. The pump would buy her time, maybe up to twelve months, but in truth there was no telling, and the risk of death was always there. She was, however, in the best place. The Cardiothoracic Centre at St. Thomas's Hospital, on the banks of the Thames in Central London, was one of the most advanced treatment centres in the world. With state of the art equipment, a suite of private high dependency rooms, and some of the best trained staff in the world, the centre was barely five years old. It was up there with the best in paediatric cardiac surgery, and for Sam, working under one of the world's foremost surgeons, Professor Adil Khan, it was a dream job.

'Thought I'd find you here.'

Sam looked up as Louisa approached and pulled up a chair. Louisa, with her hippish, flowing dress sense, corkscrew curly red hair and freckled face, cut a distinctive figure in the otherwise uniformed, groomed hospital environment. Far from unattractive, she turned heads among both staff and patients. Always jovial, she was a popular clinical psychologist who did a lot of good work with patients and family on the wards. She was a master listener and, where necessary, imparter of advice.

'Hello there,' Sam said.

'I had a few minutes between consultations,' she explained, 'so I thought I'd come up and congratulate the main man in person.'

'Thanks,' Sam said, receiving a hug and peck on the cheek.

Although it would be some weeks before they would make an announcement about Anna's pregnancy to family and friends, Anna had told Sam he could tell Louisa straight away. She thought he might need someone else to talk to about it while she was away. And Louisa wasn't just any friend. Following Cathy's murder, Sam had cut ties with his childhood friends, moving to London to study medicine. But he had remained in contact with Louisa, who in many ways took on the role of his surrogate little sister. She didn't have any brothers or sisters, and like Sam, was left alone by the tragedy. She had also been good friends with Marcus before that fateful trip – they had been next-door neighbours – so she felt the same sense of betrayal. Having trained as a clinical psychologist, she'd worked for a time in Liverpool before a job came up at St. Thomas's. Sam was surprised but delighted when she went for it, explaining that she needed a change of scene and new challenge. And although she was a constant reminder of Cathy, her presence and friendship was a great comfort.

'I bet you're higher than a kite,' she added.

'I am,' Sam replied. 'I'm not sure it's sunk in yet, but it's going to be fantastic.'

Louisa squeezed his arm. 'I was so excited when you told me. You'll make great parents, I just know you will. And I can't believe I'll be an aunty.'

Sam smiled. 'Aunty Louisa has a certain ring to it.'

'And how is the mum-to-be?'

'Emotional. I'm not used to Anna breaking down in tears, but she couldn't stop crying when I said goodbye.'

'Understandable,' Louisa noted. 'It's a massive life-changing moment. Not that I'd know, of course.'

'You will,' Sam said. 'Maybe this new boyfriend of yours will turn out to be The One.'

'Maybe,' Louisa agreed. 'Early days yet though – it's only been a few weeks.'

'Well, I've never seen you as happy as you've been since you met him, so whoever he is, he must be pretty special.'

266

'He is – but enough about my love life. How is the little golden girl?'

'She's still doing okay,' Sam replied, watching Sophie sleeping, her small body rising and falling with each breath. 'She's very tired, sleeping lots, but that's to be expected.'

'You still hopeful?'

'We have to be,' Sam said. 'But it just depends on whether she can hold on until we find a suitable donor.'

'Any news?'

'No,' Sam revealed. 'She's top of the list, but hearts suitable for two-year-olds aren't easy to come by.'

It was a sad truth that more than twenty percent of paediatric heart transplant candidates died whilst waiting for an organ to become available.

'I guess not,' Louisa said. 'It's sad that we're here, hoping that a heart becomes available, yet for that to happen another child will have to die. It's really horrible when you think about it, isn't it?'

'Some good comes from tragedy, I suppose.'

Louisa nodded. 'I can't really imagine what it must be like to see your own child like this. I mean, I've spoken to parents who have had sick children, counselled them, but until it's your child, I don't think you can ever really understand.'

'No,' Sam agreed. 'The expression in Tom and Sarah's faces over the past few days, you can see how much it's hurting.'

'Are they around now?'

'They're taking a rest. It's pretty much the first time they've left her side since she came in here. They're exhausted, mentally and physically.'

For a minute or so they both sat there, watching the fragile-looking little girl.

'And how are you?' Louisa said finally. 'I thought you were going to take some time out to recover from your near-death experience.'

'I was going to,' Sam replied. 'But I wanted to see Sophie and check the latest on the donor situation.'

'I hope you're not working today. You should be taking it easy.'

'Mr. Khan gave Miles my list.'

'Bet Miles is happy about that,' Louisa joked. 'I can just imagine his reaction. That guy is a total idiot.'

Miles Churchill and Sam were colleagues – or more accurately rivals. Both thirty-four years old, both senior registrars in the speciality of paediatric surgery, and both in competition for a consultant post at the hospital that had just been advertised. The atmosphere between the two had never been great, in their four years of working together – Miles had already been working at the hospital for two years when Sam arrived, and Sam sensed that Miles saw him as an invader on his patch. But last year things had cooled to glacial proportions, when one of the junior doctors working under Miles had confided in Sam that she felt bullied by him. Wanting to nip things in the bud, Sam had delicately raised the issue with Miles. But his intervention provoked a furious response, with Miles accusing Sam of trying to undermine him. The junior doctor moved on, but the incident dealt a fatal blow to what was left of their working relationship.

'He probably sees it as a promotion opportunity,' Sam commented, prompting a laugh from Louisa.

'Seriously though, Sam,' Louisa added, 'why don't you get away from this place for a few days? Take a total break. You need time for everything to sink in – the crash, Cathy's commemoration, the baby news.'

'Is that what you'd tell one of your clients?'

'It's something that I'd tell anyone.'

'I'd rather be here, trying to be useful.'

Louisa put up her hands to signal surrender. 'Fair enough. Who I am to argue with my adopted big brother, eh?'

'Now you're talking. And as your big brother, I want to vet this new boyfriend of yours – make sure he's good enough for you.'

Sam was only half-joking. Louisa's track record in relationships wasn't the best, and she'd dated some strange men in recent years, most of whom she'd met via internet dating websites. While some had obviously been unsuitable, a bad match, others had been plain weird, like the guy who created scrapbooks with newspaper cuttings from high-profile murder trials (he'd claimed he was just interested in the law). And playing the big brother role, Sam truly did want to see her with someone who was right for her.

'All in good time,' Louisa replied, patting him on the knee. 'So, how are you really coping with yesterday's events? Have you booked that appointment with the counsellor?'

'You're as bad as Anna.'

'You need to talk to someone about what happened,' she insisted. 'We should talk about Cathy too. I'm really sorry I couldn't be there, Sam. I was thinking about you all Saturday, wondering how it went.'

'It was okay. And don't worry; it just wasn't possible for you to be there. Everyone understood.'

'So you'll talk about things?'

'I'm not convinced I need it.'

'It will help. Talk to me about it. Not as a psychologist, as a friend.'

Sam met her hopeful smile and nodded. 'Okay, but not here. Let's go grab some coffee.'

Just as they stood up his phone started to vibrate. He pulled a guilty face. 'Shouldn't really have this on in here.' He retrieved the mobile from his pocket. It was a text message from an unknown number, and it contained just one word.

"Hero?"

'You okay?' Louisa asked, leaning in to look at the screen.

'Spam message.' Sam snapped the phone shut. 'Come on, coffee time.'

They got as far as the main doors.

'Damn,' Sam said, glaring at the pager.

'What is it?' Louisa said.

'The Board want to see me.'

'Now?'

Sam nodded. 'Right now. Said it's urgent.'

***

He picked up the note and stared at the scrawled writing and accompanying telephone number. Since receiving it the previous night his heart hadn't stopped racing. Had he been stupid to believe that everything would work out? Walking over to the telephone he grabbed the receiver and dialled the number, his hands shaking as

269

sweat coated the handset. As it started to ring at the other end, he thought his heart was about to burst out of his chest. And then the call went through to the answering service and he relaxed slightly. It would make it easier.

'I just called to say, the answer's no.'

He put the phone down, and moved into the bathroom to wash his face. His skin was ashen, his eyes red and swollen from lack of quality sleep. He couldn't take much more of this.

But maybe that last call would be enough.

He spent the next two long hours trying to pass time, watching crap daytime TV, on pins that they would call back or, worse, arrive in person. When they didn't, he dared to believe that maybe it was all over. But then, before hope could really take hold, the phone rang, breaking through the silence of the flat with a shrill cry for attention.

He moved slowly over to the phone, just watching it for twenty or more seconds, hoping that it would stop ringing. But it continued, so he brought the receiver to his ear.

An hour later, as the clock turned eleven, he sat staring into space, now knowing that he would never be allowed to move on.

5

Sam stepped into the waiting lift, but just as the doors were closing, Miles Churchill darted between the shrinking gap.

'Miles,' Sam nodded. The stench of over-liberally applied aftershave filled the space, and for a moment Sam wondered mischievously whether Miles was trying to hide something. Was the alcoholic waft coming only from the cologne?

'Sam,' Miles responded, rearranging his pale pink shirt and tie in the mirrored wall as the lift started its ascent. 'I hear that you were involved in a spot of bother last night.'

'News travels fast,' Sam noted.

'Khan told me.' Miles caught Sam's eye via the reflection. 'Just before he gave me an extra four patients this afternoon.'

'Yeah, sorry about that,' said Sam, for the first time pleased at the Professor's decision to relieve him of his afternoon list. Although he knew it was for the best, he had still found it difficult to relinquish the patients, and especially to Miles – not that Professor Khan, or Anna for that matter, had given him any choice. 'I'm sure you'll manage though.'

'Of course I will,' retorted Miles. 'But it doesn't mean that I'm happy about it.' He started on his hair now, brushing thick, floppy dark strands away from his eyes. He was like a preening bird. 'So,' he said, finishing the makeover by brushing his lapels, and addressing Sam to his face, 'if you're not up to operating, what are you doing around here?'

'Couldn't keep away from the place,' Sam replied.

Miles nodded as if that was the answer he expected. 'Afraid that people will forget you.'

Sam kept quiet, not dignifying Miles's jibe with a response. The lift pinged and the doors slid open at the fourth floor – the level for the cardiothoracic centre. Miles stepped out then turned around, surprised, as Sam stayed in the lift. Sam suppressed a smile as the doors closed between them. That would get Miles wondering.

He took the chance to examine himself. Thankfully he didn't look as bad as he felt, although the reddish tinge smudging the blue of his eyes betrayed the lack of sleep. Then of course there was the angry bruise that circled around his left eye. His blonde stubble, now flecked with white, was deliberately thicker than usual – he'd recently cut his fair hair shorter and Anna had said it made him look five years younger, so this was a way to counter-act that effect. For a doctor to look young wasn't particularly desirable, especially when aiming for a consultant position. He straightened himself to his full six foot three inches, brushed his tie, collar and suit jacket – and looked himself in the eyes. It would have to do.

Glancing at his watch, he thought of Anna. She would be just over two hours into the flight now, somewhere over Southern Europe. He knew exactly what she would be doing: trying to lose herself in one of the in-flight movies. Ironically for someone who had visited all but one of the planet's continents, she was a reluctant flyer. While Sam would gaze down at the landscapes below, revelling in the bird's-eye vantage point, Anna would use any possible method to try and forget there was thirty thousand feet of fresh air between their seat and the ground. Sam thought of his wife on her important mission, and of the unborn baby developing inside, hitching along for the ride. He still couldn't quite get his head around the news that he was going to be a father, although it felt just as wonderful, exciting and daunting as it did at the moment of Anna's announcement.

The lift pinged again as it reached the top floor. Sam turned around and stepped out onto the plush royal blue carpet. This was the world of senior management. Perched at the highest level of the hospital it seemed far removed from the activities below – the smells, the shouts of patients, the non-stop activity. Here, money ruled, or at least that's how it felt. It wasn't an environment in which he was at all comfortable. He strode down the corridor, wondering whether his summoning really was about last night, as he'd assumed. Reaching his destination, he knocked firmly on the oak door and took a step back.

'Come in,' said the voice of Carla Conway, the Chief Executive of St. Thomas's, from inside.

Sam counted out three seconds before pushing at the door. To his surprise, the board table was empty. Carla stood at the window on the opposite side of the room, looking out across the London skyline towards Westminster. She turned around and smiled. Dressed in a figure-hugging black suit, with her jet black hair pulled tight back in a bun, Carla Conway cut an impressive and imposing figure. She had a reputation for being a tough operator, but Sam knew from first-hand experience that she was also a fair person. Fifty years old, Carla had been at the hospital for three years, following a career in the financial sector, including most recently the position of executive director of the London offices of UGT, the American investment bank. The appointment of someone from the City had caused a stir, especially among the senior clinicians, who feared that a CEO without any public sector background would think only of money and nothing of patient care. But their fears had been largely unfounded. Carla had in fact been a champion of patients' rights, a legacy of her own family experience in which two of her three sisters had died from a genetic form of breast cancer. As she had said in her opening statement, she wanted to make a difference after years of just making money.

'Nice to see you, Sam.'

'Carla,' Sam replied. 'You sent for me?'

She nodded, beckoning him over with her eyes. He moved up towards the window and looked out at the Thames. A tourist cruiser passed by, sharing the water with several other boats, including a small coastguard dingy. The blue light on the back of the dingy flashed as it skimmed across the tops of the waves like a polished stone.

'I wanted to congratulate you about yesterday,' said Carla. 'What you did was an amazing thing.'

'Thanks,' Sam replied, thinking back to the whereabouts of Alison. There had still been no word from the police. 'I did what anyone else would have done in the situation.'

Carla raised a disbelieving eyebrow. 'I don't think so, Sam. Not everyone would have risked their life the way you did.'

Sam shrugged, not wanting to dwell on the event.

'How are you? That's a nasty looking bruise.'

'I'm fine,' he replied. 'A little bit sore, but I was really lucky.'

Carla nodded. 'You're a hero, Sam.'

'Well, I wouldn't say that. I was just in the right place at the right time.'

'Like on board the plane last year?' Carla smiled. 'You're making a habit of being in the right place at the right time.'

'That was different,' Sam replied.

'Different circumstances,' Carla agreed, 'but it still demonstrated something special, Sam. It's something that people wanted to hear about. People should hear about last night, too.'

'The story is in today's papers. People already know about what happened.'

'I've seen them.'

'So that's okay,' Sam added. 'People know.'

'The basic story is there, Sam, but not the details. You aren't even mentioned by name in any of the articles, unless I've missed it?'

Sam shook his head.

Carla looked off towards the city. 'Then I think that more does need to be done, Sam. The general public will want to know more about the human story behind what happened.'

'Just because people want something, it doesn't mean you have to give it to them.'

'True,' Carla replied, 'but sometimes it's the best thing to do.'

'I don't want to speak with the media,' Sam said. 'I don't want any more coverage, and I don't want my name mentioned. Surely you can appreciate that, after last time. I didn't run onto the track and save those children because I wanted my name splashed all over the papers.'

Carla turned to face him. 'I do understand, Sam. I really do. And I know that it was difficult last year with some of the coverage, but we've learned lessons and this time it will be different.'

Sam shook his head.

'Sam, this is a great opportunity.'

'For who?'

A mother had died. It was a tragedy, not an opportunity.

Carla blinked. 'For you and the hospital.'

Sam smiled and shook his head. 'I'm in surgery, not public relations.'

'I realise that. That's why I called you up here. We can help.'

Sam doubted that. 'Help? In what way?'

'We can draft a press release, and put in a quote from you. The press will be happy with that. They can run their story and they'll leave you alone. And by the day after tomorrow you'll be yesterday's news, free to get on with the rest of your life.'

'I was hoping the press wouldn't be interested after today,' Sam said.

Carla let out a laugh. 'Do you know how many enquiries from the media we've had this morning about you? Twenty – and that was the latest update, an hour ago. We've managed to put them on hold for now, promising them a press release later this afternoon. But if the press release doesn't materialise they'll come knocking on your door for the story instead.'

Sam gripped the hair on the back of his head, considering his options. This changed things. Carla was right; if the press were so keen, they would track him down, quiz him, and then write whatever they wanted. So this way would be better, despite his genuine reticence to engage. He thought for another few seconds, fighting against his instincts. 'Okay,' he conceded. 'I'll do it.'

'Good, that's good.' Carla's relief was evident. 'Sam, I know you probably think that I'm some sort of vulture, taking advantage of this, but the reality is that good news stories for the hospital really matter when it comes to decisions at the highest levels – especially with the kicking we've had in the press during the past eighteen months over the infection rates.'

'You're just doing your job,' Sam replied.

'I'm not sure if that's a veiled criticism, Sam.' Carla smiled. 'But you're right; I am just doing my job – which is to ensure that this hospital is a success. And by being a success I'm not just talking about money. I mean improving patient care. We're all chasing the same goal here.'

Sam nodded. 'I know.'

'That's good to hear, because I want to ask you one last favour.'

'Go on,' Sam said, wary as to the way this conversation was going.

'We got a call this morning from the BBC. They want to do an interview with you this afternoon on Radio Five Live.'

This was a step too far. He had been interviewed on the radio the last time, and it had been a really stressful experience. 'No way.'

'We have people who can help,' said Carla. 'Melanie Grace is our new communications manager. She'll be able to advise you, and she'll also liaise with the BBC to make it clear where the boundaries are.'

'I really don't want to do this.'

'Please, Sam, I would really appreciate it; the board would really appreciate it. You have no idea how much this could help the hospital. Just for fifteen minutes of your time. Your story can make a real difference, believe me.'

What choice did he have? He'd ceded control of the situation, giving Carla a yard and now she was taking a mile. 'What if I say no?'

Carla shrugged. 'Then it doesn't happen. We call the BBC and tell them we can't do it.'

Sam thought it over. It was a foolish man who went against the wishes of the Chief Executive, even a fair one. Carla had been highly supportive of the cardiothoracic centre, giving the go-ahead for the expansion of the team and acquisition of several expensive bits of equipment, and they needed to keep that support. And then there was the important fact that she would be on his interview panel. 'Fifteen minutes? And then that's it?'

'A quote for the press release and a fifteen minute interview,' said Carla, the hope rising in her voice. 'Then that's it.'

'Okay,' he conceded. 'But on one condition. I do this one interview and then that's it: no more interviews, no more comments. Nothing.'

Carla held out her hand and smiled. 'You have my word, Sam.'

6

'You're doing what?'

'I didn't feel I had a choice,' Sam admitted, as Louisa shook her head. They were in a quiet part of the hospital cafeteria, out of earshot from the other staff and patients. 'I know it sounds terrible, but in two weeks I'm going to be facing Carla Conway across an interview table, and I don't want to make an enemy.'

'So you do whatever she says.' Louisa's face was flushed with anger. She didn't often get angry, or at least she hid it well, and the strength of her reaction took Sam by surprise.

'I've got more than just me to think about, Lou,' he explained. 'If everything goes to plan I'll have a family to support in just under nine months. And it's just fifteen minutes.'

Louisa shook her head again, unconvinced.

'They have helped me today, dealing with the media enquiries. And Carla's right. If I don't go along with this, the press will come right to my door. At least this way there's some control.'

'I'm just worried about you, Sam,' Louisa said, softening.

They paused for a second as someone approached them. The white-haired late-to-middle-aged man was wearing a distinctive neon yellow puffer style coat, like something you'd expect to see on a roadside worker. He fixed his sights on Louisa.

'Miss Owen, I, I, I'd like to speak, to, to...'

'Richard, now isn't a good time,' Louisa interrupted with uncharacteristic abruptness. 'We're seeing each other on Friday. Remember what we agreed?'

The man's face pursed as if in heavy contemplation. 'Of c, c, course,' he said, his eyes drifting to the floor. 'Sorry, to, to, bother you, Miss, Miss Owen.'

He turned, his head lowered, and moved off more quickly than Sam had expected, obviously agitated. They both watched his journey, as he weaved around the tables and chairs and then disappeared out of sight through the main exit doors.

'He's a patient?' Sam asked.

Louisa nodded. 'Richard Friedman. I'm having a few problems with him. I really hate being like that with people, but sometimes you have to be quite firm.'

'Want to talk?'

'It's okay,' Louisa dismissed. 'The guy is struggling to come to terms with a bereavement. He's just a little clingy. I can handle it. Anyway, you're not changing the subject on me, Sam. We're talking about you and this silly radio appearance.'

'Fair enough.'

'I'm worried about you, Sam. I just don't think that this is a very good idea when you're still coming to terms with what happened. Yesterday was a massively traumatic event, even for someone like you who deals with death every day.'

She was right, of course. 'I'll be okay.'

'But will you? You were nearly killed yesterday – yesterday, for goodness sake. And today, instead of speaking to a counsellor about things, or speaking to your friend, who just so happens to be a clinical psychologist, you'll be talking to a DJ on national radio.'

'I know, I know,' Sam admitted, recognising the irony of the situation. He still wasn't at all comfortable with the decision, but he'd made up his mind.

'And after what happened last time, I just don't know how you can even contemplate putting yourself through that again. I know how much it affected you last year when the papers were full of your life story. It affected me too; it affected your parents, and Anna. Journalists dredging through your past, gossiping about Cathy, speculating about what happened. Do you really want to risk that happening again?'

'They've promised that they won't ask me any questions about Cathy.'

'But can you really guarantee that?'

'No, I suppose not.'

'The media might not be able to resist it, Sam. Marcus has just been released from prison; Cathy would have just celebrated her thirtieth. You can see how it might be too tempting?'

Sam nodded; he'd thought the same himself. 'I know, but if they do start asking questions about that, I'll stop the interview there and then.'

'If you say so.'

Sam glanced at his watch. 'I'd better go. They've got a taxi coming to get me in a few minutes.'

Louisa just stared at her coffee.

Sam tried again. 'Look, Lou, I know what you're saying, and I do agree. But I just think that this could be the best way of getting the press attention out of the way, in a more controlled fashion. It might backfire, who knows. I don't want this any more than you do, but I've decided it's the best thing to do under the circumstances. Will you support me?'

Louisa looked up. 'Just be careful, Sam.'

***

During the ten-minute taxi ride over to the BBC radio studios, Sam dwelled on what Louisa had said. He just hoped they would be true to their word, and steer well clear of anything to do with Cathy. Louisa had been right – the media coverage the previous year had hurt Sam terribly. It had also really affected his parents, pushing his father back into depression. After over a decade of them trying to shut out the pain and horror, it had all come crashing back into their lives, as fresh and raw as ever.

By the time he reached the studios, had registered at reception and was waiting on the comfy green sofa, he was full of trepidation. He was close to walking out when a young girl of Asian appearance approached, clipboard in hand.

'Hi, it's Sam, isn't it?'

Sam nodded, and followed her along a corridor. She talked as she walked, explaining what would happen, but distracted by his own thoughts, Sam only heard bits of it. They went down a flight of stairs, passed through a set of double doors and emerged into one of the main broadcast areas. Three goldfish-bowl-like recording studies, fronted by glass, led off from the central waiting area in which they now stood.

'You'll be interviewed by Simon Saunders,' the girl said, looking over to the only occupied studio. 'He's covering the afternoon slot while Mike is away.'

Sam could see Simon at the control desk, headphones on, talking to the sports reporter sat opposite him. The broadcast was being piped over the speakers. At the moment they were speculating about the latest rumours on the football transfer market. He wasn't familiar with this presenter – he tended to listen to Radio 4 – but Sam was grateful to be spared the confrontational well-known regular host, Mike Bennett.

'You'll be on in a few minutes,' the girl explained. 'Just after the news. Take a seat and we'll come and get you.'

***

'We've got time for one more caller. Richard from London, what's your question?'

Sam looked over at Simon and wished he were somewhere else. The presenter had been fine, asking some standard questions about the previous night. But he hadn't reckoned on a full-blown phone-in to follow. For almost ten minutes now he'd been quizzed by callers about the crash. Some had wanted to know the basic facts of the event. Others had sought to reflect on the nature of what it meant to be a hero. It was like a backstreet psychiatry session in front of an invited audience. He should have listened to Louisa. But one more caller and it would be all over.

'Hi Simon,' the caller began. 'Hi Sam, how are you?'

The sentence was slow and deliberate, as if each word was being stretched.

'I'm fine, thanks,' Sam lied, gazing down at the console that curved around him. The headphones were starting to irritate and he longed to rip them off and end this now.

'But you're not,' the caller replied, in the same slow drawl. 'You're not fine at all, Sam.'

For a few seconds the comment just hung in the air, as Sam decided how to respond. But before he could speak, Simon stepped in.

'How do you mean, Richard?' He glanced over at Sam as he spoke, and the excitement in his eyes was clear as he waited for a response.

'I mean that Sam isn't as fine as he's making out. We've not heard the truth.'

Sam shook his head. Louisa had been right. This had been a terrible idea.

Simon moved closer to the microphone, keeping his eyes fixed on Sam. 'You're not accusing Sam of lying?'

'I'm not making any accusations,' the man replied. 'Just an observation, that's all. I'm interested to hear what Sam thinks about it.'

Simon looked over at Sam, giving him an opportunity to respond that Sam felt unable to turn down.

'I've answered the questions as honestly as I could,' he said, trying hard not to sound defensive.

'Ah,' the caller replied. 'But that's different.'

Sam met Simon's gaze as he moved back towards the microphone – the guy was captivated. 'I don't see how.'

'Tell me about what she said, Sam.'

This was getting totally out of order. Couldn't the station just cut this guy off? He looked again at Simon. 'I don't understand what you mean.'

'I think you do,' replied the caller. 'Tell me about what she said to you, just before the train hit. That's what I want to hear.'

'Err, I think we've heard enough,' Simon said. 'Thanks for your call, Richard…'

'No,' Sam interrupted, putting up a hand and leaning into the microphone. He'd changed his mind, and now wanted to challenge this individual. 'I want to know why you think you've got the right to ask that, Richard.'

Simon nodded, taking a symbolic move away from the control console.

'Because I want to be entertained, and you're not giving me the full show.'

Sam laughed in disbelief. 'This isn't a show.'

This time it was the caller's turn to laugh. 'It's entertainment, Sam. And you're the star attraction.'

'I don't have to listen to this.'

'You think you're a hero, Sam, don't you? But you couldn't save your sister from Marcus Johnson.'

Sam just sat there, stunned. It felt like someone out of nowhere had just delivered a sharp blow to his gut.

Simon stepped in. 'Thanks for all your calls. And thanks to our guest in the studio, Sam Becker. It's clear from the vast majority of calls we've had that he's a true hero, and a testament to the staff of the health service. Thanks for coming in today Sam and sharing your experience with us. I know it must be really difficult talking about this. Thank you.'

Sam nodded, the words of the caller lodged in his brain.

'And now time for the traffic and travel with Claire Davies. Over to you, Claire…'

'I'm really sorry about that last caller,' Simon said, as they both took off their headphones. 'You get those sorts of people sometimes. We try our best to screen out people like that, but every now and again one slips through the net. You'd be amazed by how many crazies there are out there.'

'It's okay,' Sam replied, placing the headphones on the desk in front of him. In truth he felt anything but okay, but he wasn't about to discuss this with someone from the media. 'Really, it's fine.'

Simon nodded, seemingly unconvinced.

***

'Sam. It's Doug. Sorry to call you out of the office.'

'Doug,' Sam said, as he emerged from the BBC building onto the busy pavement. The heavens had opened and the rain was bouncing up from the pavement, so he sheltered in the entrance. 'Did you hear the interview?'

'I caught the end of it. They had the radio on in the staff room and everyone who could was listening. That last caller was something else. I mean, talk about deranged.'

'Tell me about it.' Sam rested against the wall of the building and watched as taxis and buses splashed by. He'd spent the past few minutes since the interview reflecting on the caller and his words.

What sort of person got their kicks out of that sort of thing? 'What's up?'

'It's not good news,' Doug replied. 'I was going to tell you when you got back, but I thought you'd want to know straight away.'

'Go on,' Sam said, moving out into the heavy rain, already looking for a free taxi. It had to be something at the hospital.

'It's that young patient of yours, Sophie Jackson. She's gone downhill, and they've rushed her into theatre. Sister Keller told me that it's not looking good.'

'No.' Sam scanned the road – all the cabs were taken. 'Who's operating? Mr Khan?'

'Miles,' Doug replied. 'Prof Khan is on his way.'

This was not good. Miles was technically a good surgeon, but not in the Professor's league, and Sam only wanted the best for Sophie. 'I don't believe it.'

'You can see why I called.'

'Sure, thanks, Doug, I appreciate it. I'll be there as quick as I can.'

Author's Note

Thank you to all those who have read and enjoyed my novels, and in particular those who have taken the time to get in touch with me, via email, Twitter and Facebook. It means a lot to me, and makes writing worthwhile. If you would like to get in touch, you can contact me via:

www.paulpilkington.com
www.facebook.com/paulpilkingtonauthor
Twitter: @paulpilkington